Secrets That Hold Us

A novel

By

Manjula Pothuri

Cover design by Manjula Pothuri
ISBN: 979-8-9990340-1-4
First Edition
Published by: Ramadia Publishing

For more information, visit: www.manjulapothuri.com.

For those who hold on to hope—even when the world forgets their name.

To my Nana,

The late Mr. N. J. Prabhakar

My greatest cheerleader—Your faith in me lit the path. This book carries your spirit on every page.

Acknowledgments

This book was born from grief—but carried forward by love.

To my dad, the Late Mr. N. J. Prabhakar, your presence continues to guide me, even in your absence. You were my biggest hero, and this story is a tribute to your spirit.

To my Maa, for love and memories we shared.

To my husband, Raghu Pothuri—your quiet strength and unwavering support gave me the space to write, even when I doubted myself. Thank you for believing in me, always.

To my daughters, Ramya Pothuri and Divya Pothuri—you remind me every day why stories matter. Your love anchors me, your faith lifts me, and your light inspires everything I create.

To my father-in-law, Mr. Gopal Rao, whose encouragement helped me begin this journey—you gave me the courage to believe my words were worth sharing.

To the friends who listened, encouraged, and stood by me in the most difficult moments—you made this journey possible.

And finally, to every reader who has found this book—thank you for letting these characters into your life. May they offer you a moment of reflection, hope, and healing.

Chapter 1

Her in the fog

Jason pushed the diner door open, holding it as Eaton stepped out. The fog had thickened since they'd come in. It curled around the pavement, smudging light and shape.

As Eaton ran ahead, Jason caught sight of a figure near the edge of the lot.

A woman—or the silhouette of one—barely visible through the haze. Just a shape carved from fog, blurred and still.

But something in him paused. His mind twitched, too well-trained to hope.

Even now, seven years after she'd vanished without a trace, he still looked for her in strangers. A tilt of the head. A shape in the fog. Anything that might be her.

"Dad, are you coming?"

"Hold on, buddy."

Jason stepped off the curb, eyes fixed. The figure shifted.

But, as the fog parted, it wasn't her. Just another older woman moving slowly towards a parked car.

He exhaled and turned back.

Eaton was waiting by the curb.

Jason joined him, resting a hand on his son's back. But before they crossed the lot, he looked over his shoulder—just once.

The space was empty now.

Still, his eyes lingered.

The elevator hummed as Dr. Jason Carter descended to Apple Creek General's main floor. Below, the morning rhythm had taken hold—nurses moved fast, monitors beeped, and voices merged into the day's first wave of chaos.

As he stepped out, a young intern nearly collided with him, her eyes widening. "Dr. Carter," she said, straightening her posture. "Welcome to Apple Creek."

Jason nodded politely. He was used to the reaction—years in war zones had a way of leaving stories behind.

A nurse glanced his way, then stepped aside as he headed toward the administrative wing. Coffee and pastry scents cut across the hallway—an oddly warm note in the hospital's sterile air.

"Jason! Over here!"

Dr. Berry Harper approached with an easy grin. Sharp cheekbones, dark-rimmed glasses, a disheveled charm—he looked like a man who knew the punchline before anyone else. He clapped Jason's shoulder.

"Still playing the 'brooding hero, huh?'"

He snorted. "Someone must maintain the reputation."

How was the flight?"

Jason didn't bother hiding his weariness. "Long. Eaton talked nonstop—he's seven and has endless questions about the town, his new school, everything."

"Sounds about right," Berry's grin softened as he gestured towards the door. "Let's get you introduced."

They entered a sleek conference room, and conversation fell quiet. Twenty doctors turned to face them.

Berry gestured, "Everyone, this is Dr. Jason Carter, our new Director of TMT."

Jason nodded. Quietly scanning the room.

Dr. Bethany Ross, Head of Surgery, stood first. "Dr. Carter, it's an honor. Your work in Afghanistan and Palestine is legendary."

"Thanks, Dr. Ross. I'm hoping to learn just as much as I share."

Dr. Moher, Chief of Pediatrics, nodded. "We're lucky to have you. Apple Creek's a long way from the trauma units you're used to."

Jason shrugged. "Figured I'd try a place where 'incoming' doesn't mean helicopters and sirens."

Laughter rippled around the room. The tension eased.

When the meeting ended, Berry nudged Jason.

"Team dinner at Golden Oaks Diner this Friday—you'll meet everyone, and I heard they have the best pancakes in town."

"Yeah, I was there on the way from the airport." He raised a brow. "A team dinner, my first week? Efficient."

"Small-town hospitality," Berry said. "Dinner at my place tonight, too. Bring Eaton—my kids are ready for him. I've already called your parents, Margaret and Robert, and invited them. "Jason smiled. "We'll be there."

Later, as the room emptied, he lingered by the window.

Apple Creek stretched below—quiet, understated, undeniably charming. For a moment, he let himself believe peace might finally be within reach.

But peace had a way of slipping through, no matter how far he ran.

Berry shoved his hands into his coat pockets as they crossed the hospital parking lot after rounds.

"Feels almost like the old days," he said lightly. "Afghanistan… minus the dust storms and bomb drills."

Jason gave a nod. "Yeah. Almost."

They walked a few more steps in silence before Berry spoke again, quieter this time.

"I wonder where she is," he said, almost to himself.

Jason didn't answer.

His shoulders stiffened just slightly—a shift so subtle most people would have missed it.

But Berry saw it.

And instantly regretted opening old wounds he hadn't meant to touch.

He looked down, the weight of guilt cinching tight in his chest.

Some things, he thought grimly, should have stayed buried.

At the Harpers' home, the aroma of garlic-and-rosemary chicken roasting mingled with the yeasty warmth of freshly baked bread.

Jen Harper, Berry's wife, poured warm apple cider into the mugs, the spice tangling in the air as laughter echoed across the open living area.

After dinner, the adults settled onto sofas by the stone fireplace while the Harper children and Eaton raced downstairs for a game of ping-pong.

"Feels good having everyone in one town," Berry Harper said, sinking into an armchair beside Margaret, Jason's mom. "Family nearby—it makes this feel complete."

Robert nodded. "Apple Creek doesn't usually pull names like yours."

"Maybe they're just desperate." Jason joked, softening the line with a crooked smile as he raised his mug. "You and mom set the bar high. I'm just trying to keep up."

Berry clinked his mug against Jason's, amused. "With parents like yours? No pressure at all, huh?"

Jason let out a soft laugh. "None whatsoever."

Jen Harper leaned forward. "So what exactly will you be doing?"

"We're building a unit to train doctors worldwide in trauma management," Jason explained. "Helping set up crisis-ready teams—war zones, disasters. Not just skills, but resilience too."

"Sounds intense," Jen said. "Saving the world or training the ones who will?"

Jason's eyes brightened. "Hopefully both. But mostly training—so I don't have to be the guy anymore."

With a gentle tilt of her head, Margaret said, "It's important work. And you're the right person to lead it."

They settled into easy conversation and shared stories, the room filling with the comfortable rhythm of old friends. Occasionally, Jason glanced toward the basement door, where Eaton's flushed face reappeared before he curled into Margaret's side.

He watched him—grounded, for now, in a steady calm.

Apple Creek was supposed to be a fresh start. But his past clung to him, refusing to let go.

Chapter 2

Echoes of laughter

Over the next few days, life blurred into motion. Between settling into his parents' home and unpacking boxes, Jason accompanied Eaton to his school orientation.

The boy met the day with a mix of excitement and jitters. At the classroom door, Eaton approached his new teacher with the seriousness of a diplomat. Ms. Page, in her mid-twenties, knelt to meet him at eye level and offered a warm handshake.

"I hope you'll make lots of new friends here and enjoy the school," she said kindly.

Eaton reached for her hand, smiling sweetly. "You're very pretty. Are you married?"

The room fell silent.

Jason's ears warmed, and he rubbed the back of his neck, gaze dropping to the floor. "I'm sorry," he managed, voice tight. "He's... very observant."

Ms. Page laughed, brushing it off. "Don't worry, Dr. Carter. I've heard that question more times than I can count. Thanks for the compliment, Eaton."

As they exited, Jason muttered, "Next time, let's save the flirting for recess."

Eaton tilted his head to one side, voice calm and sincere. "I was wondering if she'd go on a date with you."

Jason halted mid-step. "How many times do I have to tell you—I don't date your teachers."

Eaton shrugged, unbothered. "I remember. I just don't want to deal with switching classrooms if things get weird."

A groan escaped Jason. "I'm raising a tiny, matchmaking menace."

As they walked to the car, Eaton skipped ahead, humming.

Jason watched him—shoulders relaxed, face lit with that trademark Eaton brightness. Sometimes it stunned him how light his son had become. How joyful. How open.

Proud didn't begin to cover it.

Eaton was a happy-go-lucky kid, all elbows and laughter, full of wild ideas and impossible questions. But his early days had been anything but happy—or lucky.

Lucky he'd survived. Lucky they both had.

Jason still remembered the panic that swallowed those first weeks after his mother vanished. The nursery's silence. The ache that seeped into every corner of their life.

He had loved her. Married her. Held their child in her arms. And then—just like that—she was gone. As if someone had torn out a chapter from the book they were still living.

Grief had almost swallowed him. Bitterness nipped at his heels, whispering that he'd been left behind. But he'd tried—tried hard—not to let it win. He didn't want to become the kind of man whose pain poisoned everything he touched. Especially not Eaton.

He poured everything he had into being a father. Every diaper, every midnight cry, every lunchbox note. When he couldn't, Margaret stepped in—quiet and strong. She never asked. She never hesitated. She just became Eaton's other parent.

And Eaton? Eaton became a joy. A reason to smile. A reason to get up and keep going. He might not have had all the answers—but he was proud of the boy Eaton was becoming. And proud, too, of the man he was trying to be.

Driving through Apple Creek now, the golden leaves glowed beneath the afternoon sun. Eaton pressed his nose to the window.

"Why is everything so small? Even the trees?"

"That's called cozy," Jason said. "Those short trees are older than both of us combined."

Eaton made a face. "You're home late tonight?"

"Probably."

Eaton smirked. "Going on a date?"

Jason shot him a look. "Are you actually seven?"

"I'm just saying—you're dressing nice, meeting people, eating good food. Sounds like a date."

Jason sighed, tugging on his jacket as they reached the house. "Okay, fine. But for the record—I don't need your help with dating."

Eaton's grin widened. "You should ask her out. You know, for me."

Jason hesitated as Eaton darted toward the kitchen, already hatching his next matchmaking plan. A brief warmth touched Jason's face—then a quiet, undeniable ache rose to meet it.

Eaton didn't see a man too closed off or too stubborn to love.

He just saw someone… alone.

Not broken. Not bitter. Just… incomplete.

And Eaton—bright, loyal Eaton—was trying to fix that emptiness the only way he knew how. With laughter. With plans. With hope.

To Eaton, love wasn't complicated. It wasn't heavy or tangled in conditions. It was something his dad deserved—something missing that needed to be brought home.

Jason's chest tightened—not with pain, but with something more fragile. Gratitude. Wonder. And a fierce, aching kind of love.

Later, over coffee, Eaton mimicked Jason's horrified face for his grandparents. Laughter erupted across the table.

Margaret wiped at her eyes, shoulders shaking with mirth. Then, looking at Jason, her smile softened—a knowing curve only a mother could give.

Once, his laughter had been different—freer. Now it came quieter, as if he had to measure joy before letting it in.

She said nothing. But the thought lingered, quiet and present: When had his laughter last felt like it belonged to him?

After Eaton fell asleep that night, Jason walked past his room and paused.

It was quiet—just like it had been after she left. Only now, the silence didn't ache. It waited.

Chapter 3

A flicker in the fog

Alley pushed open the door to Golden Oaks Diner, where the scent of warm butter and maple syrup wrapped around her like a memory she couldn't quite grasp.

Morning prep buzzed in the air—tea brewing, grills heating, the clatter of pans threading through it all, the whole place echoing the sound of a town waking up.

Golden Oaks Diner had a way of claiming people, folding them into its rhythm like they'd always belonged,

It didn't ask where she'd come from or what she had lost. It treated her as its own—even when she wasn't sure who she was.

The thought barely settled before a voice broke through the clatter.

"Morning, sleepyhead," Adam called from behind the counter, his grin as familiar as the scent of fresh coffee.

Alley tugged her sleeves down over her hands and offered Adam a sleepy nod, rolling her eyes as she headed to the bar.

"Morning, Adam," she murmured.

Emmy's cheerful voice rang out from the kitchen, bright and teasing.

"Pancakes and bacon?"

"Yes, please!" Alley's tone brightened at the thought.

A moment later, Emmy emerged, balancing two plates stacked high with pancakes, hash browns, and bacon. Alley's face lit up. She eagerly doused the pancakes in syrup and dug in.

Emmy, who had known Alley all her life, was always amused by her appetite—especially given her petite 5'4" frame. Her heart-shaped face, framed by soft curls, bore a faint scar on her forehead—something Emmy thought added to her striking charm.

Emmy still remembered the first day Alley returned to Apple Creek—seven years ago, almost to the very day.

She'd walked into Golden Oaks before sunrise, not as the firecracker girl Emmy had once run wild with, but as someone smaller. Hollowed out. A shadow in a familiar shell.

She hadn't offered an explanation. Just that quiet voice asking for coffee and a booth by the window.

And Emmy hadn't asked questions. She'd just poured the coffee and made pancakes—knowing it was the only thing she could offer.

She never forgot how Alley had looked that morning—like someone trying to remember who they used to be.

The little bell above the door chimed cheerfully, though the low murmur of conversation and clatter of dishes nearly drowned it out.

Alley waved at Maggie mid-bite, who breezed into the diner, her heels clicking against the worn hardwood floor in a perfect, no-nonsense rhythm. A gust of crisp autumn air followed her inside, carrying the scent of dried leaves into the warm, butter-scented space.

Maggie never arrived quietly. Her brisk, purposeful energy sent a ripple through the diner's morning routine.

A color-coded planner was clutched in one hand, a bold cobalt-blue handbag in the other, loud enough to announce itself before she did. She nudged the door shut with her hip, eyes narrowing in thought.

"Alright, people, let's get moving! I've got exactly twenty minutes before my next crisis," she announced, opening her planner with a practiced flick, her highlighter already uncapped.

"We've got a full plate—festival prep, TMT dinner meet, baby shower. And surprise, surprise: everything was due yesterday."

Alley's fork paused midair. "TMT?"

Adam glanced at the form. "Trauma Management Training. A bunch of doctors from the hospital are attending."

Alley stopped chewing, staring at Adam as though he'd said something unfamiliar. Her fingers clenched tighter around her mug, knuckles paling against the ceramic.

The room stilled—Alley felt as if a single word carried the weight of everything. She forced a smile, but her grip betrayed her.

Trauma Management Training. The irony stung. Her memories were still scattered—some locked behind doors she feared reopening. The phrase hit harder than expected, brushing a nerve she hadn't known was still raw.

Adam didn't notice.

"Room full of doctors," Emmy quipped. "You'll love that."

"Don't remind me," Adam muttered.

Maggie barely looked up. "And I need someone to prep the baby shower orders by Thursday. Volunteers?"

"Caffeine," Alley said. "Just mainline it into my veins."

Adam slid a fresh cup toward her with a knowing grin. "Already ahead of you."

With a thoughtful nod, Maggie took a sip from her mug. "It's going to be a full week, but we'll manage."

Born and raised in Apple Creek, Maggie was the heartbeat of the diner, proudly carrying on her family's 75-year legacy.

She set down her mug and turned to Alley. "If you have the order ready for Victoria Ski Resort, I can take it with me. I'm meeting Steve there to discuss a wedding reception. Dale's even skipping the fishing trip to join me. It's a full family affair. Want to tag along?"

Alley arched a brow. "Dale missing a fishing trip? Either the world's ending or he's finally run out of bait."

Maggie chuckled. "Well, you know him. The only thing he loves more than fishing is giving his expert opinion on everything."

"Thanks, Maggie, but I'm drowning in work here. Rain check?"

Maggie nodded. "Alright, your loss—it'll be a feast." She paused, her gaze warming. "Your mom and I used to sneak off to that old resort when we were kids. I still remember the thrill of it."

Alley leaned on the counter, curiosity bright in her eyes. "I bet you two got into all sorts of trouble."

Maggie's grin broadened. "Oh, you have no idea. Your mom was the mastermind—I was just along for the ride." A warm light passed through her eyes as nostalgia curled her lips.

"We grew up together: same school, same terrible taste in fashion, same dream of getting out of Apple Creek—until she met your dad."

Alley's expression softened. She'd heard these stories before, but in Maggie's telling, every memory felt like a treasure she couldn't let go of.

Maggie drummed her fingers on the counter, her voice quieter now. The usual sharpness in her eyes dulled, giving way to something gentler.

"When your mom came back after..."

She hesitated, just for a second. But it was enough.

Enough for Alley to feel the shift—the way Maggie's voice faltered as if stepping too close to a memory she hadn't planned on confronting.

Enough for Alley to know exactly where this conversation was going.

She didn't mean to look away, but she did. Her fingers curled around the cup, clinging to its warmth as emotion rose inside her.

Maggie caught it.

She sighed, shook her head just a little, and reached for her handbag, hiding whatever was left unsaid.

"Anyway," she said lightly, flipping a page, "I'd better get going."

Alley didn't interrupt, watching Maggie busy herself with notes. The silence between them felt heavy—an echo of gaps in her mind.

I wish I remembered. It was like chasing a whisper through fog. She closed her eyes and let the quiet hold what memory could not.

Alley had never lived in Apple Creek. Her only ties were the summers and Christmases spent at her grandparents' farmhouse— visits wrapped in warmth, cinnamon, and porch swings. After everything she'd endured, it wasn't home that called her back, but the memory of someplace that had once felt like it could be.

She'd returned to Apple Creek at thirty, a shadow of herself, carrying fragments of a past that felt more like someone else's story. For a while, she drifted through the town like a visitor trapped between timelines.

"Now, at thirty-seven, she had built a quieter life—piece by piece. The diner's steady rhythm had become her anchor, its familiarity a buffer between the world and whatever truths lay hidden in the folds of her memory."

But in the hushed hours before dawn, when the town still held its breath, she often wondered if this life truly belonged to her.

Beyond the diner, the wind brushed the maple leaves, bringing with it a shift in the air she couldn't quite name.

Golden Oaks had seen seasons come and go, each offering its truths. But this time, something else stirred beneath the surface— something that felt like spring breaking through the frost, quiet, certain, and impossible to ignore.

Chapter 4

Between heartbeats

The diner's clatter faded into the background, but her mind stayed stuck on those three letters. TMT. Even the name made her want to disappear.

People didn't just eat at Golden Oaks---They found something they didn't know they were missing. A rhythm. A belonging.

It absorbed people, wrapped them in its rhythms like a secret too precious to lose. It never asked where they had been and never pried into the ghosts that followed them. That's why Alley stayed. That's why she needed it.

Everywhere else, she felt like a fish in a glass bowl—watched, studied, waiting for the inevitable tap on the glass, especially by the doctors.

She had spent enough time around them to last a lifetime. Not by choice. Never by choice.

She glanced at the schedule pinned to the wall.

TMT.

The letters landed like a gut punch.

Trauma...

Her mind recoiled—bright white halls, smoke-filled rooms, hushed voices behind curtains. The past, forcing its way in.

She caught her breath.

For a second, she was back there.

Then, just as quickly, she made herself breathe. In. Out.

The scent of vanilla cake and fried chicken drifted through the crack in the door—a reminder that the lunch rush was just around the corner.

She sighed, pressing her fingers lightly against her forehead. Maybe a five-minute break wouldn't hurt.

Just as she reached for her phone, it buzzed against the desk.

Seeing the caller ID, her expression shifted, a quiet ease settling in. Perfect timing. Steve.

"How's the day treating my sweetheart?" came the smooth, familiar voice—steady and warm, with the kind of ease that made his words feel deliberate.

"Oh, you know, just peachy," Alley replied, mock-cheerful. "The fish vendor delivered something that looked like it was auditioning for a horror movie. Joe thinks amaranth and spinach are interchangeable—because nothing screams 'appetizing salad' like blood-red leaves—and Emmy tried flambé pancakes. Set off the alarms."

There was a brief pause—then laughter burst out.

"So... a normal day at the diner?"

"Pretty much. I'm thinking of rebranding—Golden Oaks Circus: A Culinary Spectacle."

"You're wasting your talents if you don't start charging admission," he teased. "Though it sounds like I'm missing the show of the year."

"Oh, definitely," she said, grinning. "But don't worry—I'll save you some of Joe's special salad."

"Thanks, but I think I'll pass." He hesitated, then offered, "Come here for lunch? Mom's bringing sandwiches, Dad's joining us. Later... we could get your favorite dessert."

"Hmmm," Alley pretended to deliberate. "Your mom already invited me, but coming from you? Irresistible."

She spun her chair in a circle, a grin stretching wider.

"I'll be there in an hour."

Alley pulled into the parking lot, her tires crunching over fallen leaves scattered like golden confetti. The crisp autumn air bit at her cheeks. She tugged her coat tighter as she stepped out.

Inside, the warm glow of the reception area and the faint scent of woodsmoke wrapped around her like an embrace.

Dale was waiting near the entrance, his face lighting up the moment he saw her.

"Alley! There's my favorite girl," he said, pulling her into a bear hug. His embrace radiated a quiet affection that came from history, not habit.

"How's life at the diner?"

"Eventful, as always," she said, laughing.

Dale chuckled. "Maggie says you keep that place running like clockwork. She's proud of you, you know."

Before Alley could respond, Steve's voice chimed in.

"I think I deserve some credit for keeping her sane."

Alley turned—and the rest of the room melted away.

Steve grinned, but his eyes shone with a tenderness only she could see.

She crossed and reached for him, looping her arms around his neck.

"Missed me, sweetheart?" he murmured.

"Like crazy," she teased.

Dale patted Steve on the back. "Leave her alone, son. She's had a long morning."

Maggie swept in, carrying a tray of sandwiches. Her eyes brightened when she saw Alley.

"Oh, look who it is! My long-lost best friend of five hours! Did you miss me?"

Alley laughed, hugging her back. "You were all I could think about."

"Well, obviously," Maggie beamed. "Now sit! You're just in time to grab the best sandwich before Dale hogs it."

The private dining room was set with thick sandwiches, steaming bowls of soup, and a decadent chocolate cake that practically glowed at the center of the table.

"You're spoiling her," Maggie teased.

"She deserves it," Steve said simply. "Besides, I've got a reputation to uphold."

"For what?" Dale asked. "Being a show-off?"

"For being a gentleman," Steve countered, winking at Alley.

Laughter bloomed easily, filling the room.

As the others talked, Alley found herself watching the way Dale leaned back in his chair, how Steve stole a second glance at her when he thought she wasn't looking, how Maggie snorted when she laughed too hard.

This—this warmth, this easy rhythm—wasn't something she took for granted. Not anymore.

Shadows still tugged at the corners of her thoughts, but in moments like this, she didn't feel broken.

She felt... chosen. Loved.

Maybe healing didn't come all at once. Maybe it came in pieces. Laughter. Soup. Sandwiches made with care.

The way someone said your name like they meant it.

She let herself soak it in.

Watching her from across the table, Dale felt something shift in his chest.

He'd seen survivors before—held their hands, studied their patterns, dissected their pain. But Alley... Alley was something else. Her progress wasn't clinical. It was human.

He thought of the new trauma team—their lectures and theories—and wondered if they would understand what it meant to witness this.

She still lived in the in-between—forgetting, remembering, healing in bits and pieces.

Her past was still a locked door. But her future, Dale thought, was starting to open—quietly, imperfectly, beautifully. And for now, that was enough.

Chapter 5

When the past walks in

It was a bustling evening at the Golden Oaks Diner, where orders flew fast and adrenaline pulsed through each step. Dinner shifts weren't Alley's usual territory; she preferred the quiet precision of mornings, where the pace was steady and the chaos predictable.

But tonight was different. It had the cursed energy of a Friday the 13th—everything that could go wrong did. And to her own annoyance, she'd been called in to help.

Maggie had accidentally booked two large parties for the same night—thinking one was scheduled for the following Friday. The double booking threw the schedule into chaos. The kitchen buzzed with frantic energy as cooks shouted orders back and forth, the clang of pots and pans punctuating the rising din.

"Table six needs their appetizers now!" Emmy hollered, balancing two trays as she navigated the narrow aisles.

"We're out of the special!" Adam called from the front. "What do I tell them?"

"Tell them the chef recommends literally anything else!" Alley shot back, her hands flying as she tied an apron around her waist. She rarely stayed for dinner shifts, but tonight, her absence wasn't an option.

To make matters worse, the oven was entirely occupied. Three cakes meant for the bookings had to be outsourced at the last minute, and Alley couldn't shake the nagging worry about whether they'd arrive on time.

"Where's the courier with the cakes?" she asked, scanning the flurry of activity. Her heart raced as she mentally calculated everything still left to do.

"Relax, boss," Emmy said as she passed by, her grin mischievous. "You've got this."

Alley forced a smile, but her shoulders remained tense. Nights like these reminded her of the unpredictability of the diner—how it could swing from cozy refuge to absolute chaos in the blink of an eye. Yet, as exhausting as it was, it also reminded her why she loved this place. It wasn't just a job; it was home.

The bell above the door jingled just as the clock struck 5 p.m. A gust of cool evening air swept in. Alley glanced up, barely registering the newcomers as she barked orders for fresh coffee and side dishes.

But then she paused, her eyes snagging on one of the groups stepping inside—a cluster of professionals in sharp blazers and badge lanyards, all chatting easily as they followed the hostess toward the back.

Alley's stomach did a weird little flip.

No. No, no, no. Not the TMT team.

Just then, the cake courier called to say that a car was parked in the docking area. Alley grimaced. It was hers. She ran out from the kitchen door and quickly parked the car at the far end of the guest parking area.

She walked briskly to the diner's entrance, navigating her way through a group of joyful people loading gifts from the baby shower party.

She saw a pregnant Stacy wearing a crown and a blue sash that read Mom-to-be. Alley smiled at the group and turned to head back inside.

But just before she reached the door, something flickered.

A flash—no more than a heartbeat—of someone placing a wreath of flowers on her head. Fingers brushing her hair. Laughter. Sunlight. Then gone.

She blinked, the present snapping back into focus.

Brushing the thought aside, she shoved through the kitchen doors, the diner's clatter drowning everything else.

She hurried inside, quickly passing the TMT table. Just as she reached the counter, she turned and noticed a man with a mop of curly hair making a toast. He looked up briefly, and their eyes met.

He froze. It was Berry Harper.

The words vanished before he could speak. The air shifted. Time stalled.

Seven years.

He stared, stunned, then darted instinctively to Jason across the diner—still halfway to the table, holding two menus. Jason had stopped in his tracks too, staring at her like he'd just seen the dead rise.

Was it really her? Berry's heart thudded painfully.

He looked back at Alley, whose face had gone pale. She gripped the counter like it was the only thing tethering her to the earth, her eyes wide and unblinking. The chaos of the diner faded into a surreal hush.

Alley felt sick, gripping the counter for dear life. She saw flashes of Stacy outside, laughing and loading the presents. Memory twisted, she was laughing—but not here, not now, with people she couldn't name in a place she could not place.

Berry set his glass down, the weight of the recognition propelling him forward. "Alley?" he said.

She looked at him, brows slightly drawn, eyes searching—but said nothing. Then, ignoring him, she turned and hurried into the kitchen. Emmy was screaming, and the gas-lit stoves seemed to be on fire.

Alley gasped, breath catching as she scurried back out. Just then, Dale Rivers came out of the restroom. Spotting Berry and Alley by the counter, he walked towards them. In his jovial voice, he said, "Ha, Dr. Harper! I see you met Alley. She's the lovely—" Dale's voice faltered as he caught sight of Alley's face.

The color drained from her face, her eyes wide, her breath uneven. "Alley?" he said more gently now, stepping forward, the shift in his tone immediate. "Are you alright?"

Alley's grip tightened on the counter as the world twisted and blurred. Greasy air filled her nostrils.

The diner's noise melted into a high-pitched whine in her ears. Her vision tunneled. A wave of brightness pulsed behind her eyes, spattering white blotches across her vision.

Then—boom. A blast, distant but deafening, cracked through her senses and dragged her back to smoke-filled corridors and shattered glass.

Her chest locked up. Time thickened. Panic surged—sharp, relentless. The room spun. Light fractured like shattering glass.

Someone called her name—Emmy? Dale? But it echoed from miles away, warped and watery. Her knees buckled.

And just before everything went black, her eyes locked onto a face across the room.

Jason.

The coffee cup in his hand slipped, shattering on the floor.

He didn't move. Couldn't.

Everything inside him muted as he faced the woman he'd spent seven years trying to forget.

Alley, his wife.

The woman who had disappeared without a word.

Now, she was collapsing in front of him.

And suddenly, the space around him felt hollow—like the oxygen had been pulled from the room.

Like a prayer, he whispered, "Alley."

The Golden Oaks, once a haven of routine and small-town comfort, would never sit quietly again—not until each piece of the story had surfaced, every truth had been named, and every secret unburied.

It had begun.

Chapter 6

Buried in silence

Emmy took charge instantly, her words sharp and clear above the chaos. "Call the EMTs!"

Dale was already beside Alley, checking her pulse. "She's stable," he said, calm but focused. As he leaned closer to examine a cut on her forehead, Jason saw something—barely visible beneath her hairline.

Scars. Thin and pale, trailing down her forehead. A chill gripped him.

Emmy lingered near Dale, casting him a glance. "Has she... remembered something?"

"We won't know until we assess her properly," Dale replied, not looking up.

The EMT arrived moments later, moving swiftly. One knelt to check vitals, and another unfurled the stretcher.

Jason stepped aside to give them space, though his eyes never left her.

"She's breathing on her own," one medic confirmed. "But her blood pressure's elevated—162 over 108."

They lifted her carefully. Jason stood rooted to the spot, the years pressing in on him all at once.

She looked fragile in a way that didn't fit his memory—her hair, her face, the way her fingers clutched the blanket. Everything felt familiar, yet slightly out of reach.

Then, as they moved her legs, something else: faint scarring along her soles. He didn't stare, but the sight caught in him like a splinter.

There was no time to ask. Just the sound of sirens.

As the ambulance doors shut, Dale climbed into his car. Berry and Jason followed quickly, engines firing in unison.

Jason stayed silent all the way to the hospital. And even then, the air felt thick in his lungs.

They rushed through the hospital's emergency entrance. Just past the automatic doors, a nurse stepped into their path, lifting a hand.

"We need five minutes," she said kindly. "Let us assess and change her clothing."

Further down the hall, Dale was on the phone, his back turned to the wall. His other hand pressed hard against the back of his neck.

Berry leaned against the wall, his hands buried deep in his coat. It had been seven years since he had seen her face, yet the impact landed like no time had passed.

He had seen the way her body curled inward, like she was shielding herself from a world too loud.

And then—A different Alley surfaced in his memory. Laughing over his stolen lunch tray during a med school shift.

"Told you not to leave your sandwich unattended!" she'd teased, hoisting it over her head like a trophy. "That's not a rule!" he'd shouted, chasing her down the hallway.

And later—Standing in the hospital chapel in Afghanistan, a radiant bride with no veil, no bouquet—just a hospital gown and a smile worth a million dollars. Jason had looked at her like he was the luckiest man in the world.

Berry blinked hard. "God, Alley," he murmured. "What… what happened to us?"

There was no answer.

Jason stood by the nurses' station, tension coiled through him. Nothing had prepared him for this.

Then—The sharp squeak of sneakers against polished tile, the low thud of hurried footsteps echoing down the passageway.

A tall man stormed in, flanked by an older woman. "Excuse me," the man said quickly. "The woman brought in by Dr. Dale—where is she?"

The nurse checked her chart. "Name of the patient?"

"Alley Rivers," the man said.

"And your name?"

"Steven Rivers."

The nurse tilted her head, eyes on the chart. "And your relationship?"

"I'm her husband."

Jason went still. The words hit the chest like a blunt force. He staggered back.

Husband?

The hospital lights blurred. The walls felt too close.

Berry's voice reached him, distant. "Jason? You okay?"

He couldn't respond.

Her husband. The word repeated, looping like static.

Berry gripped his shoulder, grounding him. "Breathe."

But Jason couldn't. He turned and stumbled to the restroom. The door slammed behind him.

He reached the sink just in time.

Berry followed, alarm written all over his face. "Jason? What's going on?"

Jason gripped the sink. "I don't know," he said—barely above a whisper. "I don't know."

Chapter 7

Between the silence

Hours passed in fragments—sirens, paperwork, and the sterile chill of waiting rooms steeped in disinfectant and dread. When the chaos dulled to a quiet hum, reality settled in like a weight. That's when the stillness began to speak louder than anything else.

That night, Alley lay motionless in the hospital room, her body pale under the dim glow of the monitoring equipment. A soft breeze carried in the scent of damp earth, settling gently into the still hospital air.

The steady beeping of the machines underscored the hush around her—familiar, clinical, and ominously calm. But beneath the sheets and the unyielding atmosphere, she held secrets—secrets that clung to her like shadows in the room.

Outside in the lobby, the lights blinked once before settling into a steady glow. Maggie sat stiffly at the edge of the bench, her hands folded. She kept glancing toward the hallway, then back at the floor, where the toe of her shoe tapped out a nervous, uneven rhythm.

Steve hunched beside her, elbows braced on his knees, gnawing at the inside of his cheek. His gaze was fixed on a scuffed tile, as if answers might rise from the grout. Between his feet, a forgotten cup of coffee sat cold. The silence wasn't calm. It hummed with words neither dared speak.

The quiet between them wasn't comfortable. It buzzed with questions neither wanted to ask aloud.

"She just collapsed," Maggie whispered.

Steve didn't lift his eyes. His jaw moved, slow and tight, chewing through tension. The scent of her perfume barely masked the sharp tang of antiseptic.

"Steve." The name trembled as it reached him. "She was doing so well…. Why now?"

"I don't know, Mom. I thought we were past this. I really did." He paused, the words catching. "She hasn't had a relapse in years."

Dale flipped through Alley's medical records down the hall, his face tense with focus. Labs. Neuro scans. Trauma notes. Each one a fragment. But the part that mattered—the piece locked behind memory's door—still held her hostage.

Berry and Jason sat quietly in the hospital parking lot, the cracked window letting in a breath of cool air.

The weight of the night settled between them, heavy and unspoken. Words felt useless—both too drained to speak. Only the distant wail of sirens broke the stillness.

"Jason," Berry said, voice low. "I just remembered something."

Jason turned, the tension in his frame undeniable. Exhaustion clouded his eyes. "What?"

"Last month, when I moved here... I was preparing for the trauma program. I met Dr. Dale Rivers. He mentioned a young woman—one of the toughest PTSD cases he'd seen. He was tracking her recovery."

Amber light slid across the dashboard as Jason leaned in, jaw clenched. "You think he meant Alley?"

Berry nodded. "It fits. The way he spoke. The way he looked at her."

Jason blinked. "PTSD?" The word hit harder than he expected. "Alley?" he said, the name catching in his throat.

Berry watched him closely. "You think it could be from Afghanistan?" His tone was quiet, gentle, not pressing.

Jason peered at the sidewalk but saw only the flash of fluorescent lights and the drip of crimson on the tile. The hospital hallways haunted him, replaying every echo of that fateful night in Afghanistan behind his eyes.

"The maternity ward was one of the first to be evacuated," he said, his voice low. "I remember watching the helicopters take off. The chaos."

Berry tilted his head. "But airlifting can still be traumatic. For someone not trained for war zones—"

"The rest of us—doctors, nurses—we've done this before. If Alley was part of that evacuation, it should've followed protocol. But something was off—something didn't add up."

"We know what to expect. It's chaotic, yes, but it's still managed."

He paused. "This doesn't make sense," he muttered, almost to himself. "Unless something else happened—something I never saw."

Berry didn't say it out loud, but the thought clung to him—Jason had already been to hell and clawed his way back. What if chasing the truth pulled him under all over again?

Jason shifted in his seat, his voice low. "I don't know, Berry. But I'm going to find out."

The stillness returned, thicker than before. Fingers tapped against the steering wheel, eyes fixed on the hospital entrance.

He couldn't stop seeing her face—the stunned hush, the scars he hadn't known were there.

He'd imagined arguments, shouted accusations, the string of old wounds ripped open.

Maybe even apologies—maybe forgiveness.

But not this silence.

What happened to you, Alley? The question sat heavy in his chest.

Chapter 8

No coincidence

By the time Jason came downstairs the next morning—fresh from the shower and a little more put together—the rich aroma of coffee filled the air. Eaton sat at the kitchen table, animatedly chatting with his grandmother, his hands slicing through the air in wide, excited gestures.

Jason leaned against the doorway, arms folded, taking in the scene with a flicker of warmth that didn't quite reach the tension in his shoulders.

Eaton spotted him first and straightened. "Hey, Dad. So… there's been a slight change of plans."

Jason raised an eyebrow. "Oh?"

Eaton glanced at Margaret. "Grandma says she's free to take me to the zoo today. And Grandpa really wants to see the giant dinosaur."

Margaret smirked over her coffee. "It's true. It's been too long since we had a day out with him."

Jason pretended to weigh it. "And school supplies? Didn't we say we'd tackle that today?"

Eaton grinned. "Dad, school's still six days away. Please?"

Jason let out a theatrical sigh. "My own son, ditching me for dinosaurs and Grandma."

Laughing, Eaton launched out of his chair and wrapped his arms around Jason's waist. "You're the best."

Jason ruffled his hair. "Go have fun."

Jason watched Eaton's excitement, but the name "Alley" echoed in his chest like a drumbeat he couldn't quiet. Not now. Not yet.

As Eaton dashed upstairs, Jason turned to his mother. Her expression had shifted—steadier now, tuned to his mood. He sank into the chair across from her, the warmth of the moment already fading.

"Thanks, Mom," he said. The words landed heavier than he expected, dragging grief and the memory of a name he hadn't stopped whispering in dreams.

Margaret studied him. "You okay?"

His jaw worked slightly. "Last night was… intense." He rubbed his face. "There's something I need to tell you. About Alley."

Margaret's fingers paused on her mug. "Alley? As in… your Alley?"

He met her gaze. "Yes."

Just then, Robert entered, newspaper tucked under his arm. He stopped short, sensing the tension. "What's going on?"

Jason leaned forward. "She's here—in town. I saw her at the dinner."

Margaret's eyes widened. Robert eased into a chair.

"She collapsed," Jason said. "There were scars. And… a man. He said he's her husband."

Margaret's hand flew to her chest. "Jason… are you sure?" she whispered, voice trembling with a certainty she dared not admit.

His voice cracked. "I'd know her anywhere. It's been seven years. But it was her."

She reached across the table, clasping his hand. "You searched for her for so long."

Then, barely above a whisper: "Why here? Why now?"

Jason looked away. "I've been asking the same thing."

Robert tapped the rim of his mug twice, then spoke. "People don't return to their ghosts for nothing. Even if they don't know what they're looking for."

Robert looked at him. "You said she had scars?"

His voice dropped, taut with memory. "They're on her feet. Deep. As if she'd walked through fire."

Footsteps thundered down the stairs—Eaton, full of life and light.

Jason rose, the cold bite of the keys pressing against his palm.

At the door, he hesitated, the weight of the moment anchoring him in place.

"There's a doctor. Dale Rivers. He treated her. He knows more."

Margaret's brow furrowed. "You trust him?"

"I don't know," Jason said. "But I need to find out."

And with that, he stepped into the sunlight, toward the truth hiding in shadow.

Chapter 9

Desert whispers

As the elevator ascended, Berry and Jason stood side by side, watching the hospital lobby fade below them. Nurses crossed paths, their shoes whispering across polished tiles. The occasional announcement pierced the hum, but none of it registered for Jason.

Sunlight spilled in through the glass—warm and inviting—yet it only deepened the disconnect he felt. The ordinariness of the morning grated against the storm building inside him.

He finally spoke. "We're going to get answers today."

Berry gave a short nod. "If anyone knows the full story, it's Dale."

They'd spent the early morning going over their questions like surgeons planning a delicate procedure. What did Dale know about Alley's past? Who was Steven really? What had triggered her collapse?

The elevator doors opened. The faint aroma of coffee and trimmed hedges drifted in. The administrative wing lay quiet, ordered, and cool beneath the fluorescent glow.

Jason's hands brushed against his jeans as he walked, a vain attempt to steady himself.

Dr. Dale Rivers' office door stood slightly ajar. Soft sunlight crept in at the edge of the blinds, casting geometric patterns on the floor. Dale looked up from a thick file as they approached and stood to greet them.

"Good to see you both," he said, gesturing toward the seats across from his desk. "Thanks for making time so early."

Jason sat down, the chair cool beneath him. "We assumed it was important."

"It is," Dale said. He pushed the papers aside. "This is about Alley."

Berry sat beside Jason, his posture more relaxed, but his eyes were sharp.

Dale clasped his hands on the desk. "I need your insight. She's been under my care for a few years, but there are still gaps I can't close."

Jason studied him. "We'll do what we can."

Dale nodded. "I've known Alley most of her life, even before she married my son. Her mother, Vicky, was close to my wife."

Married my son. The words struck Jason like a punch to the ribs. A cold knot formed in his gut. He met Dale's gaze directly. "What happened to her?"

Beside him, Berry's brow furrowed. "Wait—she's married to your son?" His voice dropped, confusion giving way to something heavier. "You mean...she's your daughter-in-law?"

Dale nodded as he set down the clipboard, his fingers brushing the edge. "Yes. She married Steve about five years ago. Alley didn't just witness war—she lived through it. And she lost more than I think she's ever said out loud."

"When she returned from Afghanistan, she was different. Sleep was impossible. Sounds—any sudden noise—would send her into a panic. Dropped trays. Raised voices. Even a laugh at the wrong pitch.

"And when she wasn't anxious, she was dissociating. Like she was in the room but not really present—watching it all from the outside."

Jason's hands pressed against his knees.

"There was something more," Dale added. "Not just the evacuation. She never talked about it clearly, but you could feel it—like she was always on the edge of something unspoken."

Berry shifted slightly, casting a glance Jason's way.

Dale glanced out the window. "She had nightmares. Woke up screaming for months.

Therapy didn't help much. Meds dulled the edges.

He met Jason's eyes. "She was finally steady. Until last night."

Jason pressed his fist lightly against his mouth.

Dusty, sharp-edged memories stirred—the desert, the noise, the loss.

He shifted uncomfortably. "What about the scars on her feet?"

Dale hesitated. "We don't know. My best guess is she got them during the evacuation, but she's never explained."

Dale continued. "Her family tried. But eventually, they brought her to us. And after months of therapy, medications, and check-ins, she improved. We even thought she'd stabilized."

His voice dropped. "Until last night."

Jason looked towards the far wall, but his focus was inward. Images flickered—her hand in his, then slipping away. Half-memory, half-ache. Would she ever remember him?

Jason's gaze moved to the far wall, his voice low. "Where are her parents now?"

Dale's expression dimmed. "Eric passed away a few years back—heart condition." He paused before adding, "Her mother, Vicky, moved to California after Alley's wedding—wanted to be closer to her grandkids."

Eric, Alley's dad. Jason met him in Kandahar when he'd been there briefly, visiting Alley while on a reporting assignment—sharp-witted, kind, the kind of man who always noticed when someone was hurting. Gone now.

Dale leaned forward. "Jason, if you have any insights into what might have caused this collapse, it would be a great help. We must be careful with how we approach her recovery."

Jason glanced at Berry.

Berry gave a slight nod, nothing more.

Jason leaned back, processing. Then, quietly, "I think I know why she fainted."

Dale looked at him closely. "Go on."

Berry shifted beside him but said nothing.

"We go way back," Jason said after a breath. "Boston. Med school. The three of us—me, Alley, and Berry."

Dale froze, absorbing the words.

"You're saying you knew Alley before she moved here?"

Jason nodded once.

Berry stepped in, his tone level. "Medical school forges strange families. We were close."

Dale leaned back, his gaze sharpening. "She never brought you up in sessions. And I wasn't in touch with her during med school."

Jason felt the blow in that. He didn't let it show.

Somewhere along the way—through treatment, recovery, marriage—she had slipped away from him.

Or maybe she'd simply forgotten first.

Dale gestured to a file on his desk. "She gave permission for her case to be studied last year. It's all here—PTSD, dissociative symptoms. But now I'm wondering if it's deeper."

The file sat between them. Jason looked at it, then looked away.

Dale stood and reached for his coat. "I have a meeting with her neurologist. Let's talk again tomorrow. I think this is just the beginning."

When the door closed behind him, the quiet that followed wasn't peaceful.

Berry reached for his coffee, watching Jason. "You kept it vague. That's probably wise."

Jason stared at the folder. Alley Rivers. A name once full of promise—now heavy with everything he didn't know how to fix.

Chapter 10

A familiar stranger

Alley's eyes fluttered open, her vision blurred by the glow of overhead lights. A rhythmic beeping filled the air, blending with faint strains of instrumental music. The scent of lavender hand wash and freshly laundered sheets rooted her in the present.

Her limbs were heavy, uncooperative—but she was awake.

Footsteps approached. A nurse leaned over, her lips curved in welcome—the first clear shape Alley could register.

"Welcome back, Alley." Her tone was steady and kind, like a lighthouse cutting through fog. "We've been waiting for you."

Alley blinked, confusion edging into her awareness.

Dale, seated in the corner, rose at the sound of the nurse's voice. His usual composure faltered as he stepped closer, eyes damp with relief.

"Welcome back," he said, his voice unsteady. "We've all been so worried about you."

Alley turned her head slightly, her lips parting to speak—but no sound came. The effort drained her.

Dale squeezed her hand. "It's alright. Don't push yourself. You're safe."

The neurologist entered with a clipboard, his manner calm and practiced.

"Good to see you awake, Ms. Rivers," he said, reviewing her chart. "Let's start with something simple."

He crouched beside her bed. "Can you tell me your name?"

"...Alley," she whispered.

"And your full name?"

A pause, then clearer. "Alley Rivers."

Dale's shoulders eased.

He gave a nod. "I'll let Steve and the rest know."

In the hallway, Steve stood with Maggie and Emmy. When Dale appeared, their attention snapped to him.

"She's awake," he said, his voice rougher than expected. "She's conscious."

Maggie gasped, covering her mouth as tears welled up. Steve let out a long breath, pulling her into an embrace.

Relief spread through the group like a wave.

"When can we see her?" Steve asked, his voice thick with hope.

Dale rested his hand on his son's shoulder. "The neurologist's running some checks. Give it fifteen minutes."

Steve nodded, gaze lingering on the doors ahead, something unreadable flickering across his face.

"Thanks, Dad," he said quietly. There was more in the words than gratitude.

Dale gave his shoulder a reassuring squeeze before stepping back. Maggie dabbed at her tears while Dale's focus lingered on the door. Something still gnawed at him.

The way she passed out.

Even with the reassurance of seeing her awake, the unease remained—a quiet whisper that the past had resurfaced.

He turned to Maggie and Steve. "We'll get through this," he said. The words were meant for them—but he needed them, too.

Minutes later, the nurse returned. "You can go in now. She's a little groggy, but I think you'll be a good remedy."

The moment Alley saw them. Energy surged back into her. Her eyes found theirs like anchors in a storm.

Dale stepped aside to text Jason and Berry: She's awake.

Steve approached the bed, pausing. "Will I hurt her if I hug you?" he asked the nurse.

She smiled. "Here, we prescribe hugs more than meds."

Alley propped herself up, wincing. "Headache."

"It'll fade soon," Dale told her.

Alley's brow creased. "What happened? Why did I black out?"

Dale hesitated. "All your scans are normal. For now, focus on rest."

Steve took her hand. Emmy offered fruit, and Maggie adjusted her pillows.

"Mags, I'm fine," Alley rasped.

"You collapsed at work," Maggie replied, blinking through tears. "Let me be a little dramatic."

Alley gave a faint sigh. "Sorry."

Steve spoke gently. "You have nothing to be sorry for. We're just glad you're okay."

At the foot of the bed, Dale shrugged. "Let her fuss. It's easier than being her next target."

A fleeting ripple of relief touched Alley's features, then Dale grew serious.

"Whatever caused this," he said, "we'll go carefully. No rushing."

Alley frowned. "You think something triggered it?"

Dale glanced briefly at Steve, then returned to her. "Could be stress. Or something else. Let's not jump ahead."

But the word relapse echoed in Alley's mind. Her pulse skittered, a jolt of fear chasing through her before she could catch her breath.

Not again.

Her hands clenched the blanket. A shadow moved through her—old shame, unnamable but familiar.

A face formed in her memory—vague but recognizable. A voice she couldn't place. It flashed, then vanished.

She froze. Dale noticed the change—the narrowing of her eyes, the shift in her expression.

"What is it?" he asked, his tone calm.

Alley kept her gaze on the window. "I saw someone. I don't know who. But I think I should."

The room held still.

Dale leaned in slightly. "A memory?"

"I think so," the words wavering like the memory. "But it's like reading underwater—I almost have it, then it's gone."

"It disappears," she said, barely above a whisper, her tone edged with disbelief.

Dale nodded. "That's okay. Don't chase it. These things return in pieces. You remembered something—that's important."

Turning slightly toward the window, she stared out at the mountains. They rose like quiet sentinels against the dusk, their jagged lines softening beneath a wash of lavender light. Beautiful, she thought distantly, like Afghanistan.

The name came out of nowhere.

Afghanistan?

She stilled—but the thought dissolved before she could grasp it. A flicker of something just beyond memory, fading before she could hold on.

Dale watched, noting each subtle shift—the tension, the searching look in her eyes.

If it happened after seeing classmates...

His mind turned over the details. It wasn't just the collapse. It was who she'd seen. The timing.

Could it be recognition?

He couldn't be sure.

Trauma could bury memories, but it also let them surface—unexpected and sharp. A familiar laugh, a passing voice, a scent—tiny cues that nudged open long-shut doors.

But seeing classmates?

That was something.

Whether it was healing or warning, Dale didn't yet know.

As the music drifted on, he slipped back into the ward, already mapping out his next move.

Because if they were going to help her recover—

They needed to be ready for what would surface next.

Jason rose from his chair in the corner of his office, stepping toward the window. The sky had shifted—dusky now, streaks of gray and lavender stretching across the horizon. Behind him, Berry stood too, sensing the change in the air.

"Think Dale will talk to us today?" he asked.

Jason nodded, his voice low. "He said he would."

A pause.

"Then we better be ready," Berry said, already reaching for his coat.

Jason stayed still for a moment.

His hand rested briefly against the window frame, fingers tensing ever so slightly.

Because deep down, he already knew: If Alley was starting to remember—even fragments—They weren't just chasing answers. They were stepping back into a past that still had sharp edges.

And the past never returned gently.

Chapter 11

The morning that changed everything

The office settled into its usual background hum—the faint whisper of the vents and leaves rustling outside. Sunlight filtered through half-closed blinds, casting a warm glow across the room as branches swayed beyond the window.

Jason sat quietly, the first hints of autumn in the air—crisp and lean.

The rich aroma of coffee lingered. Medical charts, test results, and scans from Dale's email lay scattered across his desk—untouched since the text arrived.

He stared at the message that had been there for several minutes, its weight already pressing into him.

She's awake.

His fingers hovered for a moment before he finally typed a short reply:

"Thank you, Dale. Please keep me updated."

The door creaked open, and Berry stepped inside, balancing two coffee cups. Steam curled into the cooling evening air. He'd swapped his summer shirt for a light gray sweater, a concession to the dropping temperatures.

"You heard?" Berry asked, setting a cup on the desk.

Jason didn't move—the soft phone light accentuating the tension in his jaw. Berry sipped his coffee. The office felt calm but heavy—like the hush before a cold front rolls in.

"What's up?" he asked, voice low.

Jason said nothing. His grip on the phone tightened—as if she might vanish again the moment he released it.

Berry leaned in, concern knitting his brow. He'd seen the message from Dale earlier—but now Jason's expression had changed subtly, as though the words had carved deeper into him.

No need to read it again.

"It's hitting you now, isn't it?"

Jason said nothing, eyes fixed on the glowing screen. "Yeah," he said, barely above a whisper. "Because if Dale's right... she might be remembering."

Berry leaned back, offering silence instead of words, giving Jason space to steady himself.

Even the crisp air couldn't ease the weight pressing down on him. "She looked right through me."

The words landed flat—saying them only made the hurt sink deeper.

"Like I was no one."

He looked out the window, eyes unfocused.

"She doesn't remember college. Us. Anything from before..." He hesitated, eyes narrowing. "Is it just Afghanistan she's lost? Or everything that came before it?"

He blinked, almost shaking his head, as if voicing it might make it real.

He watched a leaf drift past the window. "Does she even remember giving birth?"

His voice was composed, and the words tasted foreign on his tongue—like speaking them made everything more real.

Berry let out a low whistle, shaking his head.

"Damn. That's rough."

He tilted his head, considering. "I mean, I'd joke about how it must be nice to get a fresh start with someone who forgot all your mistakes, but... this? This is different."

A tired nod was all the answer he got. "Yeah."

Berry tapped his fingers on his knee, the office clock ticking in the hush of the room.

Outside, a single red leaf scraped the glass before it spiraled downward. A breath of cool autumn air slipped through the slightly open vent.

Berry broke the silence. "So... how are you holding up?"

He brushed his fingertips across his cheek, catching the rough scratch of newly grown stubble.

"Not sure yet."

Berry watched Jason's shoulders hunch, and dread coiled in his stomach.

Seven years ago, he'd watched Jason unravel once before. And the look on his friend's face now? It was disturbingly familiar.

Berry leaned forward, eyes narrowing. "You've thought about what this means. For you... And for Eaton?"

A slight shift, a single bounce of his knee—then stillness. He opened his mouth, then shut it again, the words catching somewhere unspeakable, as he looked past Berry to the blinds.

Whatever he'd meant to say slipped away, swallowed by the weight of it all.

Berry continued, quieter now, but firm. "If she remembers... or even if she doesn't—this won't be clean. It's not just about finding answers. This brings everything back. For her, for you... for your son."

That look in Berry's eyes felt like a challenge. "Are you ready for that kind of shift? Because whatever happens next, Eaton's world will change too."

Jason's fists tightened on his knees—his body preparing for a truth he wasn't sure he wanted to hold.

He opened his mouth, then closed it again. Finally, his voice came, low and rough.

"I—I thought I had answers."

Silence.

"I don't."

His shoulders slumped, the weight of his own admission pressing down.

A few moments of thick silence passed. Suddenly, the truth hit him, sharp and undeniable.

"I'm scared."

Berry reached over and gently tapped his friend's shoulder.

He leaned back, the warning unspoken but understood. The past wasn't merely creeping back into Jason's life. It was about to rewrite it.

Outside, the office hummed with the familiar sounds of phones ringing, keyboards clacking, and conversations buzzing around him, but Jason barely registered any of it.

Memories stirred—the echo of her laughter, the curve of her lips. He could still picture her face, soft with vulnerability. When she got nervous, she'd twirl the bracelet around her wrist.

She didn't remember. He'd known it—but somehow hearing it, seeing it—cut deeper than he ever thought possible.

Chapter 12

Yesterday's price

Steve didn't like how his father sounded on the phone—measured, cautious, like he was bracing for impact. Now, standing just outside Dale's office, Steve felt a flicker of unease tightening in his chest.

Maggie stood beside him, her brow furrowed with the same concern. The air carried the aroma of brewed coffee and pine-scented disinfectant—too clean, too calm, like the pause before a storm.

Inside, Dale sat behind his desk, folders open but untouched.

"Come in," he said, rising to greet them.

"What is it?" Steve asked, his tone a blend of curiosity and something closer to dread. "You said you had good news."

"I do," Dale replied. "But it comes with complications."

Dale gestured toward the sofa.

The room was filled with the subtle scents of late August, evoking a sense of nostalgia and transition. The smell of roasted beans hung in the air, offering a quiet comfort amid the unease.

Steve raised an eyebrow, exchanging a glance with Maggie before settling into the seat. "Good news sounds great. What is it?"

Dale paused, his expression thoughtful.

"Alley might be regaining her memory."

Both Maggie and Steve stared at him, their expressions shifting from surprise to cautious optimism.

"That's incredible!" Maggie exclaimed, a note of relief in her tone. "But what's the catch?"

Steve's face mirrored her sentiment. "Yeah, Dad, why does it sound like you're still worried?"

Before Dale could respond, a knock on the door interrupted the conversation.

"Come in," Dale called.

The door swung wide. Jason moved in, reserved and steady; Berry trailed him, brows lifted in polite greeting.

Dale rose from his seat. "Steve, Maggie, this is Dr. Carter and Dr. Harper. Doctors, meet my son, Steve, and my wife, Maggie. I asked Dr. Carter and Dr. Harper to observe and advise. They specialize in trauma and memory-related recovery. I've seen what they can do in similar cases."

Steve stood, extending his hand with warmth. "It's a pleasure to meet you both. Dad mentioned your work. Alley's very lucky to have you."

Jason returned the handshake with a nod. "Thank you. We're honored to help."

Jason and Berry exchanged a glance, both aware from experience how quickly cases like this could spiral if pushed too hard.

It was Steve who spoke first, his words gently breaking the stillness.

"Dad says Alley's regaining her memory will come with complications. Dr. Carter, what are we looking at here?"

Fingers drumming lightly against his notebook, Jason hesitated before speaking—his voice steady, deliberate.

"Recovering memories isn't just remembering," he said.

"It's understanding what they mean.

He rubbed his palms together, as though weighing his next words.

For Alley, it means facing the trauma that caused her amnesia. If too much comes back too fast, it could overwhelm her—flashbacks, panic, even suicidal thoughts. It's all on the table."

"And it's not just the emotional impact," Berry added. "Regaining repressed memories can disrupt her identity.

Alley might struggle to reconcile who she is now with who she used to be. And it could strain relationships—especially if those memories bring unresolved pain."

A glance passed between Jason and Berry, their expressions weighted with quiet understanding.

"This isn't something we can rush. Alley will need time, guidance—and a strong support system to make sense of what comes back."

Steve looked up, fingers tightening around the armrests. What if those memories don't just come back... but take everything we've built?

He remembered the way she'd found her footing in Apple Creek—not quickly, not easily, but with quiet, determined steps.

The long walks. The slow trust. The way she started laughing again—not because she remembered who she was, but because she had space to become someone new.

He wasn't afraid of what she might remember.

He was scared those memories would pull her away—and leave him behind.

What if the recovery she'd worked so hard for began to unravel? What if the past didn't just come back—it pulled her under?

He just wanted her to stay whole.

"And what about us?" he asked, voice low. "What's our role in all this?"

"You are the support system. What she needs most is safety—familiar faces that won't push, but won't disappear either."

"Be patient. Be understanding. And most importantly, let her set the pace. The memories will come when she's ready to face them—not when we are."

Dale nodded, his expression resolute. "We need to proceed carefully. Alley's well-being comes first."

As the meeting wrapped up, the gravity of the situation settled over them. Each person carried the weight of what lay ahead, knowing that the road to recovery would be long and fraught with challenges.

Alley's memories were returning, but whether they would heal or break her was a question none of them were ready to answer.

But beneath it all, the implications of unraveling these memories remained uncertain—a force that could change their lives forever.

Chapter 13

The boy by the fish tank

Eaton Carter had more important things to do than answer the phone—like deciding which miniature race cars would win the championship today. But when the phone rang in the living room, he skidded into the hallway, picked up the receiver, and grinned. "Hi, Dad!

"Humm... Why? Mmmmm... When? With Grandma? Let me think... hmmm okay, Bye!" Hanging up, he looked as though he had just solved a major world crisis.

Bounding up the stairs, he nearly collided with Margaret as she stepped out of her room. "Your dad called—" she began, but Eaton waved her off.

"Yeah, I talked to him! He wants us to go to the hospital for the school thingy. He'll meet us there. You know, vaccinations! They say it's to help us live longer, but I think it's just a trick to round up kids once a year."

From the living room, his grandpa called out, "Do you know what a vaccination is, buddy?"

Eaton grinned mischievously. "Of course! It's like getting a superhero shot to protect me from germs! I mean, why else would they call it a shot? I'm basically getting my own cape!"

"Grandma, can I wear my special clothes?" he asked, flinging open his closet like a pint-sized fashion mogul.

"You're going to get shots, not an award!" his grandpa teased. "Besides, you're meeting your pediatrician, not a casting director!"

Striking a dramatic pose in the doorway, Eaton announced, "I just want to look sharp! You never know when you might meet girls from school. Or what if the pediatrician is..." He winked playfully and spun on his heel.

Margaret chuckled, rolling her eyes. "Good luck with that, Romeo," she teased as she herded him downstairs.

The hospital parking lot was alive with activity as Margaret and Eaton stepped out of the car. Clutching her hand, Eaton swung his "emergency snack pouch" in the other. "Grandma, do you think the doctor will give me a sticker? Last time, I only got a lollipop. Stickers are forever, you know."

Margaret stifled a laugh. "If you behave, I'm sure you'll get both."

As they entered the hospital, Eaton marveled at the bustling hallways. "It's like a superhero headquarters in here," he said, tugging Margaret's sleeve. "All these people are saving lives! Do you think I could be a doctor, Grandma?"

"You'd make a fantastic doctor, Eaton," she said warmly. "You've already got the confidence."

Eaton was immediately captivated by a fish tank located near the waiting area after arriving at the pediatric wing. "Look at that one!" he said, pointing at a bright orange fish darting through the water. "It's like Nemo, but cooler!"

While Margaret headed to the receptionist to fill out forms, Eaton stayed by the tank, entranced by the colorful fish. He noticed a woman on the other side of the tank watching the same fish. She watched, calm and reflective.

"Hi!" Eaton called cheerfully, his voice rising above the hubbub of the foyer.

"Are you here to get a vaccination?"

Alley turned, momentarily surprised but amused by the boy's boldness. Crouching slightly to his level, she smiled. "No, not quite. I'm here for something else. But what about you? Is this a special visit to the pediatrician?"

"Yeah!" Eaton exclaimed. "It's for a school thing—vaccinations. My dad says it's so we live longer, but honestly, I think it's just a trick to make me eat more green stuff. Especially broccoli." He wrinkled his nose.

"That's a very interesting theory."

Eaton's eyes wandered to the wristband on her arm. "Hey, do they give you wristbands instead of stickers when you come here?" he asked with wide-eyed curiosity.

Alley glanced at her wristband, her eyes lighting up.

"You could say this is my grown-up version of a sticker."

He gasped. "No way! Stickers are way cooler. Grown-ups don't know what they're missing." He paused, squinting at her name tag. "Alley Rivers? That's your name?"

"It is," Alley said, nodding. "And what's yours?"

"Eaton. Eaton Carter. We just moved here," he replied proudly.

That glint of amusement stayed in her gaze—until tension crept into her expression.

"Eaton Carter," Alley echoed, the name lingering on her lips. A glimmer of recognition stirred behind her eyes—too fleeting to grasp. She blinked.

Why did that name sound so familiar?

But the thought slipped through her fingers before she could catch it.

Just then, Margaret returned.

"Eaton, are you bothering the young lady?" she asked, her tone a mix of concern and amusement.

A gentle warmth spread across Alley's features.

"Not at all. He's been a delightful distraction."

Eaton's eyes danced with mischief.

"Grandma, I was just talking to her because she looks so pretty!"

A low chuckle escaped Alley, brightening the moment. Across the hall, Emmy and Maggie paused mid-signature, exchanged amused glances as they finished the discharge papers.

The receptionist called out, "Eaton Carter," breaking the moment.

"That's me!" Eaton said excitedly. He turned to Alley with a parting fist bump. "Hope you get a sticker next time!"

Alley smiled and matched his fist without hesitation. Their knuckles tapped in a hushed rhythm—fleeting, innocent, but to Jason, who had just stepped into the hallway, it reverberated like a bell in a cathedral.

"I'll try," Alley replied softly as Eaton turned and slipped away with Margaret into the pediatric wing.

She lingered by the fish tank, the encounter leaving her unusually buoyant. Emmy looped an arm through hers. "What's with that spark in your eyes?" she teased.

Alley pressed her lips together for a moment. "I just met a boy… Eaton Carter. His name felt strangely familiar." She murmured it again, letting the syllables roll off her tongue like puzzle pieces, the sound stirring something deep inside her—just out of reach, yet impossible to ignore.

Jason hadn't expected their paths to overlap here. He'd tried to avoid a clash with Alley's discharge, but Eaton's school had picked today for vaccinations—no rescheduling allowed. She wasn't supposed to be in the pediatric wing. And yet, here she was.

He stopped in the doorway.

For a moment, the beeping monitors, the nurses' footsteps, even the worry he'd been carrying for days—none of it reached him.

His son.

Meeting Alley.

He just watched.

Allowing himself to hope—not for the past to return, but for something new to begin.

Chapter 14

Ghosts of the present

Jason settled onto the porch, the early-September air draping him like a well-worn shawl—mesquite and cool dusk mingling in his lungs.

Inside, Margaret's teaspoons tapped porcelain in a gentle Morse code as chamomile steeped with honey's warmth.

"You've been quiet since the hospital," Margaret called, voice low—equal parts question and invitation.

He joined them at the kitchen table, fingertips grazing the grain worn smooth by years of family dinners. He rubbed the nape of his neck, a guilty habit. "I have to tell you about the woman Eaton saw this morning."

Margaret's mug halted halfway to her lips. "Yes?"

"That woman... It was Alley." The kettle's hiss died.

Her fingers locked around the cup. "After all this time?"

He flicked a stray lock of hair behind his ear. "She's thinner, hair cropped short, but it's her." His throat closed. "Dale calls it dissociative amnesia."

Margaret let out a tremulous breath. "All those years... gone."

Jason bowed his head. He'd built his life as a single dad—bedtime stories, pancakes, science fairs—a fortress. Now it felt like quicksand.

"I need to know what shattered her in Afghanistan," he said, voice rough. "What snapped the thread that should have led her home to Eaton?" His thumb brushed a chip in the table's edge.

"And Eaton still thinks Mom's off saving strangers. I dread telling him she's back..." He trailed off. "Then I dread what he'll see when she looks at him."

He pictured Eaton bounding down the hall, laughter chasing his toy car's whir—only to find an empty room.

The image knotted his chest. Robert laid a steady hand on his shoulder. Margaret leaned closer, voice calm but unyielding. "We'll face that day together."

Outside, the wind ruffled the mesquite leaves in a hush of expectation.

Alley is here.

Jason drew in a slow breath. He'd stand between his son and the woman who'd forgotten them—shielding Eaton if memory failed, guiding Alley if it returned. Hope still hurt, but it lived. And Jason wasn't letting go.

Chapter 15

The weight of the truth

Berry and Jason sat at a table by the hospital's coffee shop window, their eyes drawn to the trees outside. The leaves, touched by the early hues of autumn, shifted gently in the breeze.

The two men remained silent, lost in thought.

The barista arrived with their orders, placing two steaming cups of coffee on the table. As steam rose from the cups, the aroma settled gently between them—brief comfort in a restless moment.

Berry wrapped his hands around his cup while Jason stared into his, his face tight with contemplation.

"My parents think I should come clean with Dale," he said suddenly, his voice steady but edged with conflict. "Just lay everything out and let the chips fall where they may."

Berry glanced up, his brow furrowing as he studied Jason. "And what do you think?"

His hand hovered over the table, then dropped flat against it, tension flickering through his posture. "I don't want to complicate things. Not for Dale, not for Steve—and definitely not for Alley. What if Steve cuts me off completely? From her, from her treatment? Right now, it feels like I'm the only one who can really help her."

Berry tilted his head thoughtfully, setting his coffee down. "And what if Alley's memories return and they find out you've been lying to them about who you are?"

He said nothing—just a pause that said it all.

"That's what keeps me up at night."

"What if?"

The weight of his words lingered between them, pressing down like an invisible force. Jason stared out of the window, watching as the wind stirred the amber and crimson leaves. For a moment, neither man spoke.

Berry waited a moment before speaking. "Jason, you can't keep carrying this alone. Keeping it a secret won't make it go away. Maybe it's time to face it head-on."

The pause hung heavy. Speaking meant digging into a part of his life he'd long buried—like prying open a scar barely healed. Those years didn't return as memories, not fully. Just flashes. Glimpses.

If helping Alley meant returning to that place, he would. He'd face one truth at a time, no matter how much it hurt.

The café door swung open, drawing their attention. Dr. Sheila Raj stepped in with quiet authority, her back straight and chin lifted, her movements measured and precise.

Her dark hair was tied back in a high ponytail, not a strand out of place, mirroring the crisp professionalism of her tailored blazer. Yet the slight tilt of her head and the gentle curve of her lips hinted at the warmth beneath her sharp composure.

Dr. Raj was renowned in the field of PTSD, with a career spanning decades.

She had spent years working in war zones, helping individuals navigate trauma under the most extreme conditions. Her expertise in dissociative amnesia, post-traumatic stress, and complex trauma made her an invaluable part of Jason and Berry's trauma management team.

Today, she was here to help them chart a path forward for Alley.

Jason stood as she approached, extending his hand. "Dr. Raj, thank you for meeting us on such short notice."

She shook his hand firmly, offering a warm smile. "Of course, Jason. When you mentioned the urgency, I knew it was important. Trauma doesn't wait, and neither should we."

Berry gestured for her to sit, and she joined them at the table, setting her notebook down. "Now," she began, her voice calm but focused, "let's talk about Alley. Tell me everything I need to know."

A flicker of hope passed between him and Berry. They laid everything out over the next two hours—and six cups of coffee. Dr. Raj took notes with quiet precision, occasionally pausing to ask pointed questions or clarify a detail. Her pen moved steadily across the page, capturing not just the facts but the weight beneath them.

When they'd finished, Dr. Raj leaned back in her chair, folding her hands over her notebook. "So," she said, calm but deliberate, "you want my opinion on whether you should tell Dr. Dale about your past with Alley?"

A nod from Jason. His shoulders had gone rigid, bracing for whatever came next.

She adjusted her glasses, eyes steady. "Can I be honest with you?"

"Of course," he said—though the slight tremble in his voice gave him away.

"From an ethical standpoint, you owe Dr. Dale and Steve the truth." Her tone stayed even. "Unfortunately, the lines here are blurred—Dr. Dale, while a brilliant physician, is also Alley's father-in-law, and that dual role complicates everything. I understand why you hesitate."

Dr. Raj leaned forward, her tone calm but firm. "If it were up to me, I'd tell Dr. Dale everything. Lay out your case. If he knows anything about Alley's life after Afghanistan—something you don't—that knowledge could shape her treatment in ways we can't afford to miss. Especially since, based on what you've told me, there's no clear reason why she would've left you and Eaton by choice."

His shoulders sagged, the truth of her words settling deep.

"As for Steve," Dr. Raj continued, "it's true that he could react defensively. But patient confidentiality could work in your favor here. Before making any final decisions, I'd recommend sitting down with Dale and discussing how best to navigate this without compromising Alley's care—or her trust."

Berry nodded, thoughtful. "That makes sense. Jason, this is bigger than just you or Alley. It's about giving her the best chance to heal."

Eyes dropping to the table, Jason let their words settle. "I just want her to have the chance she deserves."

Dr. Raj offered a reassuring nod. "That's all any of us can do. The truth may be difficult, but it's often the first step toward healing. For Alley—and for you."

He stared into his now-cold coffee, his thumb tracing a slow line along the mug's handle.

The truth may be difficult.

But it was the first step toward healing—

For Alley.

For Eaton.

For himself.

The burden hadn't lifted, yet it no longer anchored him—and suddenly the path forward felt sure.

It was waiting.

Chapter 16

When the truth plays peek-a-boo

Jason and Berry stepped into Dale's office the next morning, their postures resolute, expressions unreadable. They carried the weight of the truth—both determined and uncertain about what might follow.

Dale greeted them warmly, his face lighting up as he motioned toward the chairs in the conference room adjoining his office.

Shoulders squared, eyes dulled by a weariness he no longer tried to mask, Jason clutched his coffee like a lifeline—fingers curled a little too tightly around the paper cup. His whole body was taut, bracing for something he hadn't yet found words for.

The room was cozy, lined with bookshelves of medical texts and family photos—a quiet reminder of the personal stakes at play. Outside, the autumn sun cast a pale light through the window, illuminating frost-kissed branches while a gentle rustle of wind stirred the leaves.

They sat. hands clasped, Jason leaned forward, heart thudding in the stillness of the room.

"Dale, we have to share more with you about Alley—things that are important for her care."

Dale's curious expression turned serious. "Of course. Whatever it is, you can trust me."

"The information we're about to share," Berry added cautiously, "has to stay confidential."

Measuring his words carefully, Jason said, "Alley and I weren't just colleagues from med school. We worked side by side—volunteering in war zones and natural disasters, places most people avoid. We were a team."

Dale's eyes narrowed slightly, but he stayed silent, letting the words unfold.

Leaning back, he spoke in a quieter cadence, like the words were meant for memory, not the room.

"We fell in love, Dale. We wanted to see the world, change it, even. Alley had these wild, beautiful dreams—so much she needed to do before settling down. But then one day…"

He paused, gaze drifting as if reaching for something half-lost in memory. When he spoke again, it was almost a whisper.

"Everything changed."

He could still see her, clear as day, standing in the dim light of their small Afghan apartment, looking pale and disoriented after dinner. The memory flooded back, vibrant yet haunting, as if the walls of the room were closing in on him.

"Are you okay, Al?" he had asked, his concern unmistakable as she hurriedly excused herself to the bathroom. He'd followed, hovering just outside the door as the unmistakable sound of nausea reached him.

"I think it's the fish," Alley had groaned, her face half-buried in the couch cushions.

He grabbed a damp towel and draped it gently around her neck, then handed her a ginger ale. The hiss of bubbles rising from the can broke the heavy stillness in the room.

She took a sip before leaning her head against his lap. "I feel so dizzy," she murmured, her eyes half-closed.

His hand moved gently through her hair until Alley jolted upright, eyes wide, panic etched across her face as she stared at him.

"Oh no," she said, standing abruptly. "Take me to the pharmacy. Now."

He blinked, confused by her sudden urgency. "The pharmacy? What's going on?"

"Just drive!" Alley snapped, her tone edged with urgency as she grabbed her bag, movements almost frantic.

Still trying to make sense of it all, he followed her. The drive to the hospital pharmacy passed in a haze—the world outside a shifting blur of motion and light. Alley rushed inside the moment they arrived, leaving him in the car, fingers drumming anxiously on the steering wheel.

When she returned, clutching a paper bag, her face was unreadable.

"Home. Quick," she said, her tone clipped.

He gave up asking questions, nervous laughter bubbling in his throat as he started the car, the engine's rumble filling the empty space between them.

Once home, Alley darted into the bathroom without a word, shutting the door firmly behind her. Left standing in the hallway, he pressed a hand against the door, helpless. "Alley, can you tell me what's going on?" he asked, the tension in his tone unmistakable as he stood just outside the door.

"No!" came her muffled reply. "I mean, yes. I mean... I don't know!"

He chuckled nervously. "Can I at least come in?"

After a brief pause, the door creaked open. He stepped inside cautiously, eyes locking onto the six pregnancy tests lined up on the bathroom counter—stark white against the muted tiles.

He picked one up, staring at it in disbelief. The thin plastic stick trembled slightly in his grasp, its result window unmistakable. For a moment, everything else dropped away—just him, that tiny life-altering symbol between them. He looked up, his eyes locking with Alley's—and for a second, the rest of the world dropped away.

She stood frozen, her expression a storm of emotion—fear, vulnerability, defiance, hope—all warring across her face. Her hands were clenched at her sides, and her lips parted slightly, as if she was about to explain... or apologize... or run.

"Is this real? Does this mean... we're going to be parents?" The words cracked slightly, laced with surprise, joy, and disbelief.

Alley nodded, her expression caught between excitement and apprehension. "Jay, we said we'd wait three years."

A wide grin spread across his face as he pulled her into his arms and lifted her off the ground. "Looks like nature had other plans."

"Jay, stop!" she protested, laughing despite herself. He set her down gently, brushing a strand of hair from her face. But the laughter faded as reality settled between them.

"We're in Afghanistan." Her voice thinned with disbelief. "We've still got two years left on our contract—how can we have a baby here?"

Jason cupped her face, anchoring her with the steadiness in his eyes.

"We'll figure it out, Al. We always do."

Alley looked at him, her eyes wide and uncertain. "This wasn't part of the plan."

He smiled and ran a thumb along her cheek. "We didn't plan this," he murmured, eyes locked on hers. "But maybe it's what we needed."

He fell silent mid-sentence, the end of his words lost in the air. He stayed still, fingers splayed on the table, as though bracing against the past. His focus wandered to a memory only he could see.

He didn't say anything right away.

"That was the beginning of everything for us."

Dale sat with his fingers interlaced firmly on the table, his expression unreadable. He looked at Berry, who gave a subtle nod—quiet confirmation of Jason's account.

Straightening in his seat, Jason met Dale's eyes. "I know this changes things. I know it complicates her care, and I don't want to do anything that would harm her progress. But you needed to know."

Dale pressed his fingers together, as if weighing the words in his palms. A flicker of warmth crossed his face, yet the storm beneath it remained. Finally, after what felt like an eternity, he nodded.

"Thank you for telling me. This… this changes everything."

No one said another word. The truth had already taken its place between them, solid and undeniable. Relief crept in, his pulse still drumming from the confession.

He hadn't realized the weight he carried until it finally shifted—shared at last.

Chapter 17

When the wall tears

Dale leaned back in his chair, rubbing his temple, his sharp mind piecing together the fragmented details. They knew she had lost her baby in Afghanistan—a tragedy she had carried all these years.

"She always referred to him as 'Jay.' And Vicki, her mom did too, once or twice... but it was always just a name. No details. And whenever we said it around Alley, she'd shut down. Withdraw. We assumed Jay was someone who hurt her... not someone she loved."

He glanced at Jason, the realization settling like a stone in his chest.

Dale sat rigid, shoulders tense, as if bracing against an unexpected wave. The office—familiar and orderly just moments before—now felt altered, reshaped by Jason's words.

Until now, he had seen Alley through the lens of her trauma—a patient trapped in gaps of memory, cut off from everything that once defined her.

But this... this was something no file had recorded, no parent had mentioned, no intake note had hinted at.

A life. A child. A love that stretched across continents. And now, she didn't remember any of it.

How much more was buried beneath the rubble of her missing years?

He glanced at Berry, noting the way his friend's eyes flicked between them with a quiet mix of concern and caution. There was no doubt in Dale's mind now—this wasn't just about memory loss. This was about identity. About love that had been erased like a name rubbed off a whiteboard, but never truly gone.

Dale leaned back slightly, his hands clasped in his lap. His medical instincts battled with something deeper—empathy, guilt, and the unsettling realization that he didn't truly know Alley at all.

And worse—she didn't either.

"Thank you for telling me," he said finally, his voice quieter than usual. "This... shifts everything."

Jason gave a slight nod, but Dale could see the tightness in his jaw, the way his shoulders barely relaxed. The confession had cost him something. Trust. Pain. Maybe even hope.

Dale didn't speak right away. A child in Afghanistan. A life born from chaos. A woman robbed of her own story.

He didn't know what came next.

But he knew this: if Alley had any chance of healing—truly healing—he would have to help her find those missing pages, one memory at a time.

The room felt heavier. Dale's voice was quiet as he finally spoke, breaking the tension between them.

"She called you Jay," Dale murmured, more to himself than Jason.

Jason nodded. "She never called me anything else

Dale's gaze lingered on Jason. If losing a child and the horrors of Afghanistan had shattered Alley, how had Jason survived it? How had he carried the weight of their shared grief alone all these years?

The psychiatrist in Dale wanted to analyze the layers of Jason's pain, to dissect the coping mechanisms that kept him functioning.

But the father in him saw something else—a man who had loved deeply, had lost more than anyone should, and was now trying to put the shattered pieces back together.

"Jason," Dale said finally, his voice tinged with both understanding and sadness.

"I can't imagine the strength it took for you to carry all of this. And to see her now, like this..."

A shadow crossed Jason's eyes—somewhere between gratitude and exhaustion. "I'm not sure how strong I am anymore, Dr. Dale. But I know one thing—I won't let her go through this alone. Not this time."

"Did you meet her parents?" Dale asked gently.

His expression warmed with memory as he rested an arm on the chair. "I met her dad when he was on assignment in Kandahar. Chris was... larger than life. The kind of man who made you feel like he already knew all your secrets—but never judged you for them. Alley adored him. She lit up when she talked about her dad."

A warm note slipped into his voice. "I only spoke to her mom when I decided to ask for Alley's hand; I made sure to call her. It felt right—it was important to Alley."

Dale watched him closely, the depth of Jason's love and grief unmistakable.

For a moment, he imagined Chris, the proud father, watching his daughter's happiness unfold. Then his thoughts turned to Jason, who had clearly carried the weight of that promise every day since.

"That's a beautiful memory," Dale said.

"One that clearly meant the world to both of you."

Jason said nothing, his expression unreadable, eyes fixed on a point beyond the room. "It was. It was everything. And now..." His voice faltered, the rest left unsaid—heavy with everything he couldn't bring himself to speak.

Dale's gaze lingered on Jason. "If that kind of loss—losing a child—broke Alley, I can't imagine what it did to you."

Berry, who had been sitting quietly, looked up sharply at Dale. "What did you just say?" he asked, his brows furrowed in confusion.

Dale's face remained thoughtful as he repeated, "I said... If losing a child broke her..."

Shock rippled through Jason, his face paling as he sank into the chair—like the floor had vanished under his feet.

Berry's voice was firm when he said, "Alley didn't lose the child."

Alarm flared in Dale's eyes as he turned toward him. "Jason?" His voice was cautious now. "What are you saying?"

Jason ran trembling hands through his hair, his voice cracking. "She didn't lose him," he repeated. "She... she left him."

Chapter 18

The mirage

A heavy stillness settled over the room. Dale sat rigid, his mind grappling with the revelation. Berry leaned forward, his expression a mixture of disbelief and concern.

Across from them, Jason stood slowly, the silence pressing in like fog. Without another word, he turned and walked out.

He drove home on the long, winding road that twisted like his thoughts.

Grief had twisted into fear.

Fear that she'd spent years believing their son was gone—alone, with no one to tell her otherwise. And fear that if the truth ever surfaced, it wouldn't heal her... it would destroy her all over again.

And beneath that fear, rising steadily like floodwater, came helplessness.

Because no matter how much he wanted to fix this, to protect her, he couldn't unwrite what her mind had rewritten.

The shiver he felt when Dale told him that Alley said she lost her son in Afghanistan hadn't left him. It clung to him, cold and unsettling, like a storm brewing just beyond the horizon.

Why would she say such a thing?

Why would she believe she lost her baby?

Did she truly think their child didn't make it out alive?

Questions spun through his mind, faster than he could catch them.

Why? What had made her say those words? Was it trauma? A fractured memory, distorting what she believed to be true? Or was it something deeper—something he hadn't uncovered yet?

If Alley had truly believed their son was gone, then it wasn't just her past that had been stolen from her. It was their entire future.

His heart pounded, frustration and sorrow mixing into something sharp, something raw. He needed to know what happened to her in those missing years.

He needed to know what had made her forget the one thing she could never have truly forgotten.

But first, she had to remember.

And Jason wasn't sure if the truth would set her free—or shatter them both.

Chapter 19

Licking fingers

Jason and Eaton stepped out of the car, the cool autumn air brushing their faces as a breeze stirred the fallen leaves.

They made their way across the Apple Creek Autumn Festival, the path beneath their feet crackling with fallen leaves—orange and gold hues catching the light like scattered embers.

The rich, buttery scent of kettle corn lingered in the air, blending with the warm sweetness of caramel apples.

Around them, laughter rippled across the crowd, and the strains of folk music threaded between the festival sounds.

"Whoa!" Eaton exclaimed, his eyes widening as he spotted the towering Ferris wheel in the distance.

"Dad, look! It's huge! Can we go on it first?" A chuckle escaped him as he tucked his hands into his jacket pockets.

"Let's start with something on the ground, bud. Maybe the games? Or—" He sniffed dramatically, following his nose like a cartoon bloodhound.

"Maybe something to eat?"

"Okay, but after the Ferris wheel," Eaton declared, pointing toward the ride like he was drawing a map in the air.

They headed toward the towering wheel, Jason laughing as the colorful lights reflected in Eaton's wide, excited eyes.

The line inched along, letting them soak in the festival's buzzing energy.

As they waited, a group of kids from Eaton's school joined the line behind them.

One of them, a red-haired boy, leaned forward and waved enthusiastically. "Hey, Eaton!" he called out.

Eaton turned, his face breaking into a grin. "Oh, hi, Max!" he replied, waving back.

The rest of the group giggled and jostled each other as Max stepped forward and gave an eager thumbs-up. "Do you want to join us for the ride?" he asked.

Jason crouched slightly to meet Eaton's gaze. "You know what? Why don't you ride with your new friends?" he suggested, his tone encouraging. "I'll wait for you down here."

Eaton's eyes lit up. "Really, Dad? Are you sure?"

"Go on, have fun," he said, "Just don't forget to wave when you reach the top."

"Thanks, Dad!" Eaton said, then turned to Max. "Yup, I'm in!"

The kids cheered, pulling Eaton toward the gondola line. He stepped back, crossing his arms, a quiet contentment settling over him as he watched Eaton seamlessly blend in with his new friends.

The chatter of the group and their easy laughter echoed in the cool autumn air, warming his heart.

Jason tilted his head back, tracking the wheel's rotation. As the gondola reached its peak, Eaton leaned out as far as the safety bar allowed, waving with wild enthusiasm.

He waved back with a quiet laugh. "That kid," he murmured fondly.

The air buzzed with laughter and easy conversation, wrapping them in warmth. They rose above the music and bustle of the festival—until a voice behind them pulled him back.

"Is Eaton your son?" He turned, startled to see Alley waving at Max as the gondola reached the top.

For a moment, his body went rigid, his mind scrambling to catch up. That ache—quiet for years—rose fast, like the sound of her own truth had stirred it awake.

It had been years since he'd heard her voice, but it found him now—steady and unmistakably hers.

"Yes," he replied, his tone careful but warm. "He's my son."

Her gaze followed the ride as a soft chuckle slipped out.

"Some ball of energy you've got there. He seems like a fun kid."

His lips twitched, trying to appear casual. It was the first time she'd spoken directly to him in what felt like lifetimes.

Despite the swirl of emotions her presence stirred, he pulled himself back to the moment, steadying his breath.

"He definitely keeps me on my toes." His voice was measured—too measured.

He was trying not to let the tremor slip through, trying to keep his tone steady while his insides reeled.

"Are you here with the kids?" he asked, nodding toward the group.

"Yeah," Alley said, turning back to him. "I'm here with a friend and her kids. Max is her youngest."

Before he could say more, Emmy appeared, weaving through the crowd with two ice cream cones in her hand. Her eyes lit up in surprise when she spotted Alley.

"Alley!" Emmy exclaimed, handing one cone to her. "I thought I lost you to the crowd!"

Emmy's cheerful presence seemed to put Alley at ease. Jason gave her a warm look, watching the tension lift slightly from Alley's posture.

"Thanks," Alley said, taking a cone. She introduced Emmy to him, saying, "He's Eaton's dad."

Emmy beamed, a playful glint in her eyes as she took a lick of her ice cream.

"Ah, the famous Eaton. Max hasn't stopped talking about him since the social at school."

With a light laugh, she turned back to him. "Carnival chaos. Who knew we'd be co-chaperones?"

He let out a huff of amusement, shaking his head.

The three of them stood there for a moment, the cheerful buzz of the festival surrounding them, waving to the kids laughing and shouting from their seats up in the air. The Ferris wheel turned, carrying its excited passengers back to the ground. As the kids tumbled out of the ride, Eaton ran over and waved to Alley.

"You're the lady from the hospital."

Alley waved back, laughing. "I am."

Emmy turned toward him and said brightly, "Why don't you join us for hot dogs and kettle corn? We've already got the chaos—might as well make it a party."

Eaton's face lit up with excitement. "Please, Dad! It'll be so fun!" The other kids echoed his enthusiasm, bouncing on their toes.

He glanced at Alley. "Alright, alright," he said.

"Let's do it."

Stalls brimming with pumpkins in all shapes and sizes dotted the landscape, their earthy scent mingling with the sweet aroma of cider.

Children ran about with faces painted like woodland creatures, their giggles and shouts blending with the gentle rustle of the breeze. The group made their way to a nearby food stand, the warm scent of barbecue and freshly popped kettle corn filling the air. After gathering an impressive array of food—hot dogs, ribs, and bags of sweet-and-salty popcorn—they found an open picnic table beneath a shady tree.

Laughter echoed around them, kids darting between benches with sticky fingers and painted cheeks. Jason sank into the bench, letting the lively chaos of the carnival swirl around him as he picked up a perfectly grilled rack of barbecue ribs.

He closed his eyes, savoring the first bite as the rich, smoky flavor melted on his tongue, the tangy sauce clinging to his fingertips.

"Finger-licking good, huh?" Alley watched him with a mischievous smile, her voice light and teasing.

Jason froze mid-bite, heat surging through him.

Instinctively, he licked the sauce from his fingers, a feeble attempt to steady himself.

His sunglasses hid his eyes, but the tension in his shoulders betrayed him.

There was no blink.

No shift.

He gave a sheepish grin. "What can I say? Carnival food is serious business."

Alley let out a quiet laugh, shaking her head. And then—A haze of recognition passed over her face. An image—a boy laughing, licking barbecue sauce from his fingers—flashed through her mind.

Gone before it fully settled.

She blinked, eyes momentarily unfocused, like the world had tilted just a degree off-center. Her brow furrowed, gaze darting—searching for a thread she couldn't quite grasp.

But everything remained the same—the scent of sizzling meat in the air, the distant murmur of cheerful voices, the golden afternoon sun warming the pavement.

Emmy caught the shift in Alley's posture—barely a flicker—and without missing a beat, offered, "Lemonade?"

Alley straightened, her tone just a shade too cheerful. "Yes, please."

Jason glanced at Eaton, who was chattering animatedly with the other kids, and felt a brief pang of gratitude for the fleeting sense of normalcy.

Just an afternoon like any other—except for the way hope curled quietly in his chest.

Chapter 20

Memories of beginnings

As the sun began to dip toward the horizon, painting the sky in shades of pink and orange, Jason took a moment to soak it all in. The distant buzz of the festival faded as he drove home, the vibrant energy of the day settling into a peaceful night.

In the back seat, Eaton was fast asleep, his head lolled to the side, a faint smudge of barbecue sauce still on his cheek. He watched his son's gentle rise and fall, chest tight with love even as his thoughts drifted elsewhere.

Finger-licking good.

The words echoed in his head, pulling him backward.

Years ago. The first day of medical school.

The trees on campus stood tall, their branches heavy with the last of their autumn foliage, a canopy of reds and yellows filtering light across the cobbled paths.

The air was crisp, carrying the scent of fallen leaves and fresh beginnings.

At a sticky bar table loaded with ribs and cheap beer, Jason and Berry marked the start of something new. They laughed over first lectures, monstrous textbooks, and the looming weight of what they'd signed up for. Caught up in the moment, Jason licked his fingers clean without thinking.

Amid the loud music, a bright laugh rose above the noise— effortless and full of warmth.

He looked up.

A young woman at the next table had her eyes sparkling with mischief.

"Those ribs must be finger-licking good, huh?"

Jason froze, caught off guard.

Berry burst into laughter, while Jason, flustered, managed a sheepish grin.

"What can I say? I'm a man of simple pleasures."

Her laugh rang out again, light and genuine.

"You're making me want to order ribs all over again."

Alley extended a hand to Berry, then offered Jason a teasing air fist bump.

"Alley Conor," she introduced herself, her confidence undeniable.

He met her fist with his, masking how thoroughly she'd disarmed him.

"Jason Carter."

Her laughter lingered—easy, unguarded. The beginning of something.

And it was.

Glancing at Eaton in the mirror, he felt a bittersweet tug at his heart. Ahead, the night swallowed the highway, streetlights trailing by like half-formed doubts.

Then, a thought struck him, cold and unwelcome.

What would have happened if Alley had recognized him?

His body tensed, fingers flexing around the steering wheel. The thought clawed at him, heavy and unshakable.

He couldn't bear the thought of Eaton being caught in the middle—

He pushed the thought aside with a grimace and started the music. A warm melody drifted around him, weaving together with the rush of air.

For now, he would focus on what he had.

Eaton.

And the hope that someday, somehow, things might begin to make sense again

Chapter 21

Truth seeks its price

The auditorium was dim, and the air was cool against his skin. At the front of the room, Sheila began her class, her voice steady and sure.

A vibration buzzed quietly. Jason glanced at his phone—Dale's name lit up the screen, along with a preview that caught his eye. Free this afternoon?

He moved toward the exit, careful not to draw attention. As he reached the door, Sheila's words followed him.

"In this course, we'll examine the Principle of Necessity for Trauma," she said, writing the term in bold letters on the board. "It means we prioritize their well-being over gathering details that could harm them."

Fingers resting on the door handle, he paused. Behind him, Sheila's voice grew firmer—more resolute with each word.

"It is unethical to ask for details about a traumatic incident because there is rarely a legitimate need for such information in providing care. Second, sometimes the questions cause more harm than the perceived benefit.

Trauma-informed care means we meet survivors where they are, not where we want them to be."

The room murmured in acknowledgment as he slipped out, letting the door shut behind him.

Jason thought of Alley, how every question can shatter the fragile peace she built.

He quickly typed a message to Dale: "Dr. Sheila will be joining us after lunch for the meeting. I'll see you then."

The door to Dale's office clicked shut behind him as Jason stepped inside. The older doctor hunched over a stack of files, nodding briefly in greeting.

Moments later, Sheila entered—composed and confident. Both men rose as she approached, and Dale motioned for her to sit.

"Let's begin." Dale paused before meeting Jason's eyes. "We've been reviewing Alley's case; her memory has significant gaps."

"She believes she returned to Apple Creek after an accident in a war zone," Dale continued. "The details are vague. She's reconstructed her story around that trauma, but specific places and faces are missing."

Jason leaned forward. "Did she ever come here before? When we were together, she never even mentioned this town."

"Not really," Dale replied. "She visited Apple Creek only during childhood holidays—her grandparents lived nearby—but after middle school she never came back."

Sheila tilted her head. "So, Apple Creek wasn't home."

"Not then," Dale admitted. "But since she's begun healing... maybe it has become one.

A place where her mind associates safety—a tether."

Sheila nodded thoughtfully. "That fits trauma-recovery models. Survivors often emotionally anchor to places that feel safe—even if they weren't part of their past."

"Has anyone reached out to the evacuation team that flew Alley out of Kandahar?"

Dale nodded, his expression clouding slightly. "We tried, years ago. The trail went cold immediately—no names, no access. The chain of command had shifted, and we lacked the clearance."

"I know someone," Sheila said. "He was part of the military coordination unit that managed the Kandahar airlift—organizing civilian and wounded extractions. He's retired now, so we should be able to speak with him soon."

"That helps—thank you," Jason said softly, more certain than before. After a moment, he added, "If we can reconstruct the evacuation and its aftermath, we won't just understand what Alley remembers... but why she believes it."

As the meeting came to a close, Sheila turned to Dale.

"I'd like more time with Alley—to assess her emotional state and potential triggers.

Understanding how she perceives her visible and hidden scars could guide our next steps."

"She's due for her follow-up Friday morning," Dale said. "I'll speak to her about having you join."

A quiet understanding settled in the room. Then Sheila turned back to Jason.

"One last thing," she said gently. "Whatever we uncover—it's not just Alley who might feel the impact. Be prepared. This could bring up more than you expect."

He met her gaze. The warning didn't rattle him, but it stayed with him.

He gave a short nod, already bracing for what came next.

"Also," Sheila added, "before we speak with the commander, I need your version of that day. And the years that followed."

His brow furrowed, her words landing heavier than he expected. "My version?" he echoed.

"You lived through it. Even if the details are fractured, they might help us understand how it all unraveled—for both of you."

Her request didn't feel like pressure. It felt like something inevitable.

"Your perspective. Not just the facts—the fear, the fallout, the years you carried it."

Jason's throat closed, the words refusing to come. Instead, something surfaced—vivid and sharp, cutting straight through time.

His hands—bloodied, shaking, and raw from dust and desperation. Alley's face—exhausted, sweat-slick, her eyes fluttering as her strength ebbed. The thick, acrid burn of smoke. The distant whir of rotors overhead. The chaotic churn of dust and shouting.

And then—Eaton's first cry. Fragile. Defiant. Alive.

He blinked, breath steadying, aware of Sheila's gaze.

He hadn't expected to survive that night. Let alone carry life out of it.

"Okay," he said quietly—simple words weighted by decades. "Not today… but soon."

The past wasn't behind him anymore. It had caught up—and this time, he wouldn't turn away.

Jason stepped into the hallway, the hospital noise fading. He spotted Steve by the vending machine—slumped and lost in thought.

Their eyes met across the fluorescent hum, and a heavy hush passed between them: a moment of recognition, of shared quiet understanding.

Jason gave a slight nod—no words needed—before turning and heading home.

Chapter 22

A Jedi's bedtime

Eaton spent dinner animatedly describing his triumph on the school's obstacle course—tiny hands painting his tale across the table. Jason laughed, leaning in to catch every word. But midway through, the laughter faltered. A single thought intruded—then another—until the room fell away around him.

As the plates were cleared and the chatter quieted, Jason ruffled Eaton's hair and said, "Alright, buddy. Time to get ready for bed. I'll be up in fifteen minutes to read your favorite Star Wars book."

Eaton groaned dramatically, leaning against his chair. "Do I have to? I'm not even tired!"

"You? Not tired? You were yawning through dinner, kiddo."

Eaton crossed his arms, feigning indignation, but a grin betrayed him. "Okay, fine. But you must read the lightsaber duel chapter tonight."

Jason laughed. "Deal. Go brush your teeth."

Eaton darted out of the room, his footsteps echoing up the stairs. He leaned back in his chair, watching him go with a smile that quickly faded into a thoughtful frown.

Margaret looked at her son with knowing eyes. "You've been quiet tonight," she said gently.

He shrugged, eyes dropping away from hers. "Just a lot on my mind."

Robert leaned in. "It's Alley, isn't it?"

He raked a hand through his hair, tension tightening his voice. "It's everything. Alley. The call with the commander. Eaton."

Margaret set her teacup down with a clink. "What about Eaton?"

He hesitated, pressure building behind his ribs—tight, aching, ready to crack.

"If she remembers everything... what if she wants him back? What if she sues for custody?"

The room fell silent. Margaret's eyes widened slightly, but Robert's expression remained steady, though his brow furrowed in thought.

"You really think she'd do that?" Margaret asked.

"I don't know," he admitted, frustration creeping into his voice. "She's his mother. She has every right to fight for him. And if she remembers everything—if she realizes how much precious time she's lost with him—I wouldn't blame her."

Robert leaned back in his chair, the wood creaking under his weight. With hands clasped thoughtfully in front of him, he regarded Jason with a serious expression. "But she hasn't been there, Jason," he said steadily. "You have. The courts would take that into account."

Jason's brow furrowed as he leaned deeper into the table. "It's not just about the courts," he replied, his voice rising with an edge of desperation. "It's about Eaton. How do I prepare him for something like this? How do I explain to him that the mother he doesn't even remember might suddenly want to be part of his life?"

Margaret reached across the table, her warm hand covering Jason's in a gentle reassurance. "You're overthinking this, sweetheart." Her voice remained soft. "You're trying to predict a future that hasn't even happened yet."

He met her gaze, a flicker of something protective anchoring behind his eyes. "I have to think about it, Mom…"

"You're a good father, Jason," Robert said firmly. "You've raised Eaton with love, patience, and dedication. That won't be erased, no matter what happens."

His shoulders slumped slightly, as if the weight of his fears momentarily lifted under his father's steady gaze.

After a long, quiet moment, he excused himself. He paused outside Eaton's room and listened intently to the faint sounds of his son humming the iconic Star Wars theme. Eaton's voice mingled with the sound of pages turning.

He opened the door and leaned inside. "Alright, Jedi. Ready for that duel?" he asked, lifting the mood even as the past settled at the edge of his mind.

Eaton's face lit up as he thrust the book toward him, triumphant. "I found the page! It's where Luke fights Darth Vader!" he exclaimed, his enthusiasm infectious.

He settled on the edge of Eaton's bed, the fabric soft beneath him as he leaned in, heart swelling with quiet affection. Opening the book, he let his voice carry the story—steady, animated, painting each scene with care.

Eaton listened, eyelids drooping as his father's voice rhythm tugged him gently to sleep.

By the time Luke ignited his lightsaber, he was already dreaming.

After a moment, he closed the book gently and set it on the bedside table. Pulling the covers up around Eaton, he tucked him in, contentment softening his features.

He lingered for a breath, watching his son sleep. The steady rise and fall of Eaton's chest filled him with quiet warmth—layered with a deeper ache that tugged at something old and tender inside him.

Leaning closer, he whispered into the hush, "No matter what happens, buddy... I'll protect you. Always."

He switched off the light and stepped away, his footsteps slow, careful—as if afraid to disturb the fragile peace between them.

Back in the living room, his parents waited—still and steady, their presence a quiet anchor.

"I'll be meeting Sheila tomorrow to go over the evacuation," he said finally, his voice even—though the tension beneath it lingered.

Margaret tilted her head, her eyes clouded with concern. "That day... It's not going to be easy to talk about, is it?"

Jason looked down. "No," he admitted quietly. "I haven't talked about it. Not the details. Not with anyone. But if I don't tell her everything—if I don't face it—how can I expect Alley to face what she's forgotten?"

Robert leaned forward, his voice steady. "You shouldn't do this alone."

A frown crept in. "I don't see how you could help with—"

Margaret cut in, her tone calm and unwavering.

"Jason, we're both doctors... She doesn't know what we saw."

"If you're going to relive that day, you need a safe space to do it. Sheila is brilliant, yes—but she doesn't know you the way we do."

He hesitated, glancing between them, his defenses starting to slip. "You don't have to do that," he murmured.

"We do," Robert said, unwavering. "Because you're not just a doctor, Jason. You're our son. And whether you want to admit it or not, this is going to be harder than you think."

Margaret placed a hand over Jason's, her touch warm and steady. "We'll make sure you feel supported. No judgment. No pushing. Just us creating a space where you can talk about what happened—if and when you're ready."

He nodded, emotion catching at the edges of his voice.

"Alright," he said quietly. "But don't blame me if it gets messy."

Robert shrugged, his voice patient. "Sometimes, messy is part of the process."

As he moved toward the kitchen to pour a glass of water, the memories lingered—hovering at the edges of his mind like a storm he couldn't quite outrun. He gripped the cool glass, grounding himself against the flood of memory.

For years, he'd buried the memories.

Tomorrow, the truth would come for him.

He hesitated, then spoke—softly, like the words hurt to say.

"I hope I'm ready for this."

That night, after the house had gone quiet, Margaret stepped into the suite she and Robert shared.

Stillness crept in around her, bringing with it memories she'd tried not to revisit.

But some memories don't stay buried—not forever.

Chapter 23

A mother's shield

Margaret stood in the quiet suite, her fingers brushing against the picture frame on the dresser. She lingered there, feeling the cool, smooth glass beneath her touch.

Eaton's cherubic face—sparkling eyes and rounded cheeks—looked back at her, a vivid reminder of the day he entered their lives.

She hadn't let herself go back there in years. But tonight, it rose like tidewater—inevitable and all-consuming—not the moment he was born, but the storm that followed.

The news had come in fragments, each piece more harrowing than the last. The rebel attack on the hospital had thrown everything into chaos. Margaret and Robert, still in the U.S., were frantic and worried when Berry called.

"Jason and the baby were airlifted to Karachi," he said, voice clipped but calm—the steadiness of a doctor under pressure.

"He's critical but stable. The baby's unharmed. Alley's been evacuated to Kazakhstan. Her father is with her now."

Margaret had gripped Robert's hand tightly.

"What happened?" she asked, her voice tight with fear.

"There's no time for details," Berry replied. "You need to get to Karachi. I'll meet you there."

Within hours, they were on a plane, the fear and uncertainty making the journey feel interminable.

When they finally arrived, the hospital was overwhelmed—its sterile calm shattered by a surge of urgency. Stretchers lined all passages, squeezed against walls that had never hosted so many patients at once. Rubber soles squeaked across the linoleum in frantic staccato, echoed under the fluorescent lights, punctuated by the rise and fall of voices—nurses shouting vitals, doctors barking orders, patients crying out in pain or confusion.

The air reeked of bleach, sweat, and coppery blood, thick enough to taste. IV stands careened around corners, their wheels clattering like metallic artillery.

Makeshift triage stations had been set up in waiting areas and even stairwells. Privacy curtains were drawn in haste—sometimes only halfway.

Gurneys rolled past reception desks cluttered with charts, scattered papers, and half-empty coffee cups. Phones rang unanswered. Monitors beeped in steady rhythms. Somewhere, a machine alarm blared until a nurse finally silenced it.

The air conditioning couldn't keep up—heat and panic clung to everything. A child wailed two halls down. A man clutched his shoulder, blood soaking through a bandage already red and heavy. Medics shouted for clear access to trauma bays, pushing through doors that were never meant to swing so often or so fast.

The hospital, once a place of calm control, pulsed now with raw, unfiltered life—loud, chaotic, and unbearably human.

Berry met them at the entrance, his face drawn and his scrubs rumpled, exhaustion etched into his features. Without preamble, he led them through the winding corridors to the ER.

The harsh lights cast an unforgiving clarity over everything. When they entered Jason's room, Margaret's heart clenched, and she stifled a sob.

Her son. Her vibrant, laughing boy, now pale and battered, was lying motionless on the hospital bed. Scars and bruises marred his skin, and the monitors beeped steadily beside him.

Margaret stepped closer, reaching for the chart at the foot of the bed. Her hands trembled as she scanned the notes.

"Ruptured spleen repaired. Six fractured ribs. A broken leg. Internal bleeding. Concussion," she read, her breath catching between lines.

She turned to the attending physician. "What are we looking at for recovery?"

"He's stable for now," the doctor replied. "But it'll be a long road."

Robert moved to Jason's side, his hand hovering for a moment before gently resting on his forehead.

"You're strong, son," he whispered, his voice breaking ever so slightly. "We're here now."

Margaret blinked back tears as she placed her hand on Robert's shoulder.

"You're going to be okay, my darling," she murmured, quiet but unwavering.

The words felt like a promise, one she silently vowed to keep no matter what it took.

Margaret pushed aside the fear threatening to consume her. She straightened. "Let's go," she said, her voice steady. "Let's meet our grandson."

Berry led them toward the pediatric ward, his steps brisk and voice low as he updated them. "Alley's injuries aren't serious, thank God. And her dad... he's already reached Kazakhstan."

Margaret looked up, frowning. "Kazakhstan? Why there?"

"Logistics," Berry said, glancing at her. "It's one of the closest countries with stable medical facilities. Pakistan and Kazakhstan are usually the first responders to the evac from Afghanistan."

He hesitated, then added, "They probably didn't want to overwhelm the local hospitals. With so many injured civilians and aid workers, all available beds count."

Margaret and Robert let out a sigh of relief at the news.

Berry stopped at a glass partition, gesturing toward the rows of tiny cribs.

"He's in there," he said, his voice carrying an almost reverent tone. "The nurses have been keeping a close eye on him."

Margaret pressed her palms against the glass, the coolness grounding her as her gaze swept across the nursery.

Soft light bathed rows of bassinets—some babies sleeping in perfect stillness, others squirming in quiet rebellion. Nurses moved between them with practiced grace, adjusting swaddles, checking charts, offering comfort like second nature.

Her gaze flicked from one tiny face to another—until it landed on a bassinet tucked into the far corner, slightly separated from the others. Inside, a newborn stirred. A fist emerged, waving briefly before retreating back into the folds of a powder-blue blanket.

He had been so small, so fragile—and yet had already faced more than most do in a lifetime. Margaret stood still, the weight of it all settling over her.

"There he is," she whispered, her voice trembling with emotion.

Robert stepped closer, placing a hand on her shoulder. The baby's dark hair peeked out from under a knitted cap, and even from a distance, they could see the delicate rise and fall of his chest. A fragile, miraculous rhythm.

"He's beautiful," Robert murmured, his voice thick with awe.

Margaret couldn't wait any longer. She turned to Berry, her eyes glistening. "Can we go in?"

Berry nodded. "Of course. The nurses have been expecting you."

The nursery door opened with a gentle hiss, and cool air swept over them. Margaret's heart raced, her hands trembling slightly as she reached into the bassinet to lift him.

The moment her fingers brushed the plush weave of his blanket, the baby stirred, opening his tiny eyes to reveal a deep, searching gaze.

Margaret pressed him to her, unable to hold back her tears any longer. "Hello, sweetheart," she said, her words breaking with emotion. "I've waited so long to hold you."

The baby's hand brushed her cheek, and she closed her eyes, savoring the warmth. Time stood still for a moment—the day's chaos fading into the background.

Robert stood beside her, his large hands gentle as he stroked the baby's head.

He reached out, brushing a light hand against the baby's cheek.

"Hey there, little guy. I'm your grandpa. You're safe now. We've got you."

The baby let out a tiny, drowsy coo, and Robert chuckled, moisture pooling in his eyes.

"Look at him, Margaret. He's a fighter, just like Jason."

Margaret nodded.

"He's perfect," she said, eyes shining.

But as they gazed down at the tiny miracle before them, an unspoken promise passed between them—a vow to protect and nurture him, no matter the cost.

Margaret leaned down, pressing a kiss to the baby's forehead.

"Welcome to the world, little one." She gently cradled him. "You're so loved."

With the newborn cradled in Margaret's arms, they stepped out of the nursery. Robert wrapped her in a quiet embrace, his arm a steadying anchor. Together, they walked back toward Jason's room—hearts full of love and heavy with the knowledge of the challenges ahead.

Margaret opened her eyes, the memory dissipating like mist in the morning light. She turned to her husband, who stood quietly by the window, lost in his own thoughts. His shoulders were tense, his posture rigid.

"I'll never forget that moment." She tucked a strand of hair behind her ear. Robert's eyes misted as he reached out to her.

"Neither will I. But we did what we had to, Margaret. For Jason. For Eaton."

Margaret nodded, her gaze drifting back to the picture frame.

"And we'll keep doing it."

"No one," she said quietly, "is going to break our family."

With a heavy sigh, she crossed the room to Robert, resting her head against his shoulder.

They stood together, the weight of shared memories pressing close—unspoken, but unshakable.

Chapter 24

The weight of a Dahlia

As morning crept over Apple Creek, another day began—quiet, ordinary, and unaware of the truths that would begin to surface by nightfall.

The low hum of the electric razor broke the stillness as he stood in front of the sink, letting routine guide him. Tilting his face under the bathroom's warm vanity lights, he guided the blade along the contours of his jawline—each movement practiced and precise.

He caught his reflection in the mirror, then turned toward the shower. Warm water cascaded over him, washing away the last traces of sleep.

The mirror showed a man with a square jaw and storm-grey eyes—tired, thoughtful, and carrying more than he let on.

Salt-and-pepper hair, the kind that made people pause. Refined but weathered, like someone who'd been tested by life and walked out with just enough left.

The steady rhythm of the water against the tiles was soothing, dulling his morning grogginess. He stared at the water swirling down the drain, his upcoming meeting with Dr. Sheila drifting into focus.

Taking a deep breath, he grabbed his towel and stepped out, ready to face the day.

He walked into the kitchen just in time to see Eaton slinging his backpack over his shoulders.

The boy radiated excitement, his energy filling the room.

"Bye, Grandpa! Bye, Grandma!" Eaton called, his voice bright and full of life.

Jason caught him with a grin. "Hey, bud—cool if I walk you to the bus stop?"

Eaton paused, flashing a sly grin. "Yeah. These days, it's cool to be a softy. Emotional guys are in."

Jason let out a laugh. "Oh really?"

"Totally. Girls love guys who listen," Eaton said, tossing his hands up dramatically.

Jason shook his head, laughing. "Good to know, wise guy."

They stepped into the crisp morning air.

"So," Jason teased as they walked, "with all that wisdom, got yourself a girlfriend yet?"

Eaton shrugged. "Nah. But... maybe a situationship with Lilly."

Jason raised an eyebrow. "Situationship?"

"Yeah," Eaton said casually. "Before you date—you hang out, help each other. Lilly's great at math, loves racing cars, and always has snacks. I love racing cars, I'm good at languages, and I'm always hungry. Perfect match."

Jason let out a laugh. "Sounds like you've got it all figured out."

The bus rumbled up to the curb.

"Bye, Dad!" Eaton called, bounding aboard.

A quiet laugh rumbled in Jason's chest as he watched the bus pull away, hands tucked in his pockets.

"Situationships," he muttered, shaking his head. "Why didn't I think of that back in my day?"

He stood there for a moment, the morning stillness thinning as the weight of the day began to settle. By nightfall, he'd be sitting face-to-face with the past—and with the woman who might just hold the key to all he'd locked away.

Later that morning, as the car rolled into his assigned parking spot at the hospital, the crisp air carried the faint musk of fallen leaves.

A soft mist curled around the parked cars as the golden hues of early autumn sunlight filtered through the thinning branches. Despite the brisk air, the warmth of the rising sun cast a gentle glow over the lot, making the dewdrops on windshields glisten like tiny jewels.

His attention was snagged on a flower delivery truck parked in his space. As he approached, a woman jogged toward him from the sidewalk, waving apologetically.

She wore dark jeans and a lightweight jacket, her hair swept into a loose bun half unraveled in the wind. A faint dusting of pollen clung to her sleeves, and a quick smile broke across her face despite the fluster.

"Sorry!" she called out, slightly breathless. "There was no parking—I thought I'd be in and out."

He offered a tight nod, his voice clipped but not unkind. "It's fine. I'm just in a bit of a hurry."

She nodded, already heading toward the driver's side. "Right. Totally fair. Moving now. Next time I'll park better," she called. "Might even bribe you with flowers or coffee."

He didn't look back. Just walked on—past the van, past the smile that shouldn't have lingered.

She didn't know him. Not really. But something about her—quick steps, quick smile—clung to the edges of his thoughts.

That brief moment of levity dissolved by the time he reached his office—already replaced by the heaviness of what was coming.

His hand hovered near the door, not quite ready.

He'd promised himself to do this—sit with Sheila, tell the truth, peel back the layers. But the closer he got, the more it felt like walking into a room where the air remembered everything you'd rather forget.

He'd spent years in counseling, peeling back layers of grief in sterile offices and consulting rooms. Yet discussing that day here—among people who knew him and loved Alley—landed with an entirely different weight.

It wasn't healing yet. Not fully. And talking about it felt less like closure and more like ripping a bandage from a wound that was still raw beneath the skin.

He braced himself. Then reached for the door.

He crossed the room with a nod to his parents as they looked up from the seating area.

"Hi," he said, shutting the door behind him.

Margaret stood, walked over, and placed a hand gently on his arm.

"Just take your time," she said. "We're here—for whatever this brings."

He gave a nod, but emotion swelled just beneath the surface.

Honeyed light filtered between the blinds, pooling softly on the floor.

A moment later, footsteps approached. Sheila entered first, calm and composed, followed by Dale and Berry. Jason rose instinctively, nodding in greeting.

"Thanks for being here," he murmured, motioning to the chairs. Once everyone had settled, Sheila gave him a steady look.

"Let's begin when you're ready, Jason," Sheila suggested gently. "And remember, we can stop at any time. No pressure."

He sank into the sofa. Lamplight spilled across the rug, catching in corners like echoes from another life.

The scent of coffee hung in the air, warm but distant—unable to reach the ache building inside him. He'd stayed away from this place in his mind for too long. But tonight, the quiet didn't comfort—it summoned.

He surrendered—

To the dust.

To the chaos.

To midnight walks beneath a foreign sky.

To the woman who once made war zones feel like home.

To the adventure that began before it all fell apart.

To everything before it changed.

To everything before she was gone.

Chapter 25

The beginning of everything

The bedside lamp cast a warm glow across the room, yet unease coiled tight in Jason's chest. In the distance, helicopter rotors thudded against the night—steady, relentless.

Beyond the hospital walls, Kabul buzzed with uneasy life. The honk of military vehicles merged with the distant wail of a street vendor's cry. Dust clung to the air, kicked up by wind and boots, swirling in golden plumes against sun-scorched walls.

Stray dogs barked nearby, helicopters humming just beyond the skyline.

A boy darted across the street with a bundle of bread under his arm, his eyes watchful, his steps quick.

Inside, the hospital was a brittle bubble of order—sanitized, tense, and too quiet. The contrast was jarring. It was a stark reminder of their precarious world, where hope and danger coexisted.

Jason stepped into her consultation room, the door clicking shut behind him, muting the hallway sounds.

He glanced over at Alley, who sat on the edge of the couch, her hand resting gently on her growing belly. Her expression was almost serene, as if she didn't share the weight of his concerns. But Jason couldn't shake the tight knot in his stomach—the fear that something could go wrong, that the fragile sense of safety they'd managed to build could shatter in an instant.

Concern creasing his brow, he reached for her hand. "Alley, would you consider going to your parents for the delivery? I'm just... I'm not comfortable with you having the baby here."

Alley looked up, her eyes filled with love that disarmed him even now. She reached for his hand. "Jay, it's okay. We'll be good. I promise."

Jason sighed, his worry deepening. But before he could speak, Alley continued, "Besides, I can't bail on the women here. Some of them are in their final days of delivery, they need me." She paused, her tone growing tender. "And I don't want to have this baby without you."

Her words landed heavy, pinning Jason between admiration and dread. "When you look at me like that, I don't want to let you go either," he murmured, drawing her into a tight embrace.

Wrenching himself from the memory, Jason shifted on the couch, his forehead dropping into his hand as a pained grunt escaped him.

"I should've insisted. Made her leave. Or maybe we should've left together. None of us would've been hurt. I can't believe I put my family at such great risk."

Dr. Sheila, seated across from him, leaned forward. "Jason, you couldn't predict the future. None of us can."

A hollow laugh slipped out. "Couldn't predict it, sure—but I could feel it. Something was bound to go wrong. And yet…"

His voice trailed off as the memory of that October morning returned—vivid, sharp, and unrelenting.

It had been a beautiful morning, but the atmosphere inside the hospital room was anything but calm. Alley had been in labor for eight hours, and her blood pressure was spiking. Jason hovered by her side, his hands cold and trembling despite the room's warmth.

"Alley, how are you feeling now?" he asked gently, brushing a damp strand of hair from her forehead.

Dimples formed at the corners of her mouth, a slight contrast to the tension in her voice. "I'm okay. Just… thinking about something else."

Jason tilted his head, curious. "Something else?"

Alley's lips quivered into a playful grin. "Hey… do you want to marry me?"

He blinked, caught off guard. "Al, we'd be married by now if you hadn't insisted on the entire tribe being there for your grand New York wedding," he teased, leaning down to press a kiss to her forehead.

Alley chuckled weakly, her laughter breaking the tension in the room.

"Can we marry now? Please?" Alley asked, her voice carrying a playful sweetness that reminded Jason of a child asking for more ice cream.

Jason stared at her, caught between disbelief and amusement. "You're kidding, right?"

But the look in her eyes said more than words could. He blinked, squared his shoulders, and grabbed his phone.

"Stay right here," he said, dialing quickly. "I'll be back in ten minutes."

Exactly ten minutes later, Jason returned with Berry, his best friend, grinning like a teenager. "You called for backup?" Berry winked at Alley, wheeling in the wheelchair he'd brought with him.

With the help of a nurse, Jason and Berry gently helped Alley into a wheelchair. "What are you up to?" she asked, looking bewildered but intrigued.

Jason leaned down, mischief sparking his eyes. "You'll see."

They wheeled her along the passageway, the wheelchair's quiet squeak echoing off the hospital's sterile walls. They stopped at the chapel tucked into a corner of the building, its modest interior bathed in the glow of candles.

A man in a simple robe stepped forward with a warm smile. "I'm Chaplain Owen," he said, introducing himself to Alley.

She blinked, her eyes darting between Jason, Berry, and the nurse behind her. "You're serious," she said, a hint of delight in her tone.

"Oh, we're very serious," he replied playfully.

As the chaplain began the ceremony, Berry stood behind Jason, the nurse behind Alley.

"Do you, Jason, take Alley as your wedded wife?"

Jason grinned. "I do."

"And do you, Alley, take Jason as your wedded husband?"

"I do," Alley said, steady even as tears shimmered in her eyes.

The chaplain paused, looking around. "Are there rings?"

All four shook their heads, cheeks reddening with sheepish amusement.

"No rings, no problem," the chaplain announced with a playful laugh.

"By the power vested in me, I now pronounce you husband and wife."

Berry arched an eyebrow and lifted a hand. "And what about 'kiss the bride'?"

The chaplain's eyes twinkled as he replied, "This is Afghanistan—we don't say that here. But you're welcome to… once you're back in private quarters."

"No rings, no kiss," Berry quipped, crossing his arms. "What kind of wedding is this?"

Laughter erupted, filling the tiny chapel as Jason and Berry wheeled Alley back to her room.

A soft smile tugged at Jason's lips as he glanced at Berry, who wiped his eyes with the back of his hand.

"You were there. You remember how ridiculous we must've looked—rushing through that hospital like it was a rom-com, not a war zone."

Berry nodded, his voice thick. "Ridiculous? Sure. But it was also perfect, in its own chaotic way."

He glanced toward Dr. Dale, catching the moment his hand moved for a tissue—composure slipping, just briefly.

"I didn't have rings. All I could give her was a single rose from the chapel."

Jason, what you gave her wasn't a rose or a ceremony. You gave her love. And that's what matters."

"I just hoped it would carry us through," he murmured, barely touching the couch's edge.

"Let's pause for 15 minutes," suggested Sheila.

Leaning back, Jason let his gaze rest on the amber glow of the lamp, though his thoughts had already drifted elsewhere.

Alley's laughter rose in his memory, light and unguarded. The sound caught him off balance, unexpected and sharp.

In the chaos of it all, they had found something unshakable—a love that endured, even in the most fragile places.

He didn't exhale. He sank—into the hollow ache of remembering something once strong enough to hold him together.

Chapter 26

Gone like a bubble

The group gathered again, the remnants of evening sunlight casting golden streaks across the window.

His eyes narrowed against the light as he sank deeper into memory. An hour into being married, he was sprinting beside Alley's stretcher...

Gripping Alley's hand as it was wheeled down the corridor toward the operating room. Her fingers clutched his, damp with effort and adrenaline, but her laughter still rang out—a sound that broke the tension like dawn breaking through storm clouds.

He brushed a strand of hair from her forehead. "You're doing great," he said gently.

She laughed, nudging his arm. "Just married and already on an adventure—our honeymoon's off to a flying start!"

Jason smiled, his heart swelling with admiration. Even here, even now, she was still herself—fierce, funny, unbreakable.

As the late afternoon sun spilled across the hospital floor, Dr. Rubina Khan cradled a pink, wriggling newborn in her gloved hands. A single, piercing cry split the quiet—brilliant and insistent as life's first announcement.

"It's a boy!" the doctor announced, her whole face lit with joy.

A nurse stepped forward and placed the swaddled newborn into Jason's trembling hands. The warmth of his son filled his arms, and something inside him shifted—quiet, rhythmic, real.

He turned gently to Berry, emotion welling in his voice. "Want to meet your godson?"

Berry's face, lit with awe, said everything—long before he answered.

He leaned closer, eyes wide. "Damn... he's perfect."

Alley stirred on the operating table, her eyelids fluttering as she fought the haze. Her gaze found him cradling their son, and though she couldn't speak, the curve of her lips said everything.

Dr. Khan leaned over, brushing a hand along Alley's arm. "Congratulations," she murmured. "You've just delivered the most handsome baby boy."

The baby's cries eased into soft hiccupping breaths. Jason looked from Alley to the child, his eyes glistening, overwhelmed by the enormity of the moment.

Later that night, in the stillness of Alley's post-op room, he lay stretched out on the narrow couch beside her, the joy of the day echoing in his heart like a lullaby.

Alley slept like an angel, her breathing slow and regular, while the diffuse light from above highlighted the gentle contours of her features.

Jason checked his watch: **4:02 a.m.**

He leaned in and kissed her forehead, letting his lips rest there for a beat before he quietly slipped out, pulling the door closed behind him.

The hallways were hushed. His shoes barely made a sound against the tile floor as he made his way toward the nursery. A quiet blend of hushed conversation and distant monitors filled the space, which was now familiar and almost comforting.

At the window, Jason spotted him instantly—a tiny bundle of warmth and promise, nestled among the others.

The nurse cocked her head invitingly. "Would you like to feed him?"

A grin flickered across his lips. His fingers hovered over the small bottle before he dared to take it.

"Here," she said, guiding him to a rocking chair. "I'll help."

She gently placed the baby in her arms and guided the angle of the bottle. As the infant latched on and began to drink, the gentle, rhythmic sound settled into his bones—like a memory etching itself into the present.

He chuckled, incredulously. "You're really here," he murmured.

The nurse gave a nod and backed away, her expression serene as she left him to the moment.

He cradled his son, memorizing every breath, every fragile heartbeat.

Time blurred, the world falling away until only this moment remained.

When he finally looked at his watch again, **4:47 a.m.** blinked back at him.

Reluctant to let go, he glanced at the nurse. "Would it be alright if I took him to Alley?"

"Of course," she said, placing a fresh bottle in his hand. "Just keep him swaddled."

With care, he rose, adjusting the baby in his arms. In the hallway, he murmured gentle, musical nonsense—speaking to his son as though they'd known each other forever.

The baby squirmed, scrunching up his face as if deep in thought. Jason chuckled. The corridor lights cast dappled pools of gold on the floor, wrapping them in quiet intimacy.

Back in the nursery, the nurse glanced toward the door where father and son had just left. She let out a sigh. She'd forgotten to scan the baby out.

Making a mental note to correct it, she turned to change another baby's diaper. After that, she'd head to the mother's room and sort it out. It would only take a minute.

Just as he turned to head back to Alley's room, the quiet was shattered—gunfire cracked through the air, sharp and sudden. He froze. The acrid sting of gunpowder hit his nose, tangling with something older, deeper—fear.

Muscles coiled, he burst through the fire-exit door and slammed it shut with his back.

Gulping lungful of air, his heart thundered in his chest as he fought to shove down rising panic.

From the fire-escape stairs, the horizon unfolded in dim mist— helicopters slicing the sky, U.S. Marshals in tactical gear sweeping the hospital below in synchronized precision.

He pulled the tiny bundle closer, cradling the baby against his chest. A faint whimper escaped the child, sensing the tension around them. "Shh, it's okay, buddy," he whispered, voice unsteady as he rocked him gently. "Daddy's got you. I won't let anything happen to you."

The rising sun cast a faint glow over the metal stairs as he moved, his feet pounding against the grated steps. The sound seemed amplified in the quiet morning—his breathing, the distant gunfire, the hum of helicopters—and it made his nerves crackle with urgency.

He burst into the hospital morgue at the lower level, where the air turned thick and stifling. Chaos surged around him—doctors and staff scrambled past, faces drained of color, barking frantic orders as they sprinted toward the waiting helicopters outside.

A figure sprinted toward the morgue. Berry. Relief hit him like a jolt.

"Berry!" Jason hissed. Berry's head snapped up, and his pace quickened, his face a mixture of fear and determination.

When Berry reached him, he shoved the baby and bottle into his arms. "Take him—" he said urgently, pressing the fresh bottle into Berry's hand. "Alley's still inside. I'll get her."

Berry's eyes widened, confusion and panic tightening his features. "Jason—what... what the hell—?"

"There's no time!" he snapped, already stepping away. "Keep him safe, Berry. Promise me!"

Berry nodded, clutching the baby more tightly as the door swung shut behind him, swallowed by chaos.

Inside, the cold air hit like a wall, but he hardly noticed. Instinct took over, legs moving before thought could catch up. The image of Alley—alone, unaware of the chaos erupting around her—drove him forward.

A sudden, ragged cough from Berry broke the moment. He shot to his feet and hurried out to the balcony, shoulders hunched, breaths coming in sharp, uneven pulls.

He watched him, something catching in his expression. Then he grabbed a glass of water and followed Berry outside.

The cool evening air was soothing against their skin, and the faint murmur of the town below was a distant backdrop. Berry leaned on the railing, his shoulders tense, and his head bowed. Jason placed the glass gently on the ledge beside him.

A storm churned in his chest, but he drew a steady breath.

"Take your time."

Berry nodded but didn't say anything, his breaths coming in uneven gasps.

Inside the room, his parents sat, stunned. Margaret's hands were clenched in her lap, as if holding herself together by force. Across from her, Robert remained motionless, eyes fixed on the floor, his expression unreadable.

Dr. Dale sat with them, his typically calm demeanor strained. He shifted in his chair but didn't speak. Sensing the overwhelming tension in the room, Sheila rose from her seat. "Does anyone want some coffee?" she asked, gentle but purposeful—offering everyone a way to refocus.

Margaret, startled out of her daze, quickly stood. "Let me help you." Her voice trembled just enough to betray the strain beneath her poise.

Sheila guided her toward the coffee station with a quiet, understanding nod. Margaret's hands trembled as she reached for the cups. An uneasy laugh escaped her lips—more reflex than comfort.

"Thank you," Margaret said quietly, her eyes focused on the task before her. "I just… I needed something to do."

"I know," Sheila replied gently. "Sometimes a small task can make the weight feel a little lighter, even if just for a moment."

Back on the balcony, Jason rested a hand on Berry's shoulder.

"You're not alone,"

He said. "I was there too."

Berry turned, eyes tired, voice rough.

"It comes back so fast," he muttered

"Like I'm right there again."

They stood together, the night air cool against their skin.

The silence between them didn't need filling—it held everything they already knew.

Chapter 27

Through the fire

He sat hunched forward, cradling the warm mug in both hands, his eyes fixed on the dark liquid as if searching for answers. He lifted it to his lips, the bitter heat grounding him for a fleeting second.

His parents sat across from him, their own untouched cups of coffee growing cold on the table. Margaret kept glancing at Jason, her lips pressed together as if holding back the urge to say something.

Sheila leaned forward slightly in her chair, her gentle voice breaking through the stillness. "Jason, do you want to continue, or should we stop here for today?"

He looked up. His face was pale, dark circles smudged beneath his eyes with exhaustion, but something steadied in his expression—quiet and firm. "No," he said. "I want to finish this. I don't want to do it again tomorrow."

Sheila studied him, noting the tension in his shoulders and the way his hands briefly clenched around the mug. He was running on determination alone, the emotional toll evident in each line of his body.

"All right," she said, her tone steady. "If you're sure."

He steadied his tone, though the edge didn't leave it. "Dragging it out will only make it worse."

Jason remembered racing up the stairs, lungs burning, the air thick with dust. Then—impact.

A sudden, gut-punching force slammed into him, stealing the breath from his chest. And then came the sound—deafening, all-consuming. A roar that cracked the world in two.

Instinct took over. He dove under the nearest table, heart pounding, the ground still shaking beneath him.

The air tore open with a thunderous blast. A wall to his left—solid concrete and steel—detonated into chaos, erupting into a maelstrom of dust, flame, and flying shrapnel. Chunks of debris whistled past like bullets.

His ears screamed with a high, metallic ring, drowning out everything else. The earth throbbed beneath him like it had a pulse of its own.

Crawling toward the maternity ward, covered in dust and barely aware of the cuts on his legs, he pushed the door open—only to face a gun barrel.

"**Salam-wa aleikum,**" he said, voice steady but edged with urgency.

The militant nodded at first, distracted, his rifle resting against his hip. But as he stepped past him, the man's eyes narrowed. His head tilted. His body stiffened.

He had heard it—the difference. Not the words, but the way he spoke them. The softness on the "wa," the foreign lilt curling at the end of the sentence. A Western accent, barely buried.

He froze. Then his eyes darted back to Jason's face.

He caught the shift—the way the militant's fingers tightened on the rifle, the flicker of recognition flashing in his eyes.

Jason bolted. Bullets cracked through the air as he dodged sideways, shoving a cart of medical supplies into the man's path. Glass shattered overhead, raining down like jagged arrows.

The militant turned, distracted by the sound of approaching footsteps—just enough for him to slip away.

He burst into the room where he had left Alley.

"Alley!" he called, but the chaos of nearby blasts swallowed his voice.

His eyes landed on the crumpled bed. The IV bag still hung from its stand, a needle lying discarded on the sheets. Panic surged through him.

Emerging from the smoke, he encountered U.N. marshals. Seeing his scrubs, they prepared to evacuate him.

"Wait! My wife is here!" Jason pleaded.

The sergeant shook his head. "All foreign doctors and nurses have been accounted for. We have to move."

"She just had a baby! She looks like a patient, not a doctor!" he argued, desperation in his voice.

The sergeant didn't waver. "No American doctors are left behind."

The ground trembled beneath Jason's boots before he even registered the sound. Like the growl of something ancient and merciless, a low rumble built into a sudden, concussive roar. Then— **boom**—the wall beside him exploded inward.

Time fractured.

Shards of brick and concrete hurled through the air like shrapnel. Dust surged up in a choking wave, blinding and hot. He barely had time to yell before something slammed into his side, knocking the air from his lungs. He hit the ground hard—elbow first, shoulder, cheek against dirt and grit. Pain bloomed sharp and white behind his eyes.

The weight came next.

Debris rained down, a solid, suffocating crush of rubble pinning his legs and back. A jagged beam skidded across his ribs, pinning him against a collapsed wall. The air whooshed from his lungs again, and for a moment, all he could hear was the roar in his own head—like the ocean, like static, like his body trying to remember how to breathe.

Smoke.

His throat burned. The taste of concrete dust coated his tongue. He coughed, but it hurt—deep, grinding pain like something might be broken.

He couldn't move.

Panic clawed at the edge of his mind, but he forced it back, gritting his teeth. He blinked, tried to focus. Through the smoke, a silhouette moved—the sergeant was sprawled, motionless, a few feet away, blood seeping into the fabric of his uniform.

His vision swam, his ears ringing with a high-pitched whine. But instinct shoved the pain aside.

Move.

He clawed at the rubble, dragging one arm free. Rocks scraped his skin raw. A beam shifted, and he cried out—but he kept going. He bit down on the pain and crawled forward inch by inch, like an animal, until he could hook his arm under the sergeant's shoulders and begin dragging him backward.

Another explosion rumbled in the distance. The building groaned above them, a warning.

Jason didn't stop.

The world narrowed to that task: get him out. Get him safe.

Only when they were clear of the worst of the collapse—only when other medics rushed forward and took the sergeant from his grasp—did he let himself feel it.

His knees buckled. Blood dripped from a cut above his brow, blurring one eye. His vision narrowed, color bleeding from the edges. Voices called his name, distant and muted. His body pulsed with the creeping burn of shock.

He saw a figure sprinting toward him.

Heart racing, he feared another enemy—until he recognized Berry, his face a mix of worry and determination.

"Jason!" Berry shouted, rushing to steady him.

A gasp tore from him, his voice barely holding together. "My baby?"

Berry's grip strengthened. "He's safe. I promise."

Relief crashed over him.

"Come on," Berry urged. "Let's get you inside."

As they neared the chopper, the blades' roar grew deafening. Berry helped Jason into the aircraft and collapsed beside him.

His chest rose and fell in rapid bursts, head tipping back as he fought to steady himself, to focus.

Then he saw her.

Alley.

She was boarding the helicopter.

And then—nothing.

He forced his focus back to the present, fingers curling around the edges of the chair.

The room was eerily silent.

Sheila's voice broke through, gentle yet firm. "Jason, you're here now. You're safe."

He blinked, trying to shake off the weight of the past. The scent of coffee drifted in, steadying him as he returned from the pull of the past.

His fingers circled the rim of the mug without thought, eyes unfocused. Across from him, Berry shifted, his voice rough with memory. "We got through that day, Jason. You made it."

Outside, the light faded, stretching dusk across the floor—an echo of the storm still stirring within him.

As the session came to a quiet close, Sheila gathered her notebook, offering Jason a reassuring nod. "We'll pick this up when you're ready."

Berry stood, rolling his shoulders to ease the tension. His expression was tight, but he gave Jason a firm pat on the shoulder as he passed.

"Jason…" Margaret began, hesitating.

Finally standing, he met her gaze, offering a faint smile that didn't quite reach his eyes. "I'll be home soon." He appreciated her presence, but he needed space.

Margaret nodded, giving his hand a quick squeeze. "Okay. We'll wait for you."

As the group filed out, he lingered by the window, watching the fading light stretch across the room.

Sheila paused by the door, glancing back. "You did well today."

He gave a quick nod. "Thanks, Sheila."

She smiled and left, the click of the door closing behind her.

For a moment, Jason stood still, watching the sun dip below the horizon.

Tomorrow would come.

But for now, he turned toward the door—toward home, where the lights were warm and a child's laughter waited for him.

Chapter 28

The wheels are turning

The house was still when Jason stepped inside, the kind of stillness that didn't feel empty—but earned. He set his keys on the counter with a clink and poured himself a glass of water.

He stood at the window, the glass cool in his hand, eyes lost in the night. His reflection met him there—older, wearier, but somehow lighter.

The weight of the day hadn't disappeared. The memories still clung.

More than the weight, relief hovered in the air.

Not the loud kind. Not the kind that made you cheer. But the quiet kind—the kind that settles in your bones when you've finally stopped holding your breath. Laughter from the living room drew him forward. He found Eaton curled on the couch, glued to a cartoon. Jason slid onto the cushion.

"Hi, Dad," Eaton said, looking up with wide eyes.

"Hi, buddy. How was school?" he asked.

Eaton popped a cookie into his mouth, chewing dramatically. "School is always there, Dad. Ask how I am," he replied with mock exasperation.

A soft laugh escaped Jason as he played along. "All right. How are you?"

Eaton straightened, a mischievous grin spreading across his face. "Lilly and I are in a situationship," he declared.

He raised an eyebrow, trying not to laugh. "A situationship?"

Eaton nodded, proud of the term. But before he could explain, Robert walked in and turned down the TV.

"You're in a what?" he asked, brows furrowed.

Leaning back, he answered with casual ease. "It's a pre-relationship stage. Very Gen Z."

Eaton grinned, nodding enthusiastically. "Exactly!"

Margaret appeared in the doorway with a cup of green tea, catching the end of the conversation. She raised an eyebrow.

"So, does that mean you have a girlfriend now?" she inquired.

Eaton rolled his eyes dramatically.

"Not yet. It's just a situationship!" he replied.

The adults burst into laughter, the tension of the day melting away.

"Dad," Eaton said, leaning toward Jason, his eyes bright. "Can Lilly and Max come over on Friday after school?"

Jason nodded. "Sure, buddy."

Eaton beamed. "Oh, and tomorrow is Teachers' Day," he added seriously. "I need flowers for my teacher by eight."

He groaned, "Eight in the morning? The only place I know open that early is the hospital gift shop."

"Flowers are flowers, Dad." Eaton shrugged.

The shrill beep of the alarm woke him the next morning. It was 6 a.m. Usually, he would jog before his shower, but today he remained still, letting the quiet settle over him. Morning light filtered between the curtains, brushing the room with warmth as birds chirped in the distance.

Calm settled over him—something he hadn't felt in years. He woke without the heavy ache of loss. The session had dulled the sharp edges of his grief.

Then Eaton's request for flowers popped into his mind, and Jason bolted out of bed.

Ten minutes later, Jason pulled into his assigned parking spot— or where it should have been. The florist van was there again. He sighed and dialed the number printed on its side.

A cheerful voice answered. "Buds and Petals, how can I help you?"

"There's a van parked in Dr. Carter's spot again," he said politely.

"Oh, don't worry about that," the voice replied. "He won't be in for another hour."

Jason frowned. "Dr. Carter is already here and waiting."

The phone clicked. Moments later, a woman rushed toward him, waving apologetically. She jumped into the van and backed it out, freeing the spot. She parked nearby, stepping out with a confident smile.

"Hey," he said, raising an eyebrow as she approached. "Weren't you supposed to park in the garage?"

"Yes," the woman replied breezily. "But you don't usually come till 8:30 a.m., so I figured I'd use your spot for unloading the flowers. Security doesn't mind as long as I move before you show up. I'm Leia," she added, extending her hand.

He shook it reluctantly, his expression unamused. "I guess you already know my name."

"Of course," Leia said brightly, falling into step beside him. "The offer for coffee still stands, by the way."

Jason stopped mid-step. "I'm here to buy flowers for my son's teacher," he said.

Leia's face lit up as she pushed open the door to the hospital gift shop. "Which school?"

"Apple Creek Elementary."

"Perfect! I got a delivery there at 8:00 a.m. Want me to take them for you?"

He hesitated, then gave a nod. "That would be great. Thanks."

The gift shop at the hospital entrance stirred to life in a hush. Outside, the first blush of dawn painted muted lavender and gold across the horizon, casting a tender glow across the glass storefront.

Bouquets of lilies, tulips, roses, and marigolds stood in galvanized buckets near the entrance, their colors muted by the early light.

Inside, shelves were lined with neatly wrapped chocolates, plush toys, and greeting cards promising comfort. The air smelled like morning—hopeful, fragile, and full of things unsaid.

"Just pick the flowers, write the teacher's name and a message, and I'll handle the rest," Leia said, gesturing to the floral display.

Jason chose a bouquet of dahlias and filled out the card, adding Eaton's name at the bottom. As he handed over the flowers, Leia looked at him expectantly.

"So... about that coffee," she teased, arching an eyebrow, voice light. "If I'm saving you a trip to the school, I think that earns me one."

Before he could stop himself, Jason said, "Let's go," regretting it instantly.

Leia's face lit up. "Great! Follow me," she said, practically bouncing toward the café.

Jason followed her, shaking his head at himself. This morning was not going as expected.

"Are you always this happy in the mornings?" he asked, smiling despite himself.

"Of course!" Leia replied brightly, her eyes sparkling. "Mostly, anyway. Come on."

She pushed open the café door with an exaggerated flourish, leading him in. The warm scent of freshly brewed coffee and buttery croissants filled the air, wrapping around them like a comforting embrace.

Sunlight streamed into the windows, bathing the cozy space in gold, where conversation wove between the clink of cups.

Calm loosened his shoulders, relaxing him despite himself. "I must admit, that's a pretty good trade-off for driving across town," he murmured, the morning warmth sinking into his bones.

Leia grinned and leaned closer, lowering her voice. "It's not just the coffee. It's the people watching. Best entertainment of the morning," she said with a wink.

Jason chuckled as they stepped inside. "People watching, huh? So, do I qualify as morning entertainment?" he teased.

Leia turned to him with a playful smirk. "You're getting there, Dr. Carter. You've got potential."

As they approached the counter, the barista greeted them.

Jason ordered his black coffee. Leia went with a double espresso and a croissant.

She arched an eyebrow at him playfully. "No frills? Very serious of you."

He shrugged. "I'm a serious guy."

"We'll see about that," she teased, flashing a grin.

When their drinks arrived, she raised her tiny espresso cup. "To mornings."

He clinked his mug against hers. "To mornings."

Leia leaned back, studying him with a mischievous glint. "So... Eaton's dad, huh?"

Jason nearly choked on his coffee. "How do you know that?"

She winked. "Easy. I read the card. Plus, my niece Lilly's in Eaton's class."

Jason gave a mock-serious look. "Lilly? My kid's in a situationship with her."

Leia laughed, shaking her head. "Of course he is. Lilly's dinner announcement gave my brother-in-law a mini-stroke."

A laugh burst from him, louder than he intended, and the sound caught him off guard.

They lingered, swapping stories about kids, chaos, and the weirdness of modern dating, the conversation flowing easier than he'd expected.

When Leia's phone beeped, she grimaced.

"I should go—school deliveries wait for no one."

She hesitated for a beat. Then, lightly: "I'd love to do this again if you want."

Jason smiled—a real one this time, easy and unforced.

"Yeah. I'd like that."

On the drive home, the streets still bathed in early light, the morning replayed in his mind—the laughter, the easy banter, Leia's bright, restless energy.

It felt so… normal. So comfortable that it almost startled him.

A beat passed. Then the tension left his face, replaced by something gentler.

Wait.

Was that a date?

Did I accidentally go on a date?

The realization settled into him—quiet, a little shaky, unfamiliar but not unwelcome.

Time had stood still for him.

It had been seven years since the idea of dating had even occurred to him.

Seven years since he'd last seen Alley.

He let the thought drift across the dashboard, warmed by the quiet hush of morning sun.

Maybe he wasn't ready. Maybe he never would be.

But as he turned onto his street, something lighter moved through him—a breath he hadn't realized he'd been holding.

He didn't have it figured out.

But after months of merely going through the motions, a flicker of life stirred inside him that morning.

Chapter 29

Fragments of yesterday

Alley woke to the shrill beep of her alarm, the faint gray light of dawn slipping through the curtains. A faint coolness pressed against her skin as she sat up, the night's chill lingering beneath the covers.

Careful not to wake Steve, she eased out from beneath his arm. He stirred, murmuring sleepily.

"Morning already?" he groaned, his voice muffled against the pillow.

"Yeah," Alley whispered. At the foot of the bed, Elijah, their golden retriever, lifted his head groggily, giving them a disapproving look before settling back down with a classic not-a-morning-dog expression.

Quietly, she kissed Steve on the forehead, where the faint scent of his cologne lingered from the night before, and slipped into her robe. The old wooden floors creaked under her bare feet as she made her way to the bathroom.

Outside, the wind rustled through the trees, scattering golden leaves across the yard. The sound of crows cawing mingled with the faint rhythms of life beginning to stir in their small neighborhood.

The shower sputtered, then flowed warm against her skin, chasing away the morning chill. Alley closed her eyes, resting her forehead against the cool tile. The scent of citrus rose with the steam, curling gently in the air.

Her thoughts wandered to the day ahead. She was meeting the oven salesperson at eight, then the pumpkin and apple vendors. Fall was the busiest season for her bakery, as the scent of cinnamon and nutmeg drew customers in for pies and pastries. This was where she belonged—her sanctuary, her home.

But at ten, there was Dale—and the doctor she'd briefly met earlier that week. A flicker of unease twisted her stomach. *I must have really scared Dale if he's bringing in a specialist,* she thought. She exhaled deeply, letting the water soothe her nerves. It wasn't the doctor that unsettled her; it was what the doctor might uncover.

Turning slightly, the scars on her shoulder caught her eye. Faint and silvery in the dim light, they were permanent reminders of a life she struggled to piece together. For a moment, her hand lingered over them, tracing their edges as a memory surfaced—not of the scars themselves, but of a familiar face.

The water blurred her vision, but she could almost see him, his laugh echoing in her mind. His boyish grin, his teasing voice—He resembled someone she knew, though the details drifted away like dust on a breeze.

She shut off the water abruptly, the memory slipping away. Alley wrapped herself in a towel and stepped in front of the mirror. Wiping away the steam, she caught her own reflection, her eyes shadowed with uncertainty.

Will this new doctor see beyond the scars? Will they see who she was now—or who she used to be, the one even she struggled to remember?

With a sigh, she patted face cream onto her cheeks, the faint floral scent clinging to her skin. She forced herself to push the fleeting face from her thoughts.

Her mind returned to the day ahead, and she whispered to her reflection, "Time to get moving, Alley. Let's hope this doctor has answers—or at least doesn't ask too many questions."

When Alley stepped into the kitchen, the aroma of freshly brewed coffee greeted her. Steve was leaning against the counter, holding two mugs, his hair still tousled from sleep. Elijah had followed her, plopping down by the table.

Steve lifted her onto the counter, handing her a mug.

"Can I come with you? At least to the hospital?" he asked carefully. "I promise I won't come into the consultation room."

Alley pretended to ponder, the corners of her mouth tilting in mock thought.

"Okay. But no fussing, Steve. You'll just make me more nervous."

"Agreed," he replied with mock solemnity.

Checking the clock on the stove, she hopped off the counter. "We need to leave in fifteen minutes."

Steve pressed a kiss to her forehead, but Alley wriggled away, rushing to get dressed. Her laughter echoed down the hallway, Elijah's paws tapping close behind.

As the house grew quiet, Steve lingered in the kitchen, staring into his coffee. Watching her light-hearted retreat brought him joy, but underneath it all was fear.

What if she remembered everything? She might realize she didn't belong here, didn't belong with him. She might leave, taking the warmth and connection they'd built over the years.

And then there was the possibility that the pieces might never come together for her, that she'd be haunted by fragments and her laughter forever dimmed by the weight of the unknown.

Steve gripped the mug tightly. Help her, God, he prayed. Help her find peace—whatever that looks like. And if she remembers… please let her remember loving me, too.

Chapter 30

Embers of the past

The drive to the hospital was quiet, save for the low murmurs of the radio playing in the background. Alley traced lazy patterns on the window, watching the world blur past in autumn shades of amber and crimson.

Steve noticed how her fingers curled slightly, the way they did when she was deep in thought. There was a change in her—the way she carried herself, a quiet resolve woven into her every movement.

He wanted to say something—offer reassurance, a distraction, anything—but he knew better. Some moments asked for presence, not words.

As they pulled into the parking lot, Alley loosened her grip on the seatbelt, exhaling the last remnants of hesitation.

"Are you ready?" Steve asked, his voice steady despite the uncertainty that churned inside him.

Alley was silent for a moment, staring out at the hospital. Then, finally, she nodded.

"I have to be."

Alley's gaze caught on the trees lining the lot, their leaves blazing red and orange in the golden morning light. The crisp air carried the quiet beauty of fall.

"We should have a picnic today," Alley said suddenly, her voice thoughtful. Steve turned off the ignition and stepped out of the car. A hint of amusement played on his face as he walked around to open her door. "Sure—if you get out of the session early."

Alley stepped out, pausing to look at him, her expression serious. "Steve," she began, "why don't you come into the session with me today?"

Steve froze mid-step, surprised. "Are you sure?" he asked carefully. "Will you be comfortable with me there?"

Alley's gaze didn't waver. "It's not about being comfortable," she said with growing resolve. "It's about how you interfere in the sessions.

As soon as it gets uncomfortable, you make me stop. You don't mean to, but you do."

Steve opened his mouth to respond, the reflex to defend himself bubbling up—but he stopped. He'd done it before. Pulled her out. Tried to protect her by shutting things down.

Alley held up a hand, cutting him off.

"This is important to me, Steve," she continued.

"If you promise to just listen—to be a lizard on the wall—you can come. But if you interrupt or try to pull me out when things get hard, I'll throw you out myself."

He blinked, the weight of her words settling over him. Then, after a beat, he gave a chuckle. "A lizard on the wall, huh? I can do that. Or maybe I'll be a fly on the wall," he said, but there was a hush behind the grin, like a thought had slipped in.

Alley looked at him evenly. "Really, Steve. This is serious…"

Steve looked at her for a moment—really looked at her. Strong, hurting, determined. "I know," he said finally, his voice low. "And I won't get in the way. I promise."

Satisfied, Alley nodded, and they walked together toward Dale's office. The brisk air tugged at her scarf, and she tied it around her neck.

Dr. Sheila and Dr. Dale greeted them warmly as they entered. Sheila gestured toward the sitting area, her demeanor calm and inviting. "Come in, both of you," she said. "Let's get started."

The sitting area was cozy yet professional, with chairs and a sofa arranged in a circle. A low coffee table in the center held a neat stack of notes and a vase of fresh flowers, their delicate scent filling the room faintly. The large window welcomed the fall sunlight, which painted gentle patterns across the floor.

Alley sat down first, folding her hands in her lap. Her expression was composed, though Steve noticed the way she held her fingers in a tight grip. He took the seat beside her, leaning back slightly to keep his promise of being an observer rather than an active participant.

Dr. Sheila smiled at Alley, her expression encouraging and gentle.

"Alley, we spoke earlier this week about your fainting spell," she began. "But today, we're going to take a step further back. If you're ready, we'll begin exploring some of the deeper pieces of your past."

Alley nodded, steadying herself. "I'm ready," she said, though her words were a little unsteady.

Sheila glanced at Steve.

"Steve, thank you for joining us today. To clarify, your role here is to listen and provide support. This space is primarily for Alley, and we want to ensure she feels safe to express herself fully," she said kindly, although a touch of firmness was clear in her voice.

Steve nodded quickly, sitting up straighter. "Understood," he said earnestly.

Dr. Dale leaned forward, his notebook resting on his knee.

"Alley, let's start with something simple," he said gently. "Tell us about a memory—something from your childhood that feels significant, even if you're not sure why."

Alley hesitated, her gaze falling to her hands. She twisted the bracelet on her wrist, a habit she did when she was gathering her thoughts.

Finally, she looked up and spoke, calm and quiet.

"I remember the wind chimes," she began. "They hung outside our house. When the breeze came, they'd start singing, and something about that sound… it always made me feel calm."

She hesitated. "I don't know why, but I always connected those chimes to my dad. Maybe I imagined the sound as whispers from the universe—his way of telling me he was okay."

Sheila nodded encouragingly. "That's a beautiful memory, Alley. Do you feel like those chimes were tied to a sense of safety for you?"

Alley swallowed, her gaze distant. "Maybe. I think… I don't think of them anymore. My mom was happy and full of life, keeping us together when my dad left to write about the world's suffering as a war correspondent. He was my hero."

Steve's fingers curled slightly around the armrest of his chair, but he remained silent.

Sheila's voice remained gentle.

"Would you like to talk about your dad today?"

Alley hesitated, her fingers still twisting the bracelet.

Finally, she nodded.

"I think I need to."

"Good." Sheila offered a small, encouraging smile. "Let's take it one step at a time. Say whatever comes to mind, even if it feels random."

Alley's gaze grew distant.

"I remember the hallway... the light was flickering. As a family, we gathered around the TV to listen to his reporting from different parts of the world. My mom would cut his articles out of the papers and make a journal."

Her gaze softened, touched by memory. "I wanted to be like him when I grew up, but he urged me to go to medical school and help the suffering. My sister was ten years younger than I—too little to understand what he did, but she adored him."

Her eyes softened with the memory. "He was so happy when I got into medical school..."

Steve and Dale exchanged glances, both remembering when Vicky had called to share the same news about Alley getting into medical school.

Alley lifted her gaze to Sheila. "The trip to the school for the white coat ceremony was memorable. The first day, I walked into a whole new world."

Even in the quiet therapy room, the memory of laughter under string lights seemed to fill his nostrils with smoke and spice.

"That's where I met Berry... and Jay."

She paused; her voice tinged with nostalgia. "They were my best friends—they became my family."

Chapter 31

Unraveling the silence

As Alley spoke, the memories seemed to take on their own life, unfurling like pages in a long-forgotten book.

Dr. Sheila leaned in slightly, a trace of compassion in her gaze, but her focus didn't waver.

At the mention of Jay and Berry, their expressions shifted—curiosity mingled with recognition.

She exchanged a glance with Dale, one that said more than words could. Alley's sentence had left something suspended in the air—heavy and unresolved.

"Berry and Jay... What was it about them that made them feel like family?"

Alley hesitated, her lips twitching with the memory. "They just... fit. Berry made everything feel like an adventure, and Jay... always knew what to say. I don't know, they just made the world feel smaller. Less lonely."

A glint of warmth passed through her eyes before they steeled into guardedness.

Dr. Sheila didn't push. Instead, she let the silence settle, allowing Alley the space to sit with the weight of her own words.

Steve, however, sat with his hands clenched against his knees. He had promised to be a lizard on the wall, but watching her speak about another man—one whose name had slipped from her lips with unfiltered warmth—it did something to him.

And as Alley exhaled, her gaze growing distant, Steve couldn't shake the feeling that—piece by piece—she was remembering a world he wasn't a part of.

"Jay?" Sheila asked gently, tilting her head. "Is that short for something?"

Alley blinked. "Yes... It's my nickname for Jay..." The end of the sentence slipped away, her expression clouding with doubt.

She hesitated, brows knitting. "I—I think it was…" The crease deepened. "I'm not sure," she whispered. "I don't know why I can't remember."

Sheila's voice stayed steady. "It's okay. Go on."

Alley ran her fingers along the edge of her bracelet. "I know I called him Jay," she said quietly. "But it feels… distant. Like something I dreamed, not something I lived."

Sheila nodded. "Memories come in pieces."

Alley swallowed. "I need to remember."

Dale's voice was calm, reassuring. "For now, we'll go with what comes to you."

She leaned back slightly, loosening her grip on her bracelet.

"Those first few weeks were overwhelming. The city was so different from my small hometown. Everything felt enormous—like stepping into a different world. But then… I met them. Berry and Jay.

"I was nervous at first, but they were easy to talk to. Berry always cracked jokes, making everyone laugh. Jay was quieter and more serious, but he had this warmth that made you feel like you belonged."

A quiet tension crept through Steve, but he listened silently, as promised.

"The three of us became inseparable. Late-night study sessions, long conversations about life and dreams… They were my anchor, my family away from home."

She paused, her expression clouding. "Jay… Berry and I were idealistic kids, happy-go-lucky, determined to set the mad world straight after finishing medical school."

Alley looked up at him, her expression conflicted. Her gaze moved to Steve, who sat silently beside her, tension radiating from him. She hesitated.

"I think…" she started, faltering. "I think I need a minute."

Sheila nodded with quiet understanding. "Take your time, Alley. There's no rush."

Alley exhaled. "Can we have something to eat? I'm hungry."

Steve chuckled softly. Sheila gave a slight nod. "Of course, Alley. Let's take a break."

After the break, Alley sat in the chair, fingers absently twisting her bracelet as memories washed over her.

The hospital was a whirlwind of noise and movement. As young interns, she and her classmates scrambled between patient charts and overflowing wards, the air filled with the sharp scent of antiseptic and the muffled beeping of monitors.

Cups of coffee became lifelines, keeping them awake through grueling exams. "One more cup before the anatomy final," Berry would say, grinning as he handed her a steaming mug.

In the midst of chaos, something unexpected bloomed.

"Love," Alley murmured, the word escaping her lips like a secret.

Sheila tilted her head slightly, curiosity piqued. "Love?" she prompted gently.

Alley nodded, her gaze distant. "Jay. It started quietly, and then everything shifted. He became more than a steady presence—he became everything. The person I trusted most."

Steve stiffened slightly but remained silent.

Alley's voice grew quieter. "I remember one night… It was late, and we were both exhausted after a double shift. We sat in the breakroom, eating leftover sandwiches from the vending machine, and he just looked at me. Like he could see straight through—my fears, my dreams. And he didn't look away."

She blinked, her eyes glistening. "That's when I knew. I think I'd always known, but that was the moment it hit me."

No one spoke. Her words lingered, heavy in the air.

Sheila's voice was gentle as she asked, "And how did that change things?"

Alley hesitated, twisting her bracelet. "It made everything more complicated. I couldn't separate my own feelings from what we were supposed to be. And I didn't know if he felt the same way."

She glanced at Sheila, her expression conflicted. "It was… messy. Beautiful, but messy."

Alley swallowed as if pushing down something unsaid. "In the end, it was those moments that shaped us. The late nights, the long conversations, the way we learned to hold each other up. We thought we had time."

Then, with a quiet, resolute tilt of her chin, Alley squared her shoulders.

"I don't know if I'm ready to talk about the rest," she admitted, her words steadier now. "But I think… I want to be."

Sheila nodded in understanding. "That's a good place to pause."

Alley glanced at Steve, searching his face for something, reassurance, maybe. He gave her a look—quiet, almost that didn't quite reach his eyes.

"You're doing great," he murmured.

A quiet certainty whispered that maybe—just maybe—she wasn't carrying it all alone.

Chapter 32

Love isn't about replacing the past

The air was crisp, carrying the faint scent of damp earth and fallen leaves. Steve stood on the balcony, fingers curled around a cooling cup of coffee. A shiver crawled up his spine, but he didn't move—didn't seem to notice the wind lifting the hem of his shirt.

Alley's words echoed in his mind, sharp and relentless.

Jay. She had spoken his name like a prayer—gentle and reverent.

The railing was cold beneath his palm as he set the cup down. Below, in the courtyard, a father chased his laughing child around a park bench. The boy's giggles rang out like wind chimes, bright and unburdened.

That could've been me and Alley.

The thought burned, curling in his stomach like hot embers. He dragged a hand down his face, fingertips brushing the rough stubble along his jaw. It wasn't jealousy—at least, not entirely. It was grief.

Grief for a part of Alley's life he could never touch.

The sliding door behind him rattled before gliding open. He knew who it was before the footsteps followed—steady and deliberate.

"Steve," his father said gently, his voice carrying the warmth of a well-worn coat. "How are you holding up?"

Steve didn't answer right away. He let the question drift into the air like smoke, dissolving before it could settle. The distant scent of burning firewood reached him, and for a second, he let it ground him.

Finally, he looked off to the side, irony threading faintly through his expression.

"It's not about me," he murmured. "This is about Alley. About what she needs."

Dale stepped closer, his presence solid beside him. "And yet, it's impossible not to feel it, isn't it? The weight of everything she's remembering."

Steve made a sound—something between a sigh and a laugh. It held no humor.

"It's not jealousy," he said quietly, his hand tightening on the railing. "I knew she had a past. A whole life before me. But hearing her say his name… seeing the way her eyes light up when she talks about him…" He paused, eyes fixed on the horizon, the unspoken words hanging heavy between them.

"It's not that I'm angry. I just—" He paused. "I just don't know where I fit into all of this."

Dale didn't speak right away. He gave Steve space, letting the moment settle. The air smelled like rain, though the skies were clear.

The faint scent of coffee lingered in the room, sharp and familiar. Steve swallowed hard. "I love her," he said quietly. "I always have. And I know this is what she needs to heal. But God, Dad… it hurts." His voice wavered. "It hurts to see her remember a love so deep, so all-consuming, and know that it's not me."

Dale reached out, resting a firm hand on his son's shoulder.

"You're here, Steve. You're her anchor now. What she had before doesn't erase or diminish what you share with her. The two can coexist. Love isn't about replacing the past; it's about making space for both."

Steve turned, meeting his father's eyes. They were steady, the kind of steady Steve wished he could be.

"I just want to do right by her." His gaze dropped. "Even if it means standing in the background while she pieces herself back together."

Dale gave his shoulder a reassuring squeeze. "And that, son, is exactly why you'll always matter. Love isn't about erasing the past. It's about standing beside someone as they carry it."

Steve didn't respond, but something in him shifted. His shoulders eased, his grip on the railing less rigid.

For now, it would have to do.

Below, the laughter from the father and child faded, swallowed by the wind. Steve filled his lungs with cool autumn air, its sharp sting a reminder that he was still here.

The road ahead would be fraught with memories and ghosts, but for Alley he would brave the storm.

He just prayed he'd have the strength to withstand it.

Chapter 33

Mad about you

Sheila called Steve and Dale, signaling that it was time to continue.

Steve slid open the balcony doors, letting in a gentle breeze scented with the fragrance of blooming jasmine. He took a seat behind Alley, who sat stiffly, her posture tight with tension.

"Anytime you're ready," Sheila said, her voice calm.

Alley's voice came low. "At the time, I didn't think marriage was something I wanted. Not yet."

She paused, eyes clouding.

"But that night... something happened."

Her gaze dropped, fingers still twisting the bracelet.

"That night felt like a fairytale. But I... I'm not sure what happened after that."

She hesitated, glancing at Steve, who was watching her intently. His expression was unreadable, and his hands rested quietly in his lap.

"I don't know," she admitted. "It's... hard."

Sheila nodded. "Take your time, Alley. We don't have to rush."

Her eyes grew distant, caught in a memory. The firelight, the mountains, the laughter—they lingered like a faded photograph she couldn't quite reach.

"I thought that night would be the beginning of something perfect," she whispered.

Emotion broke through as she turned toward Sheila.

"Berry... I thought I saw him the other day. And Jay... my dad..."

The words slipped away. Her face went pale.

Steve's stomach turned at her words. He stood abruptly, forgetting his promise to stay still. Kneeling before her, he gently placed his hands on her knees.

"Alley," he said, his voice trembling. "I'm here. I've got you."

She trembled into him, her head sinking against his shoulder. As he held her, the tension left her body, and her sobs echoed through the still room.

Sheila watched with a calm, thoughtful gaze. "Let's pause for a moment. Take all the time you need."

"I don't want to stop," Alley said once she'd composed herself, her eyes moving between Sheila and Dale. "What if I forget again? What if it all slips away, and I lose them all—for good?"

Sheila's tone was warm, anchoring. "I understand, Alley. But it's important to pace yourself. These memories—they can bring so much, all at once. Let's give them space. Let's give you space."

Alley's fingers danced along the armrest, restless with energy she couldn't quite name. "I'm scared." Her voice trembled. "What if I can't find the rest of it?"

Sheila gave a steady nod, her eyes calm and kind.

And in the hush that followed, something stayed. Uncertain. Unfinished. But she was still reaching for the light.

Chapter 34

Echoes in the smoke

"I don't understand," she said into the silence.

The balcony door slid open, and Steve entered the office, followed by Sheila and Dale. Their footsteps were careful, their gazes searching.

Steve's eyes locked onto hers instantly, reading her face as if trying to gauge how much of her was still in the room and how much was lost in the past.

"Alley?" His voice was quiet, uncertain. "Are you… Okay?"

She lifted her eyes to his face, full of clarity and heartbreak. Her gaze wavered for just a second. "How could I forget them? How could I let them slip away?"

Steve hesitated before lowering himself into the chair beside her. He didn't reach for her hand—wasn't sure if she needed his comfort or space.

"You've been through so much," he said carefully. "Maybe your mind was trying to protect you."

Alley pulled back slightly, frustration flashing across her face. "But why? They were everything to me, Steve. How could I not remember them?"

The moment that followed weighed between them—an unspoken truth neither had the words for.

Dale's voice was steady but gentle. "Alley, what do you remember about… what happened?"

A flicker of fear crossed her face. She looked at Dale, then at Sheila.

"Not everything," she admitted. "But enough to know that something went terribly wrong."

Sheila nodded, her tone calm and reassuring. "That's a natural response with dissociative amnesia. Your mind shielded you from something too overwhelming. Now, those memories are resurfacing because you're finally in a place where you can begin to process them."

Alley looked up, her fingers trembling against the ceramic cup. "I remember waking up in a hospital room," she said quietly, her words suspended in memory. "White walls. Curtains shifting in a breeze from a half-open window. And the beeping... steady, unrelenting—from the monitors."

She hesitated, pressing her lips together before continuing.

"The first thing I noticed was the smell of smoke and screams. It clung to everything—sharp, metallic, suffocating. Then... the noise. A bomb. An explosion. I could feel the vibration in my body."

Her words faltered.

"I tried to get up, but there were IV tubes in my arm. I ripped them out, and—" She stopped abruptly, eyes drifting to her wrist as if she could still feel the sting of it.

When she spoke again, the words barely stirred the air.

"I kept calling for them. Jay. Berry. Dad. I kept calling their names, but... no one came."

The room felt colder. Steve held the armrests like they might anchor him. He wanted to comfort her, to take away the pain—but how could he?

Alley's fingers curled around her cup as she forced the words out. "The smoke got thicker. I couldn't think straight. I panicked. And then... I heard my dad's voice."

Sheila tilted her head, a trace of curiosity in her eyes.

Alley hesitated, confusion flickering across her face. "I... I think so. I remember him sitting by my bed, holding my hand. His voice was calm, steady."

A frown crept onto her lips.

"But now... I don't know if it was real. What if it wasn't? What if he wasn't really there?"

A crack slipped into her words. She pressed a shaking hand to her mouth, her shoulders curling inward.

Steve leaned forward instinctively, his fingers digging into his jeans. The urge to pull her close gripped him, to tell her none of it mattered—that she was safe now. But she was unraveling in a way he couldn't reach.

Sheila reached out, placing a hand gently on Alley's knee. "It's okay to question those memories. Whether real or not, they gave you comfort in a moment of fear. We'll piece it together, one memory at a time."

Alley gave a faint nod, her voice barely audible. "But I need to know… If it wasn't real, then where was he?"

Steve went still, forcing himself to breathe despite the weight pressing inward. He didn't have the answers. He wasn't sure he wanted them.

Finally, Sheila spoke, her brows slightly drawn and her expression calm and thoughtful. There was no rush in her demeanor, only a quiet certainty. "We'll get there, Alley. But for now, let's take it one step at a time."

Alley's hands firmed in her lap. "I don't want to stop," she admitted. "What if I forget again?"

Sheila gave a small, measured glance. "You won't. But taking a break will help you process what you've already remembered."

Steve nodded, his voice tight but steady. "A break sounds good." Even though part of him ached to keep going—to uncover what had happened and make sure she never had to face it alone again.

Sheila stood, motioning toward the door. "Get some rest. Both of you."

She pushed to her feet. When Steve offered his hand, she blinked once, uncertainty flickering—then reached for him.

He squeezed her fingers gently. A promise spoken without words. "I'm proud of you," he said, his voice trembling despite himself.

Alley's eyes filled with unshed tears, her lips trembling with gratitude. "Thank you," she said softly.

As they approached the door, Alley turned back to Sheila, desperation threading through her words.

"Jay and Berry…Are they here?"

Sheila exchanged a glance with Dale, a shadow of doubt crossing her expression.

Steve's voice was firm but careful. "Let's go, Alley. We'll figure it out."

Alley nodded reluctantly and followed him out. As the door clicked shut, a heavy stillness settled over the therapy room—as though the walls had soaked up every unspoken word.

Sheila lowered her gaze briefly before looking at Dale, uncertainty flickering across her composed face.

"That was... intense," Dale murmured.

Sheila nodded, her expression somber. "And it's only the beginning."

Sheila's gaze followed the last traces of daylight as they slipped away. Because once Alley's memories returned, the past wouldn't just be remembered—it would demand to be faced.

Outside, the sky had deepened into burnt orange and indigo, the crisp air carrying the scent of distant woodsmoke. Sheila watched the last traces of daylight fade, a quiet heaviness settling in her body.

Chapter 35

Unsettling face

The last traces of daylight faded, giving way to the deep blues and golds of a crisp autumn evening. A cool breeze rustled through the trees, carrying the scents of wood smoke and damp leaves.

The session had ended, but its weight lingered as Steve and Alley walked to the car. Neither of them spoke. The moment felt heavy with things they hadn't said.

As they climbed in, Alley's phone buzzed in her bag, breaking the quiet. She pulled it out just as Steve started the engine. Emmy's name flashed on the screen.

"Hey, Em—"

"The cake! The bakery! It closes in twenty minutes, and Max will never forgive me if he doesn't get his dinosaur cake! Please, please, please, can you pick it up?" Emmy's voice was frantic.

Steve shot Alley a questioning glance. Amusement flickered in Alley's eyes as she fought back a laugh.

"What do you think, Steve? Can we save Emmy from a full-blown panic attack?"

Steve sighed. "A noble cause." Then, leaning closer to the speaker, he added, "But after we pick up the cake, can we swing by the house for a quick change of clothes?"

Emmy groaned. "Fine, but only if you actually pick up the cake in the next few minutes. No detours, Steve! I mean it."

Alley laughed as she ended the call. "You know, you just gave her a whole new reason to stress out, right?"

Steve smirked, hands steady on the wheel. "If saving the cake means I get to ditch this wrinkled shirt before Max's party, it's worth the risk."

They chuckled, the day's tension dissolving like sugar in coffee. For a moment, normalcy settled between them.

As Steve turned onto the main road, Alley leaned her head against the window. The session clung to her like static—unseen but impossible to shake. The memories were raw, jagged at the edges. But she wasn't ready to open them up. Not yet.

The party would be a welcome distraction—a few hours of laughter and normalcy before reality came crashing back.

An hour later, freshly changed, Steve and Alley pulled up to Emmy's house with the prized dinosaur cake in hand.

Inside, chaos reigned.

Joel—Max's dad—wrestled with a tangled roll of streamers, Emmy chased Max with a comb while straightening his shirt, and Max—being Max—squirmed away like a wild dinosaur escaping capture.

"Joel, if you don't fix that banner, I'm taping you to the wall next," Emmy snapped, waving a streamer like a whip.

Max snickered, unruly curls flopping into his eyes as Joel muttered, "Yes, ma'am."

"Stop-p-p, Mom!" Max cried dramatically, shielding his head with his hands. "Messy hair is cool!"

"It's not cool. It's chaos," Emmy huffed, wielding the hairbrush like a weapon.

Max rolled his eyes, ducked, and bolted toward Alley and Steve with a triumphant grin.

"Uncle Steve! Aunt Alley!" he yelled, throwing his arms in the air. "Tell Mom messy hair is way cooler!"

Steve crouched, setting the cake aside before ruffling Max's already wild hair.

"You know, buddy, you're pulling off this whole 'Tyrannosaurus with swagger' look pretty well," he said with a wink.

Alley laughed, handing the cake to Emmy, who shot her son a halfhearted glare.

"Fine. Be messy."

"Messy with style," Max corrected proudly before stomping off toward the kitchen.

An hour later, the house was buzzing—lights low, music up, kids laughing and darting between rooms.

Then, Eaton arrived with his grandmother.

The warm porch light illuminated them as they stepped onto the path.

Eaton clutched his grandmother's hand, his eyes lighting up at the sight of his friends.

"Go on, have fun," she urged, brushing a strand of his hair from his face. "Your dad will pick you up at seven, okay?"

"Okay, Grandma!" Eaton exclaimed, already halfway across the yard.

Margaret lingered at the edge of the porch, the golden light casting soft shadows across her face. Her gaze drifted and landed on Alley.

The warmth in her expression faded, replaced by something else. Recognition.

Her lips parted slightly as if to say something.

But just as quickly, she turned away, slipping back into her car.

At that same moment, Alley's gaze drifted across the yard.

Their eyes met.

And for a heartbeat—the noise, the laughter, the party—all of it faded.

There was something unspoken in that exchange.

Something just beyond reach.

Then, a boy dashed past, bumping into Alley with a hurried "Sorry!" before disappearing into the fray.

By the time she looked back, the woman was gone.

Her silhouette had vanished into the night.

Alley stood frozen, thoughts racing.

She had seen this woman before.

Standing beside a boy... Eaton. At the hospital.

Almost unconsciously, she looked up, her expression caught between curiosity and ache.

The scent of vanilla frosting, caramel apples, and freshly baked cookies filled the air.

A Tyrannosaurus piñata swayed gently, waiting for its turn to be demolished.

The children shrieked in delight as Max smashed the box open, sending a cascade of colorful candies tumbling to the ground.

The party buzzed with warmth and joy.

But Alley barely registered any of it.

A shiver passed through her as she rubbed her hands against the chill.

She had been running on adrenaline all evening—swept up in the comfort of normalcy.

But now, fatigue pressed down—thick and unshakable.

Steve's voice pulled her back.

"Hey," he said gently, coming up beside her. "You okay?"

Alley turned to him, trying to muster warmth she didn't quite feel. "Yeah. Just… tired."

Steve studied her for a moment, concern flickering across his face. But he didn't push.

Instead, he simply nodded.

"Let's get you home."

Alley let out a quiet breath of relief.

She didn't need to figure everything out tonight.

She didn't need to untangle the past all at once.

She could let it wait.

For now, she just needed rest.

As the party hummed around them—the glow of string lights reflecting off happy faces, the distant sound of a birthday song starting inside—Alley let herself lean into the exhaustion, into the warmth of Steve's presence. Into the simple comfort of knowing that, just for tonight, she didn't have to remember.

Chapter 36

The lady by the fish tank

Jason pulled into the Meijer driveway, headlights washing over the porch as laughter spilled into the night. Kids darted across the front yard, their sneakers crunching over fallen leaves.

Just as he stepped out of his car, another vehicle pulled in behind him. He turned slightly, squinting as the glow of headlights faded. Leia emerged, her face lighting up with a warmth he knew well—even in the dim driveway.

"So we meet again," she teased, a hint of amusement in her tone.

Jason offered a small smile, polite but distant. "Seems like we have a habit of showing up at the same places."

Leia approached, her heels clicking against the tarmac. "Are you coming in, or should I let Eaton know you're here?"

Jason slid his hands into his jacket pockets. "I'll wait here if you wouldn't mind," he said, his voice measured. The last thing he wanted was to step into a crowded room filled with noisy parents and birthday cake-fueled chaos.

Leia studied him for a beat before nodding. "Not a problem. I'll grab him for you."

Jason leaned against his car as she disappeared inside, tilting his head back. The night stretched clear overhead, stars scattered like flecks of silver across a deep canvas. A cool breeze carried the scent of damp leaves and distant woodsmoke, mingling with the lingering warmth of pavement.

Leia returned moments later, stepping lightly down the porch steps. "They need about fifteen more minutes to finish dinner," she said with a smile. "Want to take a walk while we wait?"

Jason hesitated, then glanced back at the warmly lit house. He paused, still for a beat.

"Yeah," he said, pushing off the car. "Let's go."

They strolled down the quiet street, their pace unhurried. The rhythmic crunch of gravel beneath their feet filled the spaces between words, blending with the rustling of trees in the cool autumn breeze.

Leia glanced at him, her eyes bright. "So, do you always linger in driveways to avoid socializing?"

Jason chuckled, shaking his head. "Only when absolutely necessary," he admitted. "Navigating a room full of sugar-high kids and overly chatty parents wasn't exactly how I planned to spend my evening."

Leia laughed, tucking a stray strand of hair behind her ear. "Fair enough. But I'm pretty sure Eaton would argue those fifteen kids are the best company in the world."

"He would," Jason said, a hint of amusement softening the words. "He's good at reminding me not to take life so seriously."

Leia's gaze softened. "Kids have a way of doing that."

They settled into an easy quiet, the night wrapping around them like something familiar.

Jason hadn't realized how much he needed this—the stillness, the space, a moment free from the noise, the pressure, the weight of everything else.

"Thanks for this," he said finally, his voice quieter. "I didn't realize how much I needed a break."

Leia looked over at him, her expression open, warm. "Anytime," she said, and he believed her.

The party was still in full swing when they looped back to the driveway. With some surprise, Jason realized he wasn't in as much of a rush to leave as he had been earlier.

The front door swung open, breaking the quiet. Jason turned just as Eaton and Lilly bounded down the steps, their laughter ringing into the night.

"Don't forget about our plan tomorrow!" Lilly called after Eaton.

"I won't!" he yelled back before jogging toward the car, tossing his backpack onto the seat as he buckled in. Completely unaware of the quiet exchange between the adults, he was still buzzing from the excitement of the party.

Jason glanced at Leia, her face still illuminated by the porch light. For a fleeting moment, he thought about saying something—

acknowledging the ease of the evening, the unexpected comfort of her company. Instead, he settled for a simple nod.

"See you around," he said.

She looked at him with casual warmth. "See you, Jason."

She gave a quick wave before turning toward her car.

Jason turned onto their street, his grip loosening on the wheel. The drive had been quiet, a rare stretch of peace he hadn't realized he needed.

He glanced at Eaton through the rearview mirror, watching his son stare out the window, lost in his own thoughts. "Had fun?" he asked, keeping his tone casual.

"Yeah!" Eaton said excitedly. "Max's party was awesome."

A quiet ease settled in Jason's chest as his mind lingered on the walk, the stillness, and the surprising comfort of Leia's presence. As he backed out of the driveway, a faint ripple of emotion stirred inside him—one he'd kept locked away for years.

Then—just as Jason's mind started to settle—Eaton dropped it so casually and effortlessly that Jason almost missed it.

When they pulled into their driveway, Eaton unbuckled his seatbelt, pausing before hopping out. He turned back, his face mischievous.

"Oh, by the way, Dad."

Jason raised an eyebrow. "Yeah?"

Eaton grinned. "The lady from the hospital—you know, the one from the carnival? Alley? She was at Max's party."

Jason tapped his thumb once against the wheel before steadying it again. "She was?" he asked, his voice careful, almost too steady.

Eaton nodded, then shrugged as if it were nothing. "Oh yeah. I think she's in love with me."

Jason blinked. "She is?"

Eaton stretched dramatically, yawning mid-sentence. "Yup. You know how women get when they find out I don't have a mom. They go all soft and start fussing over me like they're trying to adopt me or something."

He let out a laugh, completely unbothered. "Not complaining, though. Always works in my favor—I got extra cake and ice cream."

With that, Eaton trotted inside, leaving Jason standing by the open car door. The boy's laughter faded into the house, but Jason remained still.

Alley.

His hand lingered on the doorframe, the weight of old memories pulling at him.

Just minutes ago, he'd been thinking about Leia—the quiet, the steadiness, the ease of something new.

But now, all he could feel was the pull of the past. The past… and Alley.

Chapter 37

The truth that does not set you free

Jason and Berry waited for the elevator, coffee cups in hand, their scrubs slightly crumpled after hours of chaos in the emergency room.

Berry leaned against the wall and slowly sipped his coffee before sighing dramatically. "Another day, another near-death-by-caffeine overdose," he muttered, eyeing his cup like it had personally wronged him.

He opened the Skittles, shaking his head with a faint smile. "Hard to believe we live on the same junk we tell patients to cut out."

Berry chuckled, raising his cup in a mock toast. "Hypocrisy, my dear Jason, is the fuel of modern medicine."

The elevator chimed, its sleek glass doors sliding open. As the elevator ascended, both men looked down, the busy lobby unfolding behind the clear panes.

Alley.

The hospital doors parted, and she walked in—unhurried, but with quiet intent. The fluorescent lights caught in her hair, giving it a shimmer as she glanced around. She was just another face in the crowd for a moment—until her gaze lifted and met theirs.

Berry froze mid-sip, coffee hovering near his lips. Jason crinkled the Skittles bag in the sudden hush. The world seemed to shrink, the hospital's steady drone fading to a faint hush.

Her expression was unreadable. Did she recognize them? Jason's heart thudded the question lingering like an echo he couldn't shake.

The moment stretched, heavy with unspoken words neither of them could voice. Then, the elevator doors chimed again, breaking the spell as they slid open to their floor.

Jason blinked, his gaze lingering on her until the last possible second. Berry stepped out first, rolling his shoulders like he needed to shake off what had just happened.

They started walking down the hallway, the overhead fluorescent lights stretching pale shapes across the floor as their minds raced.

Berry glanced over. "Do you think she recognized us?"

Jason didn't answer right away. He squeezed the Skittles bag, his pace quickening as if he could outwalk the question.

"I don't know," he finally admitted, his voice low. "But she looked…"

They didn't finish the thought, didn't need to.

The image of Alley standing in the lobby lingered for the rest of the day—her eyes, calm but searching, lingered in his mind, like a name you almost remember but never say out loud. And that single, fleeting moment left him wondering not just if she had recognized them, but what it would mean if she had.

They stepped into Sheila's office, their footsteps muted against the polished floor. Dale sat on the edge of his desk, file in hand, his expression unreadable.

Jason and Berry exchanged a glance before taking their seats. The air was thick with anticipation, the kind that stretched time unbearably.

They were waiting for the phone call.

The one they had dreaded yet needed.

The commander who had airlifted Alley that morning—the morning that had torn their lives apart—was finally going to speak to them.

Jason leaned forward, elbows resting on his knees, hands clenched together. Berry sat beside him, unusually still, his coffee untouched on the table.

And then, the phone rang.

The sharp sound pierced the room, sending a chill up Jason's spine. His stomach twisted as he exchanged a glance with Sheila, who picked up the receiver with a steady hand—though her expression betrayed the weight of the moment.

"This is Dr. Sheila Raj," she said. "Yes, we're all here. I'm putting you on speaker."

She pressed a button, and the room seemed to shrink.

"Thank you for joining us, Commander Boulder," Sheila continued. "With me is a panel of doctors treating Dr. Alley—the individual you airlifted that day. We need details about that evacuation, specifically in relation to her."

A crackle of static came through, followed by a firm voice responding. "This is Commander Tony Boulder. I have Commander

John Light with me. John was the one who found Dr. Alley. I'll let him explain."

There was a pause, then another voice came through—rough, deliberate.

"Hello, everyone. This is Commander John Light. I was the one who found Dr. Alley in the maternity ward."

Jason's stomach clenched as he gripped the chair's armrests.

"She was with Dr. Rehana Khan, who was delivering a baby—in the middle of the chaos," John continued. "They begged me—just a few more minutes—to finish delivering the baby. "Rehana stayed. And Alley… she stayed too."

Jason felt a crushing weight as his mind painted the scene—the acrid scent of smoke, the distant thunder of explosions, the desperate cries of newborns trapped in a war zone.

John's voice grew heavier. "Dr. Alley bolted for the nursery as soon as the baby was delivered."

He blinked, dazed, struggling to process what he'd just heard.

"I tried to stop her," John went on, voice thick. "I told her no one was in there, but she wouldn't listen. She ran straight toward the fire. I shouted for her to stop, but then the blast hit."

The room went still.

The words sat like lead in the air.

"The nursery. The maternity ward. Everything collapsed."

Jason's breathing faltered, shallow and uneven, as his hands balled in his lap.

"She screamed for her baby. Begged me to let her go. She fought me, clawed at me, crying… but there was nothing left. Just rubble. Fire."

Jason closed his eyes, gripping the armrest.

Her screams—raw, broken—echoed in his head.

John's tone grew hushed. "She lost consciousness after that. We carried her to the chopper and evacuated her to Kazakhstan."

A hush fell across the room.

Commander Jason spoke again, voice calm and deliberate.

"We were also under the impression that the baby didn't survive the fire. All infants from the nursery were accounted for in the database—except one. There was no record of Alley's baby being evacuated. Each child who left the nursery was logged into the system after the evacuation… except hers."

Jason froze as the realization hit him like a punch to the gut. His fingers dug into the table as his face drained of color.

"Oh my God," he exclaimed.

Berry turned to him, frowning. "Jason? What is it?"

Jason's pulse pounded in his ears. His stomach twisted.

"There's no record," Jason said. "Because I never signed him out."

He looked up, stunned. "Oh God… they must have thought he died."

The system never showed that the baby was evacuated…

The room fell deathly silent.

Dale's gaze sharpened. "Jason, are you saying—"

The words scraped from Jason's throat.

"The hospital might have told Alley that the baby didn't make it."

Berry was the first to speak, his voice uncertain.

"Wait… I told Alley's dad the baby was alright. I—I thought he'd tell her."

Jason's head snapped up.

"You told her dad?" His voice carried a flicker of hope.

Berry nodded.

"I'd bet my life on it. He was her dad, Eric. Of course, he would have told her."

Jason leaned back, stunned

"Then why… why didn't she know?"

No answer came. Only the crushing truth: The words had been spoken—but never heard.

Chapter 38

When truth dares you

Dale stared at his hands as if the answer to Alley's amnesia lay within them. The weight of uncertainty pressed down on him, the memory of Vicky's call playing repeatedly in his mind.

Alley had been airlifted to Kazakhstan.

Vicky had been frantic, but said Eric had kept it vague. He was with Alley and assured her everything was fine—just some formalities before they returned home. There were no specifics, no explanations.

And then, a couple of days later, Vicky called again—this time, sobbing uncontrollably.

Eric was gone—a heart attack. On the very day they were supposed to leave Kazakhstan.

Dale hadn't hesitated. He had flown out to Kazakhstan to bring Alley and Eric's body home, leaving Vicky to make the funeral arrangements. But the moment that haunted him most wasn't the aftermath of Eric's death.

It was the hospital room where Alley lay suspended between life and oblivion.

The memory was etched into his mind with painful clarity.

The air held a faint metallic tang, bland and unsettling. Overhead fluorescents cast a glacial brightness, stripping the space of any comfort or warmth. He could still picture her—so small and adrift—her fragile form dwarfed by the narrow hospital bed, the threadbare blanket hanging limply at her sides.

Tubes and wires snaked across her body, an oxygen mask obscuring the face he had once known so well. The rhythmic beep of monitors was the only sign she was still there. Still fighting.

Alley—alive, but barely present.

Grief had settled over her like a suffocating fog. She had barely spoken. Her eyes were vacant, lost somewhere between sorrow and guilt.

Time stretched into eternity as Dale stood helpless, unable to move or speak.

Now, seated in Sheila's office, the realization hit him with the force of a freight train.

Sheila's voice pulled him from the abyss. "Dale?" she said, concern etched into her features. "What is it?"

He steadied himself, though a tremor slipped into his voice as he finally spoke.

"What if... what if Eric never got the chance to tell Alley about the baby? When I got to Kazakhstan, she was still unconscious.

"The memory hit him mid-sentence, tension winding sharp and tight through his chest.

"Oh, Lord," he whispered, his voice breaking.

"She doesn't know. She doesn't know her baby survived.

"The words sank into the room, heavy and shattering, leaving a stunned stillness behind.

He shot up from his chair. Panic clawed at him as he stumbled toward the balcony, struggling for air.

Berry and Sheila sat frozen, staring at Dale in shock, the weight of his revelation sinking in.

And then—cutting into the suffocating stillness—Commander John's voice crackled over the speakerphone.

"So that solves the mystery behind Dr. Alley's condition."

Sheila blinked, suddenly remembering the call was still in progress. She swallowed hard.

"Yes. Yes," she stammered, forcing herself to focus. "Thank you so much for your help. Oh, and—" she added quietly, "thank you for protecting Alley."

"Glad to be of help, ma'am," John responded. Then the line went dead.

The room remained still. Heavy.

Jason stumbled onto the balcony, clutching the cold railing like a lifeline. The air burned in his lungs. His hands locked to the metal, tension radiating through his body. How had it come to this? How had they let it happen?

He shivered as the memory crashed over him—the day his world tilted, the day he lost her.

He could still hear her voice, fragile and breaking, the phone's static crackling like a cruel barrier.

"I'm sorry... I can't go on. Please forgive me, Jay. Bye."

The words had been fragmented, distorted by interference, but the pain behind them had been unmistakable. It had lodged deep inside him, an ache that never truly faded.

Now, as the night air wrapped around him, he exhaled shakily, striving to steady the turmoil within.

Grief had turned to anger. His pride had refused to believe Alley had willingly left him.

Maybe she didn't want to be saddled with a baby.

The bitterness had consumed him, growing into resentment, then into something colder. Indifference.

After two years, he had convinced himself he didn't care anymore.

But now—now, the truth stood before him like a blade to the gut.

Guilt twisted inside him, sharp and merciless.

Berry stepped onto the balcony. Jason stood rigid, his body coiled with unspoken emotions. Berry didn't speak at first. He just stood beside him, offering a quiet solidarity neither of them needed to voice.

"You know," he said, voice quiet, "grief has a way of stealing time from us. One day, you wake up, and you don't even realize how much of your life you've spent carrying it."

He didn't respond, but his fingers twitched, a muscle in his jaw jumping.

Berry continued, "I used to think grief was just sadness. But it's not, is it?" He let out a dry chuckle. "It's guilt. It's anger. It's every damn what-if that keeps you up at night. It's losing time you can never get back."

His mouth thinned. When he finally spoke, his voice was raw.

"I thought... She walked away without looking back. And I—" He broke off, dragging a hand across his mouth. "I didn't hate her, Berry. I was just... hurt."

Berry nodded as if he had always known Jason didn't harbor hate—only a wound that had never healed.

Jason's voice was tight. "I searched for her. I tried to find answers. But each door I knocked on was already closed. I told myself to stop caring—to move on—but... You don't just stop."

The truth hit him hard, sinking deep into his bones.

Alley had never abandoned their son. She had never even known he survived.

The pause lingered, heavy but not empty.

Berry didn't try to fix it. He didn't say it would be okay.

Instead, he just stood beside Jason, a silent witness to everything that had been lost.

For now, it was all he could ask.

That night after dinner, Jason moved through the familiar rhythm of clearing plates and wiping crumbs from the table. The house was quiet, the kind of quiet that comes after a day full of noise—settling.

As he reached for a stray napkin, his hand brushed a sheet of paper partially hidden beneath it. He pulled it free, immediately recognizing Eaton's bold crayon lines.

The drawing showed four stick figures—Eaton in the middle, arms outstretched in a superhero pose. On one side stood Margaret and Robert, smiling, both wearing glasses

On the other side stood Jason, taller than the rest, with wild brown hair. At their feet, Pepper sat with a pink tongue hanging from a lopsided grin.

At the top, in Eaton's blocky handwriting, it read: *"My Family."*

Jason stared at it for a long moment, one corner of his mouth pulling into a faint smile.

When he asked about it, Eaton shrugged.

"Max at school said you need a mom and a dad to be a real family," Eaton said, tugging at his sock. "But I told him, 'No, you don't. You just need people who love you and a dog who listens sometimes.'"

He managed a chuckle, even as the truth in his son's words sank deep.

He smoothed the paper gently and pinned it to the fridge door with a magnet.

He stood for a long moment in front of the fridge, its quiet purr the only sound in the kitchen.

The drawing fluttered once, catching the draft from the hallway. He touched the edge of the paper lightly.

"You just need people who love you."

Maybe that was the part he'd forgotten.

Chapter 39

The cost of the truth

The rich aroma of warm muffins filled the air. Sheila and Dale sat across from each other, voices hushed, Dale's brow furrowed, Sheila flipping through the thick file. Papers and medical reports lay scattered across the table, their edges curling from overhandling.

Jason stepped inside, tray in hand; the cups of coffee sloshed slightly beside a bag of moist banana cake as he set it down.

"Breakfast delivery."

The sweet warmth of cinnamon and butter from the muffins and cake hovered between them—but provided no relief from the tension pressed into every corner.

He sank into a chair; the wood creaked beneath him. Sheila barely looked up, her eyes locked on the document.

"We were going over Alley's latest psychological assessment." She turned the page; the whisper of paper punctuated the quiet.

"Now that we know her amnesia is psychologically—rooted in trauma rather than injury—it changes everything."

"We've worked with what we had," Dale said, his voice quiet. "Back then, Alley's records were bare—no real detail about Afghanistan. And she never brought it up."

He looked at Jason. "But now, with the evacuation and your account—details, only someone who was there could give—we're not guessing anymore. We're finally working with context instead of guesswork and silhouettes."

Jason leaned forward, resting his forearms on the table. "So, what's the plan?"

Sheila tucked a loose strand of hair behind her ear. "We need to tread carefully. If we push too hard, her mind might reject the truth entirely."

He ran a hand through his hair, the clean scent of his morning shower lingering.

"But she has to know," he argued. "Knowing she has a son might actually help her heal."

Sheila nodded. "And she will. But it has to be on her terms."

Jason sipped his coffee, the warmth pressing into his palms. "So what do we do? Just sit back and hope she magically remembers?"

Dale shook his head, the scrape of his chair against the floor the only sound in the silence.

"No. We need a controlled approach—gradual exposure. Subtle cues that guide her to the truth without overwhelming her. "Tilting his chair slightly, he leaned back.

"And how long does that take?"

Sheila hesitated, tracing the edge of the file. "There's no timeline for healing trauma. But one thing is certain—Eaton is the key. If he connects with her in a way that feels safe, her mind might start to open up."

"You're focusing too much on memory," Jason said. "What if it never comes back?"

"She's tormented by the gaps in her past. Not knowing is worse than the truth. Even if she never remembers giving birth, she deserves to know who she is."

Dale exchanged a glance with Sheila.

He spoke with unwavering determination. "She needs something real to hold on to. To stop living in a reality that isn't even hers."

Sheila sighed, the sound barely audible in the quiet room.

"If we do this too fast—"

"I'm not saying we drop Eaton in front of her and expect everything to fall into place," Jason interrupted. "But let her know he's alive."

No one responded right away. The gravity of his words settled over them like a fog.

Dale repeated. His voice low and measured, "If we do this, we must be strategic. No surprises. No pressure."

Sheila nodded. We introduce the idea first. Let her process the possibility before we bring Eaton into it."

Jason gripped his coffee cup, the ceramic warm against his skin—but it wasn't enough to stop the chill creeping through his chest.

He stood abruptly and walked to the window, the movement sharp, almost restless. The thought of Alley learning about her son—without the memories to go with it—unsettled him.

He could almost see it—her confusion, the disbelief in her eyes, the unbearable stillness that might follow.

He rested his forehead lightly against the cool glass. God, how would she survive it?

That kind of truth could break a person wide open.

But it wasn't just about her anymore.

His thumb tapped restlessly against the lid of his cup.

"Eaton doesn't know he's doing any of this," he said quietly. "He just sees her as a nice lady at the hospital. If she pulls away again, what happens to him if this goes wrong?" Sheila and Dale looked up. The crack in his voice wasn't anger—it was fear.

"I've raised him to be strong," Jason continued, his voice low. "But he's still a kid. He's already lost so much. I don't want him to be part of a strategy—I just want him to be her son. I want her to want him."

The moment stretched.

"But I know one thing for sure," he added, steadying himself. "She deserves the truth. And so does Eaton."

His gaze lifted, sharp now, the conflict clear in his eyes. "I'm not reluctant. I'm scared. But I'd rather give them the chance to find each other than keep pretending time will fix this."

The air in the room had changed—thicker, weighted by everything left unsaid. Outside, the wind rattled the window. The sky hung overcast, casting a dull gray light into the room.

He rubbed his jaw, hesitation creeping in. "What about Steve?"

Sheila and Dale looked at him, their faces unreadable.

Jason sighed, tapping his fingers against the cup. "Should we tell him?"

Dale crossed his arms. "That's tricky. Steve's been by Alley's side through all of this. He's protected her, fought for her. But we don't know how he'll react to learning her son is alive."

The thought of Steve finding out later—after everyone else—made Jason uneasy. He shifted his weight, discomfort creeping through him.

"Yeah… but keeping it from him isn't an option either."

Sheila tapped her pen once before setting it down. "If we tell him before Alley, it puts him in a difficult position. If we wait too long, he might feel betrayed."

Jason pinched the bridge of his nose, then let his hand drop to the table. "We can't afford another mistake."

They all knew the truth—no matter what they decided, someone was going to get hurt.

Sheila finally spoke, steady and calm. "We tell her first."

He looked up, his pulse steady, but his mind raced. This was it. No turning back.

The truth wasn't a question of if anymore.

It was only a matter of when.

But as Jason thought of Steve—the man who had stood beside Alley through it all—another thought settled heavier than before.

They weren't just deciding Alley's future.

They were deciding Steve's too.

And when the truth finally came out, he wasn't sure if any of them would be ready for what came next.

Chapter 40

Fragments of us

The doctor's lounge lay deserted, bathed in the amber glow of an autumn sunset. Beyond the wide windows, the western horizon blazed orange as trees bent with the evening breeze. A piano's distant notes drifted softly across the room in the hush.

Berry stayed by the doorway, watching Jason and the others as their meeting continued in hushed voices.

"I'll be back in a minute," he said softly.

Jason gave him a brief nod.

Berry wasn't even sure why he needed to step away—just that he did.

Maybe he needed air. Perhaps he needed Skittles.

Probably both.

He made his way toward the vending machine in the far corner of the lounge. The glow from its screen pulsed brightly, illuminating rows of candy and chips.

He dug into his pocket, fishing out some change, and punched in the code for his favorite.

The machine whirred. The coil twisted.

And then—disaster.

His Skittles stopped halfway, refusing to fall.

Berry narrowed his eyes, carefully assessing the situation

He grabbed the sides and gave it a firm nudge.

Nothing.

Another, a little stronger this time.

Still nothing.

He sighed, placing both hands on the glass.

"Come on, man," he muttered. "I paid fair and square. Just let me have my Skittles."

The machine remained unmoved.

Berry's voice turned desperate. "This is the last one! You wouldn't do this to me. I need this."

He took a step back, rolling his shoulders, preparing to deliver the final blow—when he felt it.

A hand.

On his arm.

His entire body tensed.

Startled, he turned his head—and there she was.

Alley.

Her face was blank, unreadable, her fingers still lightly touching his sleeve.

Berry blinked. The vending machine, the Skittles, his minor candy crisis—suddenly, none of it mattered.

"Alley…" His voice came out quieter than he expected.

She didn't react. Didn't say a word.

She just stood there.

Watching him.

The music in the background was barely audible.

Berry swallowed, his mind catching up to the moment.

She had been standing there long enough to watch his entire meltdown over a bag of Skittles.

And yet—her expression didn't change.

As if she didn't see him at all.

Something pulled taut inside Berry as he studied her face. His eyes misted, the weight of unspoken words pressing against his ribs.

Then—something shifted.

A flicker of something familiar passed through Alley's vacant expression. Her lips parted slightly—the faintest movement at the corner of her mouth—recognition.

Berry swallowed, his pulse thudding in his ears. Was it just his presence she recognized? Or was her mind beginning to stitch the past back together? Carefully, he lifted a hand and placed it over hers—solid, warm, real. She didn't pull away.

His fingers curled around hers as if grounding her and himself.

Then, without thinking, without knowing what would happen next, he lifted her hand to his lips and kissed it.

His heart pounded.

Did she remember him—or did she remember everything?

Alley's eyes stayed locked on his, searching. Trying to grasp something just out of reach.

Berry went still, waiting.

Hoping.

Then, finally—her lips parted.

"Berry?"

A ragged breath escaped him, his eyes welling with tears. He nodded quickly, swallowing hard, unable to trust his voice.

Just then—

Jason entered the room.

"Are you vandalizing the vending machine or what?" Jason's voice rang out, light with sarcasm, but as soon as his eyes landed on them—he stopped.

Everything stopped.

Alley turned to face him—deliberate, unhurried.

She took one step forward, then another.

Jason stopped cold. Something inside him fractured—real, bone-deep fear.

He didn't look at her. He couldn't.

He bowed his head, fingers digging into his palms like he needed the pain to stay grounded.

His breath faltered. The room seemed to contract. The music was gone, drowned out by the heavy thud of his heartbeat against his ribs.

She was too close now.

Jason's hands trembled at his sides, guilt pressing down on him like a crushing weight.

Then—fingertips grazed his arm. a fleeting touch.

Jason flinched but didn't move.

And then—her hand rose to his face.

Fingers ghosted over his cheek, tracing his jaw, moving toward his eyes.

Searching.

He closed his eyes and let her.

He let her explore his face, as if she were trying to find something buried beneath his skin.

And then, as if a storm had hit him, Jason suddenly gathered her into his arms.

He held her tight, too tight, his voice breaking as he whispered:

"Alley… It's me. Your Jay."

He clutched her, his body shaking, and wept into her shoulder.

Like a child desperately holding onto home.
After what felt like an eternity, she whispered—
"Jay."

Chapter 41

Count on me always

As evening settled, the horizon blazed orange, its light dancing across the canopy of trees. The ground was a mosaic of fallen leaves, and behind the hospital, a secluded picnic bench awaited.

Jason approached, spotting Alley and Berry laughing—an echo of old times.

Setting down the steaming coffee, Jason slid into the seat opposite them.

Alley caught the rich aroma and let out a laugh. "I can't believe we're meeting again here," she mused. Noticing the wedding band on Berry's finger, she teased, "So, who's the lucky girl? Anyone we know?"

Berry chuckled deeply. "No, she was my neighbor in New York."

"Do you have kids?" Alley asked, taking a sip of her coffee.

"Yeah, three boys," Berry replied, his gaze drifting momentarily.

Turning to Jason, Alley remarked, "I hear you're single."

"Something like that," Jason responded, his tone evasive.

Alley's lips curved into a gentle smile.

"It's so wonderful to see you both again. If I seem a bit off, I apologize—I've been living with amnesia for a few years now. I don't recall much of our time together, only our friendship and… the fact that I had a crush on you, Jay."

She chuckled, a shy sparkle in her eyes.

"I'm so happy we've reconnected."

He managed composure, but a quiet ache stirred beneath it.

A crush. That's all she remembered—

Just a distant, harmless crush—nothing like the fierce, fragile love they had once built.

He had slipped the engagement ring onto her finger with trembling hands.

The words left him before he could stop them. "Are you happy, Alley?"

She blinked, slightly caught off guard, but then her face lit with quiet certainty. "Yeah. I am. I'm married to a really nice person—Steve Rivers. He's kind, patient... everything I could ask for." She glanced down at her coffee. "Except for my health issues, life is good."

A knot formed in Jason's throat, and he gave an absent nod.

He should be happy for her.

She had a good life now—stability, a husband she trusted. But all Jason could see was the ghost of what they'd had.

The way her eyes had lit up when he first proposed.

The way she had traced the ring on her finger in disbelief, whispering, Are you sure?

As if she couldn't quite believe he was hers.

She didn't remember any of it.

To her, he was just a college crush—an echo of youth, something easily left behind.

He kept his tone even. "That's good," he said, though the words scraped on the way out. "I'm glad you're happy, Alley."

Alley glanced at her watch, and a flicker of realization crossed her face. "I should get going," she said, standing up and brushing the fallen leaves from her coat. "Steve will be waiting for me."

She turned back to Jason and Berry, her expression touched with warmth.

"I know I lost a lot of time... and a lot of memories. I have bits and pieces, but there are these gaps I just can't fill. And you two"— she nodded toward them—"were a big part of my life back then, weren't you?"

He felt his pulse quicken, but he kept his face neutral.

Berry nodded. "Yeah, we were."

Alley's eyes lit with hope. "Then maybe you two can help me remember—fill in the blanks."

Jason hesitated, not because he didn't want to help her—he'd fought for this, pushed Dale and Sheila to move forward. He had insisted that Alley deserved the truth, that she deserved to remember who she really was.

But now, sitting across from her, hearing her talk about Steve with such calm certainty, it struck him differently.

The reality wasn't abstract anymore—it wasn't just strategy or therapy notes. It was her—laughing over coffee, calling their history a crush, looking to him as a friend.

Helping her remember meant reopening wounds she didn't even know she had. And standing by while she pieced together the love they once shared, knowing she might never feel it again.

Could he handle that?

Berry, sensing the shift in Jason, answered for them both.

"Of course, Alley. Whatever you need."

Jason gave a quiet nod, unable to find the words.

He would do it. He had to.

Even if it broke him all over again.

Alley beamed, relief and gratitude shining in her eyes. "Thank you. That means a lot."

She adjusted the strap of her bag, then turned to leave, her silhouette glowing in the last hues of daylight. Jason watched her walk away, feeling like he was losing her all over again.

Berry placed a hand on his shoulder. "You okay?"

Jason exhaled slowly, eyes fixed on the fading horizon.

"No," he said. "But I will be."

And as the light faded into the trees, he knew he would be there—whatever pieces she reclaimed, whatever she forgot, even if it meant remembering alone.

Chapter 42

A forgotten proposal

The last light of day slipped behind the trees, bathing the bench in twilight where Jason and Berry sat, wordless.

Berry's shoulders sagged. "This isn't fair, man."

Jason said nothing. He just stared down the path where Alley had disappeared, her words still echoing in his mind.

A crush.

That's what she had called their love. A passing fancy. A fleeting memory, no more significant than a childhood infatuation.

Jason drew a breath, then let it go through gritted teeth. "What was I supposed to say, Berry?"

Berry's voice was sarcastically edged with frustration. "I don't know. Maybe something. Maybe 'Hey, Alley, actually, we were engaged once."

Jason didn't answer right away. The memory was still sharp, impossible to forget. His mind pulled him back to Kandahar.

The jeep rattled along the dusty hillside road, tires kicking up clouds of earth as they wound through the Afghan mountains.

Jason lurched slightly in his seat, one hand gripping the door as the scenery blurred past. "Alley, slow down."

She grinned, blond hair whipping in the wind, blue eyes alight with excitement. "What's the matter, Jay? You scared?"

Jason just shook his head, his other hand bracing against the dashboard. "Scared is a strong word."

She just laughed, completely in her element.

Her dad, Eric, had just arrived in Kabul, and she'd been talking about him nonstop on the way to the airport. Jason had expected to feel nervous meeting him—after all, the man was a renowned war correspondent, sharp-eyed and no-nonsense.

But the moment they shook hands, Jason liked him. He had a way of making people feel at ease, and his approval had come easily— almost too easily.

"You must be the man who's been keeping her out of trouble," he'd said, shaking Jason's hand firmly. "I owe you one."

The fire crackled between them that night, sending embers spiraling upward—tiny sparks dissolving into the dark.

The air was cool and crisp, carrying the faint scent of pine and smoke.

Somewhere nearby, Ali—the chauffeur—played a slow, soulful tune on his harmonica, the notes threading gently through the hush of the evening. Jason sat back, his gaze fixed on Alley as she laughed. The firelight flickered across her face, catching in her hair like a halo of warmth.

God, she was beautiful.

The thought hit him hard.

She wasn't just his best friend. She wasn't just the person who challenged him, who pushed him to be better, and saw parts of him that no one else ever had.

She was everything.

He stood abruptly, brushing the dirt off his jeans, and stepped toward her. "Dance with me."

She blinked up at him. "Jay, there's no music for dancing."

Jason grinned. "Since when have you needed music to dance, Alley?"

She hesitated for only a second before slipping her hand into his.

They swayed in the firelight, slow and unhurried, the warmth of her body pressed against his, the quiet crackling of the flames the only sound between them.

His chest rose with a slow, steadying breath.

He had no idea if she was ready for this.

But he was.

His fingers found the cool metal in his pocket, and before he could overthink it, he pulled back slightly—then dropped to one knee.

For a moment, Alley just stared at him, her wide eyes reflecting the flickering flames.

His pulse thundered, but his voice held firm.

"Alley… will you marry me?"

A nervous laugh escaped him. "Put me out of my misery."

The world stopped, waiting for the space between them to collapse.

Her breath caught. She opened her mouth, but no words came. Jason caught every detail—the lift of her chest, the faint tremble in her fingers.

And then—

Tears.

Jason's stomach twisted. He couldn't tell if that was a good thing—or a terrible one.

He wrapped her in his arms, afraid the moment would dissolve if he let go.

Slowly, wordlessly, she folded into him.

Berry let out a yell, and suddenly, they were being swarmed. Ali tapped Jason on the back, while Berry hugged them both at once, shouting something about finally.

And then—her father stepped forward.

Jason met his gaze, ready for anything.

After a long silence, her dad placed a hand on Jason's shoulder.

"Just promise me," he said, the words rough. "Don't ever stop protecting her."

Emotion surged, unspoken and heavy. He held her tighter, as if that alone could anchor the moment.

His voice didn't waver.

"With all my heart, sir."

And when he looked down—

Alley was still crying.

But this time—

She was smiling too.

The fire faded. The stars disappeared.

Jason blinked—and just like that, he was back. Sitting on a cold bench as darkness gathered overhead, eyes unfocused, seeing nothing at all.

Jason could feel it—the weight of Berry's gaze, the unspoken understanding in his eyes.

The silence between them was thick, grief-laced. Only the hum of distant traffic tethered him to now.

Berry asked quietly, "So what now?" Jason's eyes sharpened. There had never been a choice. No matter how much it hurt, he had to help her remember. He looked straight ahead, voice steady.

"Now?" he echoed. "Now, I help her remember."

Chapter 43

A bond beyond

The lights blurred as Alley drove, but she barely noticed them. Her mind was stuck in the past, replaying the evening over and over again.

She hadn't expected to see Jay and Berry tonight. Hadn't expected the rush of emotions that hit her the second she saw their faces.

She recalled how happy they were to see her.

The way Berry laughed, his eyes lighting up like they had rewound time. The way Jason had held her tight, like he was afraid she would disappear all over again. And the way he had cried.

She stared straight ahead, her hands rigid with tension.

Jason had cried.

She cried with him.

His shoulders trembled, his body shaken, and his hands clung to her like she was something precious and fragile.

And at that moment, she felt the exact same thing.

Because hugging Jason had felt like coming home.

The realization hit hard, rooting her to the spot.

It was so deeply familiar—so safe, so right—that she realized she had been waiting for this moment all along without even knowing it.

She had called Jason a crush tonight.

But the truth was—she had been in love with him.

She just hadn't wanted to say it. Didn't want to embarrass him.

She didn't mean to, but the question surfaced: why had they ended things?

After all, he'd moved away, had a child, and built a life. What good would it do now to admit what she'd once felt?

She let out a deep sigh as she pulled into the driveway. She was happy now. Wasn't she?

She stepped out of the car, locking it behind her, and walked toward the warm glow of the house.

The strains of jazz music greeted her as she entered, the candlelight flickering against the walls, making the space feel cozy, intimate.

Tonight was their anniversary. For a moment, she simply existed—this life, this love, a safe harbor after chaos. Yet deep down, something stirred—gentle but insistent—like the tide tugging at her anchor. It didn't threaten the harbor; it merely reminded her there had once been another shore.

She had thought they'd go out to celebrate, but clearly, Steve had other plans.

A hint of calm passed over her face.

She kicked off her boots and made her way to the bedroom, the sound of running water drifting from the bathroom. She didn't hesitate—she stripped, opened the door, and stepped inside.

Later that evening, they sat by the patio as a breeze stirred the branches, the scent of grilled steak hanging in the air.

Steve sat across from her, his features illuminated in the soft glow of the candlelight. He was watching her.

Alley took a sip of wine, trying to focus on him, on them, on this life they had built together.

She looked at Steve—the man who had pieced her back together when she had been too broken to stand.

She owed him everything.

A wave of emotion washed over her, and a memory surfaced— unbidden, unexpected.

Alley crossed her arms, arching an eyebrow as she sat in her wheelchair. "I swear, Steve, if you push me down a hill, I will haunt you forever."

Steve grinned, stepping behind her and gripping the handles. "Haunt me? Princess, you already live rent-free in my heart."

She rolled her eyes, but the corners of her lips twitched.

Steve leaned down, his breath warm against her ear. "Hold on tight."

Before she could react, he sprinted forward, pushing her wheelchair down the path.

The cool mountain air rushed past her face, and despite herself, she laughed.

A full, unrestrained laugh, the kind she hadn't let herself feel in months.

She had forgotten what it felt like to be free.

Steve steered the wheelchair effortlessly, spinning her around in circles, dipping her back dramatically like they were dancing.

"This is completely irresponsible." The words spilled out in a laugh.

"But fun, right?"

She rolled her eyes lightly, a grin slipping through.

"Yeah. Fun."

A warm grin spread across Steve's face. "I missed hearing you laugh."

Something in the way he said it sent a flutter through her heart.

She remembered how he pushed her at physical therapy. She dreaded seeing Steve more than the therapist. She could remember all too well the painful days.

She gritted her teeth, pain shooting up her legs.

"Again," Steve said firmly, standing in front of her, arms crossed.

Alley stood rooted, every nerve coiled tight. "I can't."

"Yes, you can."

His voice was strong, unwavering, and safe.

She could feel frustration boiling inside her—the anger at herself, the exhaustion, the hopelessness.

"Why do you even care?" she had snapped.

He had only stared at her, his eyes both tender and fierce.

"Because you deserve to walk again. And I'm not giving up until you do."

She hated him at that moment.

But when she finally took one step, then two, his arms were there to catch her.

And when she cried, not from pain but from pure relief, he had just held her.

No teasing, no banter. Just Steve—steady, unshaken, willing to fight for her when she had no strength left to fight for herself.

She never would have made it without him.

The memory faded, but the warmth lingered.

Alley blinked back to the present, finding Steve laugh over something she hadn't caught.

He had been her anchor, her strength, her home.

She reached for his hand, squeezing it gently.

He looked at her, a hint of warmth in his eyes. "What's that for?"

She hesitated. "Just… thinking about everything you've done for me."

His fingers curled around hers, warm and reassuring. "I'd do it all again, Alley. In a heartbeat."

Her expression softened, but her heart was heavy.

Because for all the love she had for Steve, Jason's arms still lingered in her mind.

Still made her feel like home.

And she had no idea what to do about that.

As Alley yawned, Steve tilted his head slightly, studying her. "Tired?"

She stretched, nodding. "Yeah. Today was an emotional day."

Steve chuckled. "How so?"

Alley waved a hand. "I ran into two of my old friends today—Jason and Berry."

Silence.

For the briefest moment, Steve froze.

His fingers curled around the glass, the corner of his mouth lifting, yet his eyes held an inscrutable depth.

Alley didn't notice.

She stood, gathering their plates and glasses, heading to the kitchen. "I'm hoping they'll help me fill in the lapses in my life."

Steve didn't follow her immediately.

He sat motionless, his wine glass forgotten in his hand.

The glow of the candle played over the table, carving shifting shadows on his face, but he stayed still.

She remembered Berry and Jay.

The names echoed in his mind, stirring something deep inside him—something he didn't want to name.

He had spent years watching her rebuild herself, loving her without expectations, being the one who stood by her when everything else had been lost.

Now, she actually recognized Jay.

Jay, the one she had loved in medical school.

But it was only the name. Only the surface.

Not the man she had promised forever to. Not the man who once held her heart.

And that, somehow, hurt more than if she had remembered everything.

Steve's fingers coiled tighter around his glass.

She didn't remember the love.

She didn't remember the pain.

She didn't remember the choice she had made—him.

But even as unease settled deep, Steve made a decision.

He wasn't going to fight her memories.

He wasn't going to beg her to forget.

Because he had never been the kind of man to hold her back.

The past was returning.

It was going to shake the foundation of everything he and Alley had built.

But he would face it.

Because he loved her.

And when the past finally caught up to her, he could only pray that she'd still find her way back to him.

Chapter 44

A memory in waiting

She let her fingers drum against the steering wheel, an unconscious rhythm echoing the quiet melody on the radio—a tune she didn't recognize yet somehow felt familiar.

Lightness settled over her at last. Hope bloomed, and she felt on the edge of discovering something—herself, perhaps.

Jay and Berry.

The names no longer felt distant, no longer echoes of a life she couldn't grasp. She knew them now, and that meant something. Maybe they held the missing pieces. Maybe they were the answers to the questions she hadn't even learned to ask yet.

As the hospital came into view, she took a steadying breath.

Today, she would begin to remember.

The sterile scent of disinfectant and freshly brewed coffee greeted her as she entered the hospital lobby. The air hummed with quiet conversations, the shuffle of nurses between patients, and the rhythmic beep of a distant heart monitor.

She walked toward the therapy wing, the weight of anticipation pressing against her.

Dr. Dale's office was at the end of the hall—a familiar space now. Inside, the atmosphere was warmer. A yellow light glowed from the lamps, contrasting with the sharp, clean lines of the medical charts stacked neatly on the desk. A faint trace of mint tea lingered in the air—Sheila's preferred drink.

The room wasn't cold. It wasn't impersonal. It was designed to feel safe.

Jason and Berry were already there when she arrived.

Berry, with his easy grin, sat slouched in the chair, a disposable coffee cup balanced between his hands.

Jason, on the other hand, sat still, his back straight, fingers interlocked. He wasn't tense, exactly, but there was something about the way his gaze slid toward her as she walked in—something unreadable.

She didn't know why, but it made her pulse quicken, just slightly.

Dr. Dale greeted her warmly.

"Morning, Alley." He set down the folder, his steady presence as reassuring as ever—no longer a patient, she was firmly in charge of her own recovery.

Sheila nodded toward the chair across from her. "How are you feeling today?"

Alley eased onto the seat, smoothing the sleeves of her sweater. "Good, actually," she said, relief threading her voice. "Lighter."

Berry smirked, sipping his coffee. "That's the caffeine talking."

She let out a laugh, but Jason didn't. He was watching her. Not intensely, not uncomfortably—but with a quiet kind of carefulness, like he was studying every word, every breath.

Dr. Dale leaned forward. "Alley, I'm so glad you could remember Jason and Berry. That means you're progressing, and the sessions are helping."

She nodded, absorbing his words, feeling the reassurance settle in her.

"Did you have any specific concerns you want us to address?" Dr. Dale asked.

Alley paused, fingertips resting lightly against her knee as she steadied herself.

"I feel like Jay and Berry could help me trigger my memory," she admitted, her voice clear.

Berry straightened slightly, setting his coffee down. Jason, though, remained still.

"If they have any pictures from our college days, from internships—anything," she continued.

Then, taking charge, she pushed forward.

"You can tell me," she said, looking directly at Dr. Dale. "Even if I don't remember it, I can process it. I need to."

There was a pause.

He shifted slightly, tension coiling beneath his stillness.

She turned to Dr. Dale again, her gaze steady.

"After months into therapy, I was told my dad passed away while I was in a coma. A heart attack. I processed it, I accepted it—even though I was very close to him."

She spoke without wavering, yet the weight of the words hung heavy in the room.

A flicker of sadness passed through Jason's expression, but it was gone just as quickly as it had appeared.

Sheila nodded. "That was a painful memory to absorb, but you handled it."

Dr. Dale leaned forward, his voice calm but probing.

"Are you saying you feel ready for more?" Alley hesitated, then nodded. "I think so."

Berry spoke. "Alley, you had an episode when you saw Jason and me at the dinner. We can't take another risk."

She shook her head. "It wasn't just because I saw you and Jay. In fact, I didn't even recognize Jay at the time. It was because I saw a pregnant woman…" She trailed off. "It… it was like deja vu. I saw the same scene in my dreams…"

Dr. Dale nodded, his hands loosely folded in his lap. "Tell me about it."

Sheila leaned forward slightly, always careful to let Alley lead the conversation.

Jason's fingers dug into his knee.

Alley licked her lips, trying to find the words.

"There were flowers. And music. And…"

She frowned.

"…A sash. It said 'Mom-to-Be.'"

Jason's posture locked.

Berry sat up straighter.

Dr. Dale, however, remained unfazed.

"That's very specific." His voice was neutral. "What else do you remember?"

She rubbed her temple as if trying to coax the memory forward.

"A flower crown. Someone was placing it on my head. The weight of it felt so… real."

Her hands trembled slightly as she mimicked the motion, fingers brushing against her hairline.

He remained silent, though something in his face had gone rigid.

Dr. Dale paused before speaking. "Did you recognize anyone in the dream?"

Alley frowned. She could feel warmth, happiness, voices blending together—but the faces were blurred, like looking through fogged glass.

She looked away. "No."

Sheila's voice was calm. "How did it make you feel?"

She blinked at her. "…Like I belonged there."

The second she said it, something inside her sank.

Like the memory wanted to break through, but something was holding it back.

Jason shifted slightly, the tension ebbing—but only just.

Dr. Dale clasped his hands together. "Alley, noticing familiar faces like Jason and Berry—that's exactly the kind of progress we hoped for."

As he spoke, a flicker crossed his face—something more personal than professional. Relief, yes, but also a trace of hesitation. His gaze held on her a moment longer as if a thought pressed behind it he didn't want to name.

She was healing. Remembering. And that was good. That was what they all wanted.

But even as a doctor, Dale couldn't ignore the quiet truth creeping in beneath the progress—that memory didn't just change the patient. It shifted everything. And in this case, it might upend the balance of his own family.

Still, he nodded once, his voice gentler. "Really… It's a big step forward."

Sheila's tone was reassuring. "You're doing really well."

Alley closed her eyes and focused.

Flower crown. Music. Laughter. A hand resting on her belly.

She inhaled sharply.

Dr. Dale didn't push. He let her process.

Alley's fingers flexed on the armrest, and she let out a shaky breath.

The edges of the memory were still blurred, but something was different now.

It wasn't just a dream.

It spoke of real loss—a piece of her life snatched away.

Her gaze lifted.
Her eyes landed on Jason.
In that instant, she realized he was afraid.

Chapter 45

The past at her feet

The door slammed shut behind him.

Jason barely made it two steps into his office before the files in his hands went flying.

Papers scattered. Charts and folders hit the floor.

Frustration surged through him.

Goddamn it.

He had almost done it.

Almost told her.

The words had been right there, ready to spill out—he had been ready to watch the pieces fall into place for her, even if it hurt her.

Even if it shattered her.

But then—

She'd seen the pregnant woman—and Jason had seen the flicker of something behind her eyes. No recognition. Not yet. But something close.

Jason pressed his hands against the desk.

He could still see it—that day, etched into him like a scar.

He couldn't afford a fancy baby shower in that tiny village in Afghanistan.

There was no time, no decorations—but he had wanted her to have something.

So, he had made one.

A sash—stitched together from the blue hospital scrubs he had stolen from the supply room.

The words "MOM-TO-BE" were written in bold, uneven marker strokes.

And a flower crown—woven from wildflowers he had picked himself.

He had placed it on her carefully, nervously.

She laughed.

And God, he had thought he would never love anyone more than he loved her in that moment.

Jason tilted his head back and let out a bitter laugh, dragging a hand through his hair. How much longer could they drag this out? How much longer was he supposed to watch her suffer? She was so damn close now. She had felt it.

Her hand had gone to her stomach. A reflex. An echo. For a split second, he'd thought she might be remembering—but no. It hadn't reached her mind. Not yet.

And he had let it.

Jason dropped into his chair, his head falling into his hands.

The truth that he wasn't allowed to give her, threatened to drown him.

Every day, she forgot—he lived it for her.

Every memory that had faded for her—remained sharp as hell for him.

He wasn't sure how much longer he could keep this up.

Because whenever he looked at her, that flicker of memory surfaced—

Air jammed in his throat. A soft knock broke the silence. He muttered a curse, willing the intruder to leave.

The door creaked open anyway, and Jason jerked his gaze up, nerves still raw. Alley stood in the doorway.

For a split second, he froze, fingers still curled against the desk.

She shouldn't be here.

Not right now.

Not when he was still wearing his emotions too close to the surface.

Jason stood up, dragging a hand through his hair, trying to pull himself together.

"Just keep it together."

He forced his voice to be even, casual.

"Hey." He nodded toward the mess on the floor, the scattered folders and pens. "Uh, come in. Sorry about the disaster."

A moment later, Berry appeared, stepping inside with his usual easy presence.

He looked at the mess on the floor and let out a low whistle.

"Damn, Jay. A tornado paid you a special visit?"

Jason huffed, kneeling to shove the scattered papers back into the file.

Alley crouched down, picking up one of the magazines that had landed near her feet.

"Don't worry, I'll take care of it," Jason muttered, reaching for it.

But she handed it to him anyway, her expression unreadable.

She didn't mention the mess or ask why his office looked like a war zone.

Berry crouched down to gather some pens.

"Looks like a tantrum—or a breakdown. Which one are we dealing with?"

Jason shot him a flat look. "What are you even doing here? Don't you have a wife and kids to go to?"

Berry just arched an eyebrow, unimpressed.

"I was leaving, but I wanted to check in on you." He stacked the folders together and set them on Jason's desk, crossing his arms. "Good thing I did."

His expression shifted—something knowing.

Berry gave Jason a look only a best friend could give.

The look of a disapproving mother, mixed with a guy who knew exactly what was happening.

Jason turned back toward Alley, trying to act like his skin wasn't crawling with tension.

Trying to act like she wasn't the exact reason he had lost control of his emotions just minutes ago.

He nodded toward the chair. "Sit down?"

She hesitated, just for a second.

Then she moved, settling into the chair across from his desk.

Jason swallowed.

"How about pecan pie?" he said, too casually.

Berry blinked. "What?"

Jason grabbed a plastic container from the side of his desk and held it up. "A patient brought this in this morning. Thought you'd appreciate a bribe before you start lecturing me."

Alley tilted her head slightly, eyes still studying him.

He walked toward them, stepping over the scattered papers he still hadn't cleaned up.

Berry smirked, taking a spoon. "Bribery. Smart. I respect it."

Jason handed Alley a spoon next, avoiding her eyes.

She didn't take it.

He looked up then.

She was watching him too closely, too intently.

Not amused.

Not playing along.

Jason forced a smirk. "It's good pie, Al. I promise."

Berry was still smirking, completely oblivious, licking a bit of pecan filling off his spoon.

Jason, still gripping the plastic container, felt his stomach clench.

And then he looked down—

He saw what she was holding.

Photographs

He didn't move. Couldn't.

The photos were from the hospital. From that day.

She was holding the baby—Eaton. Just minutes old.

The file sat at her feet, open slightly, revealing the edge of a photograph.

A picture he knew too well. He'd given that photo to Dale just days ago—after Sheila had insisted he share his version. He hadn't meant for Alley to see it yet, not like this.

A jolt of dread locked him in place.

The air around him thickened, suffocating.

The picture was slightly faded from time, but it didn't matter.

He remembered every detail.

Alley. Exhausted but radiant.

A newborn baby wrapped in hospital blankets, nestled in her arms.

His tiny face, still wrinkled from birth.

Jason had been the one to take the picture.

Berry stood still, helpless.

He'd seen patients cry. Survivors shake. He'd watched grief unravel families from the inside out.

But this... this was Alley.

She was shaking in front of him like her body couldn't hold everything it suddenly remembered.

He turned slightly away, blinking hard. His throat burned.

There was nothing to fix. Nothing to say.

Only the ache of watching someone you care about fall apart—knowing you'd give anything to carry the weight for them and realizing you can't.

So, he stood there.

Quiet.

Shattered.

Chapter 46

The weight of the photographs

Alley's hands gripped the file. She flipped to the next picture. Then the next. Her pulse quickened. She froze on the third.

The woman in the photo—It was her.

Not just a resemblance. Not maybe. It was her.

Hair messy. Skin flushed. A hospital gown clinging to her shoulders. And in her arms—

A baby.

Tiny. Wrinkled. Wrapped in a blue blanket printed with cartoon ducks. She was cradling him close, eyes full of something she couldn't name. Joy? Love? Grief?

Her stomach flipped.

She turned to the next photo. Still her. Still the same baby.

Her face was calm, but tension coiled through her frame.

With every turn of the photograph, her grip grew tighter.

Her gaze snapped between Jason and Berry—accusing, searching, demanding.

And neither of them said a word.

She glanced at Jason.

He refused to meet her eyes.

She glanced at Berry.

He had the same expression she'd seen on a kid caught sneaking a beer at a high school party—half guilt, half panic, and absolutely no plan to get out of it.

She turned back to the pictures.

Then back to them.

The way they said nothing—it roared louder than words.

It made her blood boil.

Her voice, when it finally came, was too calm.

"Explain."

Jason looked away.

Berry bent his head.

Jason rubbed his jaw, still refusing to look at her.

Berry opened his mouth—then closed it.

She slammed the file shut.

"One of you say something."

No one answered.

A muscle in Jason's jaw ticked.

She turned to Berry. "You always have something to say."

Berry scratched the back of his head. "Yeah, I'm gonna be real honest with you, Al."

He gestured between himself and Jason.

"We're currently in a 'who talks first' situation, and I really don't want it to be me."

Jason shot him a glare.

Alley slammed the file onto the desk.

"Jay."

His head snapped up.

His eyes met hers—and at that instant, she saw it clearly.

Not just hesitation.

Not just guilt.

Fear.

He was afraid of what she would remember.

And that realization sent a chill down her spine.

He glanced at Berry.

Berry looked concerned, his lips pressed into a tight line.

Then, Jason turned to Alley.

He approached her cautiously, like he might break the moment if he moved too fast.

"Alley, we need to talk."

His voice was steady, but not emotionless.

He gestured to the chair. "Please sit down."

Berry hesitated, shifting on his feet. "Jay, maybe—"

Jason shook his head firmly.

Berry sighed, raking a hand through his hair before sinking onto the carpet.

Jason joined him, settling across from Alley.

"This might be intense," he said, his voice low.

He met her eyes.

"But you can take it."

Alley's heart pounded.

Jason's eyes were heavy, like they carried the weight of everything she had forgotten.

Then, he reached for her hand.

His grip was gentle, steady.

"Those pictures." his voice was quiet.

"The sash. The baby shower. The wreath…"

Alley didn't breathe.

His fingers pressed lightly around hers.

"It was you.

It was your baby shower."

His words hung in the air.

Alley stared at him.

She blinked.

And then—

Nothing.

No rush of recognition.

No sudden flood of memories.

Just quiet.

Like the words had been spoken into an empty void.

Berry stayed silent, his face shifting—hardening beneath everything he left unsaid.

Then, he turned away.

Like he couldn't bear to see what was coming next.

Alley felt cold.

Her fingers trembled slightly as she reached for the photograph—the one of her, the baby, in the hospital.

She held it between her fingers.

Turned it slightly.

Studied the exhausted but glowing woman in the picture.

Her gaze moved to Jason.

Silent. Questioning.

Asking him without words.

Is this my baby?

Jason's face broke.

And then—

He answered with a firm nod.

His lips were pressed so firmly together, they were turning white.

Tears gathered in his eyes.

Overflowed.

Spilled down his face.

And still—he didn't speak.

Alley's grip on the picture grew firm.

She sucked in a sharp breath.

Something about the baby's face—the warmth in her own expression captured in the picture—carried an uncanny familiarity.

And then—

Her hand fell to her stomach.

She had always noticed the small stretch of skin that felt different—slightly looser, softer, marked in ways she couldn't explain.

Subtle changes she'd dismissed.

Weight fluctuations. Hormones.

Life.

But now…

Now she knew.

She had carried a child.

She had given birth.

And she had never known.

Berry watched her carefully, his body tense.

Not saying anything.

Just watching.

Making sure she didn't break completely.

Alley should have felt suffocated by their attention.

By the way Jason sat across from her, hands clenched in his lap, while Berry sat nearly motionless beside him, his usual lightheartedness nowhere in sight.

But somehow—

She felt safe.

Safe because Jason was here.

Her fingers trembled as she flipped through the pictures.

One by one.

Tears slipped down her cheeks, warm and unstoppable.

Each photo stared back at her like a stranger's life.

But it was her life. The most beautiful moments of her life.

Her pregnancy. Her baby.

But she didn't remember.

Not the swollen belly.
Not the soft kicks beneath her ribs.
Not the nervous excitement before delivery.
Nothing.

Chapter 47

The empty room

The hush between them wasn't quiet at all—it pulsed with memories too jagged to touch, too sacred to name.

Alley's eyes searched his face, not for comfort, but for truth. Her mind was a battlefield—one part clinging to fragments, the other terrified of what might come next.

She could still feel the ache in her lower back, the phantom pull of something torn too soon.

The photographs had unearthed something profound, but the truth behind them—the real memory—had cracked open a door she wasn't ready to face alone.

And yet, here she was standing on the edge of a truth too big to carry, too cruel to ignore. She needed to hear it—not gently, not carefully. Just honestly, from him.

The blast hit before she opened her eyes. Even now, surrounded by the soft stillness of Jason's office, she felt it—raw and immediate. The kind of soundless pressure that rips through your ribs before sound even registers. BOOM. The floor trembled.

The walls pulsed. People were screaming. Not here. There. In the field hospital. Somewhere in Afghanistan.

She could smell it again—smoke, blood, diesel. Hear boots pounding, mothers wailing, metal trays crashing, someone yelling in broken English. Her shoulders locked.

"I remember," Alley said suddenly, eyes fixed on nothing.

Both men stared at her.

Her words cracked open.

"The light was swinging. Rehana was crouched beside a woman, guiding her through delivery. I was there—I was helping. I held the baby... cut the cord... tied it off with surgical glove tubing."

She blinked.

"I remember her hands—covered in blood. And mine. The sound he made when he finally cried."

Berry leaned forward but didn't speak.

"I thought I was helping someone else. But..."

She closed her eyes. The memory twisted—too fast.

"No." The word slipped out, thin and unsteady. "No, that wasn't her baby."

She swallowed.

"It was mine."

Jason flinched, barely.

"I remember pushing," she said, disbelieving now.

"Screaming. God, it was so loud. The blast had just hit— everything was chaos. I was screaming his name—yours, Jay. I wanted you there."

Her hand fell to her lap. "I remember the blood...how cold it felt on my skin. They told me not to move. Someone held me down. I think—Rehana. Maybe a nurse. I don't know."

Tears slid down her cheeks, but she didn't wipe them away.

"I asked if he was okay. The baby. I asked again. No one answered. And then it went dark."

She opened her eyes. Jason's face was pale. Still.

"I wasn't in scrubs. I wasn't there as a doctor."

She looked at him then, really looked.

"I was the patient."

A long pause. "And when I woke up... you were gone."

Jason didn't move.

"Tell me," she said quietly. The tremor was gone from her words.

"Did I have a baby?"

Jason's jaw tightened, but his eyes didn't waver. Whatever walls he'd built to survive this moment—he let them fall. He reached toward her, his hand hovering, then retreating, unsure if he had the right.

"I didn't know how to tell you," he said at last, voice low and rough.

He rubbed a hand over his throat, then looked up at her, steady, hopeful.

"I thought... maybe it would come back on its own. That you'd remember, and then we could talk about it together.

Maybe it would hurt less if it was your memory, not just my confession."

Alley didn't blink. The silence stretched between them, heavy enough to touch..

"Say it," she pressed. "Did I have a baby?"

Jason closed his eyes. His shoulders rose and fell on a shudder. When he looked at her again, he had nothing left to shield himself with.

"Yes."

The word shattered whatever hope she hadn't dared admit to carrying.

Chapter 48

Truth is savage

A sharp knock split the room. Jason whipped around, body taut. Berry exhaled. "They're here."

Dr. Dale and Sheila strode in, taking in the scattered photos and Alley—rigid, clutching one like a lifeline. The moment they stepped in, a quiet ease settled over him.

"We came as soon as we saw Berry's text."

Sheila remained composed, posture perfectly steady.

Jason had never been this relieved in his life. For the past few minutes, the room had felt like a ticking bomb, seconds from detonating. Now, with Dale and Sheila here, he wasn't sure if it had been defused—or if they'd simply stepped into the blast.

But at least he wasn't facing it alone.

The relief was short-lived. Sheila's gaze landed on him—sharp, searching. The question was in her eyes, in the slight tilt of her head, in the way her arms stayed at her sides instead of reaching for the chair: It was clear what she was thinking—what the hell had happened in here.

Jason's muscles tensed. How the hell was he supposed to explain?

Berry shifted. "She found the pictures."

Sheila turned to Alley. "I might have to monitor you for the night."

Alley's head snapped up. "No. I don't need—"

"Alley," Dale cut in smoothly, voice calm but firm.

"You can leave as soon as we run a few tests. That's it."

Her tired eyes tightened with frustration. Her gaze drifted—almost involuntarily—to Jason.

His lips curved in a quiet, knowing way—no words needed. For some reason, that single gesture unspooled her composure.

A weight settled inside, pressing like something unspoken she couldn't swallow. She looked away, gripping the photo harder.

Dale crouched. "Alley, can I check your pulse?"

She nodded, but her fingers stayed locked around the photograph. "Sweetheart, I need your other hand." Still, she held on. Dale's eyes flicked to Jason.

Jason paused, then offered his hand—just presence. After a moment, Alley let go of the photo. He gently placed it on the desk while Dale clipped a pulse oximeter onto her finger.

Sheila leaned in, reading the numbers. Her lips thinned. "Blood pressure's too low. I need to start fluids."

She faced Alley. "Have you eaten anything today?"

Alley lifted one shoulder in a shrug.

Berry rubbed both hands over his face and exhaled loudly. "Okay, this is officially the heaviest room I've ever been in."

Jason shot him a flat look.

"No, seriously," Berry said, leaning forward. "If I don't make a dumb joke, I might pass out from secondhand stress."

The room held still. Then, to everyone's surprise, Alley let out a tired laugh. It wasn't much, but it was something. Berry grinned. "There she is. Thought we lost you."

Jason rolled his eyes. "You're an idiot."

"And yet, you love me."

Before Jason could respond, another knock at the door shattered the moment. A nurse and an aide stood with a wheelchair, their faces professional, expectant.

The hospital waiting area was nearly empty, save for the quiet shuffle of nurses behind the reception desk and the occasional murmur of distant conversation. The lights buzzed overhead, casting a cold, sterile glow over the hospital lobby.

Jason sat forward, elbows on his knees, hands clasped so tightly his knuckles were white. Berry leaned back beside him—one ankle over a knee, arms crossed, fingers tapping his bicep, leg bouncing.

Across the room, Dale stood near the hallway, voice low and clipped on the phone. Jason didn't know who he was calling—and wasn't sure he wanted to.

Between him and Berry, the quiet thickened. Words hovered, but neither reached for them. Frustration flickered across Jason's face. "I should have waited," he muttered. "Dale was right."

Berry sighed. "Yeah, well… should've, would've, could've. We're here now."

Jason didn't answer.

Just then, Sheila entered, calm and professional. He snapped upright.

"How is she?"

"I gave her a mild tranquilizer," she said.

"Just enough to keep her mind calm."

Berry straightened. "Is that necessary?"

"It's not to sedate her, Berry—just to let her rest without racing thoughts."

Jason dipped his head, eyes shadowed. "How long?"

"As long as she needs." Sheila folded her arms.

"When she wakes, everything will feel real again. The least we can do is let her have peace first."

Jason leaned back, raking a hand through his hair; his fingers still trembled.

Berry looked toward the hallway.

"So we just… wait?"

"We wait," Sheila said—gentle, final.

Jason closed his eyes, inhaling, willing the tightness inside him to ease. It didn't. Because no matter how long they waited—tomorrow would come. And with it, so would everything Alley had lost.

Chapter 49

The calm before the storm

The automatic doors whooshed open as Steve strode into the hospital, his movements clipped, precise—urgent.

The sharp sting of antiseptic hit him the moment he stepped inside, but he barely noticed.

His heart pounded. Tension pressed hard across his face. Dale's message still echoed: Sheila had recommended keeping Alley under observation. That was all—but it still shook him.

As he pressed the elevator button, Steve caught a glimpse of his own reflection in the brushed metal doors—drawn, tense, jaw set like stone.

He hadn't realized how much his body remembered this floor.

The scent. The static in the air. The hush of voices behind closed doors.

And then, without warning, the memory surged forward—unbidden, whole.

He'd been standing right here the first time he saw her after she returned to Apple Creek.

Not just Alley, but that version of her —the one who didn't know her own name, the one who stared at the floor as if she didn't trust it would hold her.

She was being wheeled down the hallway, her posture rigid, arms folded tightly in her lap, as if trying to keep herself from coming apart.

She wore a white cotton dress, which looked borrowed—slightly too big in the shoulders, summery and gentle, entirely at odds with the fog in her eyes.

And yet—even through the silence, the paleness, the vacant expression—he had known her.

Alley, from long ago. The girl who used to jump into creeks fully clothed. The one who raced in the rain. But she wasn't that girl now.

She didn't look at him. Didn't see him at all.

Her eyes were wide and far away, locked on something only she could see, as if she were stuck in a story the rest of the world couldn't hear.

And all he could do was stand there. Watching her vanish down the corridor without a word.

That moment had never left him.

It haunted the quiet between his breaths.

The elevator dinged now, pulling him back into the present. The doors slid open.

He stepped inside, fists clenched at his sides.

He wasn't sure what he'd find at the top of the ride—but the memory still echoed inside him, sharper than the steel walls around him.

The elevator doors slid open, fluorescent lights overhead burning too bright against his eyes. He stepped out, the rhythmic tap of his shoes on the polished floor the only sound anchoring him.

He wasn't running. Not exactly. But every step dragged. Every hallway stretched too far. He rounded the corner sharply, and the waiting area came into view.

Jason.

Sitting forward in his chair, his elbows on his knees, his fingers woven together.

Berry.

Beside him, legs crossed, arms folded. His usual glint of amusement was gone.

Sheila.

A few feet away, her expression was unreadable.

They all looked up at the same time.

Suddenly, Steve wasn't sure whether to explode in anger or walk away for good.

Jason's posture shifted, his muscles visibly tensing.

Berry muttered under his breath, "Oh, shit."

But Steve didn't waver. He headed straight for the nurses' station. Jason and Berry watched him exchange a few words with the nurse, saw her nod, then led him toward Alley's room.

"Come on," Berry said, nudging Jason toward the exit. "You need caffeine before this goes nuclear."

Jason lingered a second longer, then followed.

They walked quietly, the weight of that room—Alley's withdrawn gaze, Steve's arrival—still pressing down on Jason's shoulders, tight and unmoving.

The café buzzed with conversations, the clinking of cups, and the occasional hiss of the espresso machine.

The air smelled of freshly brewed coffee and pastries, a tempting mix that made Jason momentarily forget the chaos in his life.

Jason scanned the room, searching for an open table when—

"Jason!"

Leia's voice cut through the crowd.

She was already seated, waving them over like they were longtime friends instead of brand-new acquaintances.

Berry, walking beside Jason, smirked. "Man, we just walked in, and you're already getting summoned? "

Jason ignored him and made his way over. Berry followed, grinning like a guy who just sensed an opportunity for entertainment.

Leia gestured at the open chairs. "You can sit here."

Jason slid into the seat with a nod, already bracing for Berry's commentary.

Berry, however, paused and gave Jason an exaggerated look.

Jason sighed. "Berry, this is Leia. Leia, this is Berry."

Leia offered a polite nod. "Nice to meet you."

Berry raised a brow, still looking between them suspiciously.

"Leia. As in Eaton's girlfriend's …" He trailed off, tilting his head.

"Aunt," Leia confirmed, taking a sip of her coffee.

Berry's eyes widened dramatically. He leaned back like someone had just hit him with breaking news.

"Damn. Our guy moves fast, huh?"

Leia, clearly amused, didn't bother to hide the curve of her mouth. "It's a competitive field," she said smoothly. "You place bets early."

Berry blew a low whistle, shaking his head like he was deeply impressed.

"Damn. Ruthless."

Jason closed his eyes briefly—probably counting to ten.

"Can we not—"

He rubbed his temple. "Are we done?"

Berry grinned wider. "Oh, not even close."

A low grumble escaped him, mostly to himself. "Why do I have friends?"

Unbothered, Berry stretched out like he owned the place and grabbed a menu. "Alright, Leia, since you seem to know how this whole game works—what's the best thing on the menu?"

As Jason handed her the menu, their fingers brushed—just for a second. She didn't flinch or rush; she simply smiled, a genuine, kind smile, and kept talking.

A spark of mischief lit Leia's face. "Depends. How competitive are you feeling?"

Berry leaned in, already sensing a challenge.

Meanwhile, Jason was staring into his hands as if they might teleport him out of this entire conversation.

And for just a second—before Berry launched into another teasing quip—Leia let herself look at him. Not as Eaton's dad. Not as the guy with a haunted past.

He tilted his head and let a faint grin slip through—measured, expectant. Kindness shone in his eyes, yet a soft echo of isolation lingered beneath it, setting her pulse racing.

He was handsome. Not in an obvious way. But in the quiet confidence of someone who carried too much and still stood tall.

She tucked the thought away before it lingered too long.

They ordered coffee.

Leia took another sip of coffee and then gave Berry a sideways glance.

"So, have your boys found you a future daughter-in-law yet?"

Berry groaned, dropping his menu dramatically onto the table. "Ugh, don't remind me."

Leia raised a brow. "That bad?"

Berry scoffed. "Absolute losers in the field so far. No hustle. No vision. I raised them better than this."

Leia smirked. "Maybe they're just waiting for the right moment."

Berry scoffed. "Right moment? Please. At this rate, I'll be in a retirement home before any of them make a move."

Sipping his coffee, Jason said, "Sounds like a personal problem, Berry."

Berry shot him a glare. "Don't act like you're better than me, Jay. You're the captain of the single squad."

Leia covered a laugh behind her cup. "Wow. Captain of the single squad? I love that."

A heavy sigh escaped him. "I need new friends."

Berry smirked. "Nah, you just need a competitive strategy."

Leia nodded in agreement. "Yep. Can't win the game if you don't play."

Muttering into his cup, Jason replied, "This isn't a game."

"That's exactly what a loser in the field would say," Berry said, all mock sympathy.

Leia laughed into her drink, and a rare lightness settled over Jason. It wasn't just her voice—it was the way she looked at him, as if he weren't broken, as if he were just… a man at a café.

He was still caught in the storm.

Drowning. In every unsaid thing.

Still carrying a truth too heavy to share.

But right now?

Right now, Berry was teasing Leia about her aggressive matchmaking strategies, and Leia was holding her own like she'd been dealing with them for years.

And Jason?

Jason found himself laughing.

Not the hollow kind of forced laughter that covered up everything underneath.

It was real. Effortless. And damn it, he needed this.

But as the laughter settled, Jason looked toward the window.

The hospital was still there.

And so was Steve.

This moment of normalcy wouldn't last.

He still had a storm to walk into. But for now, the rain had paused. And that had to be enough.

Chapter 50

Love is beyond romance

Jason stepped into his office, still damp with sweat from the morning's emergency drill. His muscles ached from the strain, but the physical exhaustion was nothing compared to the storm inside his head.

The room was exactly as he'd left it—a battlefield of papers, folders, and scattered debris. His desk, once a symbol of control, was now a mess of frustration and recklessness.

He raked a hand through his hair, exhaling sharply.

What the hell had he done last night?

He had lost control. Completely. He had thrown things like an angry teenager instead of the composed doctor he was supposed to be.

And now, looking at the aftermath, he wondered—

Was he even in the right mental state to be involved in Alley's care?

He sank into his chair, closing his eyes for a moment as if sheer willpower could steady him.

No wonder doctors were advised never to operate on family.

He had crossed the line.

Not just as a doctor, but as a man who had promised himself that if Alley ever remembered, he would be her anchor, not another storm.

He should have put the pictures away after showing them to Dale and Sheila.

But if she kept believing her baby was gone, if she kept carrying that silent, aching grief, she would never fully heal.

She would never truly recover.

And she would never reclaim her life.

Because somewhere deep down, in the part of her mind she couldn't access, Alley had been waiting.

Waiting for someone to tell her the truth.

And now, she knew.

And despite the chaos, despite the shattered glass of their past—

There was no doubt in Jason's mind—he'd done the right thing.

He dragged a hand down his face, then stared at the mess on his desk.

He had made his choice.

Now, he had to live with it.

And in a few hours, he would have to face the man who had been living with it all along.

A knock pulled Jason from his thoughts.

He glanced up. It was Steve.

Both men walked to the sitting area by the window.

Jason finally spoke. "How is Alley? Is she awake?"

"She slept through the night calmly. But she said she felt a little groggy this morning. Dale suggested she sleep it off."

Jason gave a short nod. "That's the tranquilizer working."

He poured a glass of water and pushed it toward Steve, finally meeting Steve's gaze. "Steve, I'm so sorry about Alley's condition. I know this opens… another dimension."

Steve's posture shifted—barely—but enough to betray the effort it took to stay composed. Hands clasped, he looked like a man on the edge of unraveling.

Jason studied him for a moment.

Steve looked tired. Not just physically, but in a way that settled deep into a man's bones. Like someone who had spent years carrying something heavy—and now, after all this time, that weight had finally shifted, but he wasn't sure if that made it any easier.

And yet—there was something else in him.

Something unshaken.

Steve set the glass of water down with a quiet clink against the table, his movements measured and deliberate. He walked toward the window, hands slipping into his pockets, shoulders rolling back—a man standing tall, but his eyes gave him away.

Too still. Too full. His lips parted, then closed again—like the truth was pressing at the edges of him, dangerous in its shape, too sharp to speak without drawing blood.

Jason remained seated, leaning back slightly, fingers loosely wrapped around the glass. He was not tense, not defensive, just waiting.

Neither spoke, but the stillness carried a shared understanding.

"Jason, can I ask you something—outside of Alley's medical care?"

He set his cup down. "Yeah."

Steve hesitated. His lips tightened, as if holding back more than just words. When he finally spoke, his voice was calm but searching.

"Alley told me once that 'Jay' was the love of her life." He turned toward Jason, eyes locking in with quiet intensity. "I figured that was you. Am I right?"

No flinch. No blink.

Jason simply nodded. "Yeah. It was me."

Steve said nothing at first. Just sat there, watching.

Jason held his gaze, offering no excuses, no elaboration.

And when Steve finally moved—it wasn't in anger or resentment. It was in understanding.

"I saw the way you look at her," Steve said finally, his tone unwavering—not an accusation, not a challenge, just observation. "And the way you've been involved in her recovery—it tells me something."

Jason looked away briefly, the tension visible in his shoulders.

"Steve—"

Steve shook his head. "I'm not looking for reassurances, Jason. I'm looking for the truth."

Jason's shoulders slumped slightly, weariness threading through him, before he lifted his gaze to Steve—clear, steady, unflinching.

"I'm not trivializing my past with Alley," Jason admitted, voice firm. "She was the love of my life. We built dreams together—traveling, growing old side by side."

He let the weight of those words sit between them.

"But fate had other plans."

Steve kept quiet, eyes steady, absorbing it all.

Jason's voice dropped slightly, but his conviction didn't waver.

"But love—real love—isn't about whether your dreams come true." He let out a steady breath. "It's beyond possession. Beyond what we wanted for ourselves."

His eyes met Steve's—steady, unshaken.

"This isn't about romance anymore."

A pause.

"My love for Alley now?" He let the words settle. "It's not about holding on—it's about helping her find her way back."

Steve turned back toward the window, hands still in his pockets, weighing Jason's words.

Jason didn't push. Didn't expect anything.

And then—Steve's voice broke the stillness, his question unexpected.

"Is this your son?" he asked, nodding toward a picture frame on the shelf—two-year-old Eaton, smiling wide beside his dog and Margaret, sunlight catching in their hair, a moment of joy captured forever.

Jason gave a quiet nod.

He had moved forward, built a life, a family.

And Alley… Alley had been trapped—suspended in the cobwebs of a past she couldn't remember and a truth no one had dared to give her.

A quiet moment passed before Steve turned, calm but focused, to face Jason.

For years, he had imagined this moment—confronting the man from Alley's past.

The ghost of a love she didn't remember.

But he had.

And yet, standing here, listening to Jason now—it didn't feel like he was facing a rival.

It felt like he was facing someone who understood.

Someone who had loved Alley once, yes.

But more importantly—someone who still wanted what was best for her, no matter where that left him.

Steve lowered his shoulders.

"You were important to her," he said finally. "Maybe more than I even realized."

Jason swallowed, nodding once.

Steve didn't look away. "But if what you're saying is true—if this is just about helping her—then I have to trust that."

Jason met his gaze.

"You can."

The words were simple. Honest. Something finally settled when Steve walked into Jason's office—not as enemies, not as rivals.

But as two men who would stand beside Alley, no matter what came next.

Chapter 51

The resurrected truth

Jason's footsteps echoed down the empty hallway, growing heavier with every step. Sheila had asked him to come to Alley's room ASAP.

The conversation with Steve had gone better than expected—maybe too well.

And yet, the weight of what he was holding back pressed down on him, tight and unrelenting.

He still hadn't told Steve that Eaton was Alley's son—their son.

Steve had seen Eaton's photo with Margaret and assumed Jason had moved on and started a family.

Jason had convinced himself it wasn't the right time. Alley's recovery came first. Telling Steve everything now—before Alley had a chance to process it herself—might only unravel what little peace they had.

He steadied himself, then pushed the door open.

The first thing he heard was her sobbing.

Raw. Broken. Guttural. The kind of sound that carved deep into the bones, that ripped through the soul, and left nothing but devastation in its wake.

A sharp pang gripped him at the sight of Alley curled forward in the hospital bed, her body trembling violently.

Dale held her hand, concern etched into every line of his face, his thumb tracing steady circles—but it wasn't helping. The storm within her refused to be calmed.

Sheila stood on the other side of the bed, composed but watchful, as if waiting—as if already knowing what needed to happen next.

And Steve—

Steve stood rigid, just a step away, his whole body locked in place as if caught between the past and the present.

Jason barely took another step when Alley's voice cut through the air, hoarse and shaking.

"I saw it."

Her breathing hitched, fingers curling into the blanket as if trying to hold on to something that wasn't there.

"I saw the explosion."

The sentence caught in her throat, her face twisted in raw memory.

"And I—I couldn't get there in time. My baby—"

A choked sob ripped through her, shaking her petite frame, and Jason felt Steve sway beside him.

Jason's hand locked on Steve's shoulder, anchoring him—because Steve looked like he might collapse.

He could feel the tremor running through the man's body. Could see the way his eyes stared straight ahead, unblinking, his mind trying to make sense of something that would never make sense.

Because Alley thought their baby was dead.

Jason braced himself. He had to fix this.

Then the door swung open again, and Berry stepped inside.

His pulse pounded—loud, insistent—but the moment his eyes found Alley, trembling and undone, everything in him snapped mute.

Color drained from his face.

He didn't have to look at him. He already knew what Berry was thinking.

The man had seen war. He had seen broken men and women cry like this—people who had lost everything, people who had been left with nothing but grief and ghosts.

And now, he was looking at one.

It was Alley, making that sound.

Berry didn't say a word. Didn't even move. But the tension in his face spoke volumes.

Alley's cries filled the room, the hospital walls feeling too small, too suffocating for what was happening here.

Jason gathered his thoughts, then lifted his gaze.

And that's when he saw them.

Dale and Sheila.

They were both looking at him now.

Not with shock.

Not with confusion.

But with understanding.

And in that moment, no words needed to be spoken.

This was it.

This was the moment.

The truth had been a dam ready to break for too long, and now, it was coming down—whether any of them were ready for it or not.

Jason shifted his weight, the moment pressing against his chest. He turned back to Alley, who still hadn't registered his presence... and still hadn't noticed the way Steve was barely holding himself together.

And then, he spoke. "Alley."

She flinched. Her head snapped up. Her eyes—wide, tear-filled, and lost—landed on him.

Jason stepped closer and gently took her hands in his. His touch was tender but firm—an anchor in the storm he'd brought. His voice didn't waver.

"You didn't lose your baby."

The room stilled.

Alley's lips parted, her entire body frozen in place. Beside him, Berry tensed.

Steve's shoulders went rigid. Sheila and Dale stood still in the background, watchful and unmoving.

Alley's head shook. Once. Twice. "W-what?" she said, barely getting the word out.

A tremor passed through Jason's hands as he held on tighter.

His voice didn't waver.

"You didn't lose your baby."

He held her gaze. Didn't blink. Didn't waver.

"You didn't lose him, Alley. You never lost him. He lived."

And then—

Everything collapsed.

Alley gasped, her hands flying to her mouth, everything she believed splintering in a heartbeat.

Steve staggered backward, eyes wide, as if the words had knocked the ground out from under him. His gaze snapped to Jason—shocked, wounded.

He didn't say a word, but the way he looked at Jason said enough. You knew. All this time, you knew.

Berry closed his eyes, the lines of his face stiffening, as if bracing for impact.

And Jason—

Alley's scream knocked the wind from Jason's lungs.

Because it wasn't just the truth breaking now.

It was her.

And there was no coming back from it.

The weight of the revelation suffocated the room. No one moved. No one spoke.

The only sound was Alley's broken sobs. She stumbled forward and collapsed into him, burying her face against his chest, her sobs breaking loose all at once.

Jason drew her closer, feeling the tremble in her fragile frame. He shut his eyes briefly, anchoring both of them in the moment.

God.

He should have told her sooner.

Should have given her these lost years back.

But now, all he could do was hold her together as she fell apart.

Dale took a step forward, looking like he wanted to say something, but he didn't.

Because what could anyone say?

This was a mother realizing she had been grieving a child who had never died.

This was a woman understanding that her worst nightmare had been a lie—one she had lived with for seven years.

Steve had yet to move.

Jason could feel the way the tension rolled off him.

Sheila, composed as always, gave a steady nod, her gaze meeting Jason's with something unreadable.

Jason could tell. She understood.

Understood that this moment—this devastation-had been inevitable.

Jason stayed still, his fingers tracing grounding circles against Alley's back.

She felt unsteady in his arms—fragile, like she might fall apart if he let go.

And then—

Her fingers fisted into his shirt even tighter.

She wavered on her feet, suddenly unsteady.

"How do you know?" she said, her words breaking mid-breath. "You're not just saying it to—"

He couldn't speak at first—his voice buried beneath the weight of it all.

"I was there when he was rescued, Alley."

A jolt shot through her, sharp and dizzying. Her legs gave way, and she collapsed into a sob that tore straight from her core.

Later that night, Jason stops by Alley's room. Silver crescent moonlight shimmers through the curtains, sketching gentle shadows across the floor. He watches her—soft, unburdened, fragile—her steady breath echoing the peace of a child at rest.

He closes his eyes. A flash: dancing beneath Kandahar's moonlit sky—her laughter spiraling through lantern-lit air. A memory reborn.

His fingers brush the doorframe as he steps away. The door clicks softly, and the room settles into stillness.

A few blocks away, Steve settled into his balcony chair with a steaming mug of tea. The crisp fall breeze drifted by, carrying soft hints of woodsmoke. Above, a silver crescent moon peeked from behind wisps of cloud, its pale glow calming the night.

Steve closed his eyes, lifting the mug to his lips. The warm scent of mint-chamomile seeped through the steam, anchoring him to the quiet moment.

Elijah curled against his side, a steady, comforting presence in the gentle darkness. They sat in silence—two souls sharing warmth beneath autumn's hush.

Below, the Golden Oaks Diner's neon sign glowed crimson-orange, its soft pulse reflected in the distant hospital windows—a silent echo of late-night hope.

Alley slept in peace.

Steve exhaled under the moon, letting the night steady his breath.

Chapter 52

After the storm

The next morning, echoes of Alley's sobs still lingered, hanging in the air like smoke after a fire. The room felt hollow—like something had broken and the pieces hadn't yet settled.

Jason didn't move, his pulse pounding in his ears as the nurse withdrew the syringe from Alley's IV.

The tranquilizer would calm her, steady her breathing, ease the tremors wrecking her body—but it wouldn't take away the truth.

Nothing could. She lay against the pillows, her body curled slightly—like she was trying to hold onto something, even in sleep. Her movements were faint and uneven, touched by the haze of sedation.

He tipped his head down momentarily, gathering himself, before looking up at Dale.

"How long will she be out?"

Dale didn't answer right away. His expression was grim as he studied the vitals monitor, the rhythmic beep marking her body's gradual return to calm.

"A few hours," he murmured. "She needed it."

Jason understood that.

But it didn't make it any easier.

Berry sank into the chair, pressing his palms briefly over his face, as if trying to wipe away the heaviness clinging to him.

Sheila stood near the door, arms crossed, her usual calm demeanor strained but steady.

And Steve—

Steve still hadn't said a word.

Jason turned his head, studying him carefully.

He looked calm, but he was angry. Holding it in.

And his eyes—

They were still fixed on Alley, but Jason could see it—the storm raging just beneath the surface.

The truth was sinking in.

Not just that their son had lived—but that Jason had known.

This wasn't over.

Not by a long shot.

But right now, Alley was asleep.

And for the first time in seven years, she would wake up in a world where her son still existed.

The door swung open.

"What are we looking at?"

A voice too casual, too bright for the room's suffocating air.

Everyone turned—as if an alien had just landed in the middle of a battlefield.

And there, standing in the doorway, was Emmy.

Jovial. Unbothered. Completely unaware that she had just walked into the aftermath of an emotional earthquake.

Her wide eyes swept the room, taking in the rigid stances, haunted expressions, and the suffocating quiet that had settled over them.

Her gaze landed on Jason first, then flicked to Steve—who looked like he was about two seconds from collapsing in on himself.

Then, finally, she saw Alley.

Her smile vanished. Her features tightened, the ease slipping away.

For a moment, she just stood there. The usual lightness in her posture dimmed, shifting into something sharper.

Then—

With a quickness that surprised everyone, she crossed the room in three long strides, moving straight to Alley's bedside.

"Oh, babe."

The words were gentle but full of something deep and unshaken.

With zero hesitation, she sat on the bed, one knee tucked under her, and reached for Alley's hand.

Jason expected her to cry. Or whisper words of comfort. Or even ask what the hell had just happened.

She did none of that.

Instead, she sighed dramatically and muttered, "Well, everyone, please leave and give me and my gal here some privacy?"

Jason blinked.

Berry choked on a laugh from his chair.

Steve—who hadn't reacted to anything in the past ten minutes—
actually turned to look at her like she had lost her mind.

But Emmy simply sighed, her fingers still gently tracing patterns
over Alley's hand.

"Seriously, all of you standing around like haunted statues isn't
going to help. You look like you're waiting for someone to announce
the end of the world. Which, I mean, I get it, but also—go be dramatic
somewhere else."

Jason lowered his gaze.

Berry stood first, stretching lazily.

"I could use coffee—and maybe a shot of whiskey... after last
night's apocalypse

Sheila shot him a look.

"You're in the hospital."

Berry grinned.

"Then two cups of coffee."

Jason hesitated, glancing at Steve, who hadn't moved or spoken.
His hands were still clenched, his gaze flickering between Alley's pale
face and Jason himself.

Emmy must have noticed, too, because she tilted her head at him,
unimpressed.

"That includes you, Mr. Tall-Dark-and-Doomed."

Steve's head jerked slightly as if caught off guard. His eyes
hardened.

"I'm not leaving."

Emmy gave him a long look.

Then she shrugged.

"Suit yourself. But if you stand there much longer, I'm going to
start monologuing about my feelings, and trust me, nobody wants
that."

Berry let out a loud laugh, his grin stretched, his eyes lighting up
as he leaned back in his chair, clearly relieved the shift in the mood.

Jason finally sighed.

She was right.

There was nothing more they could do right now. And Emmy—
for all her dramatics—had just said what none of them could.

So, one by one, they left.

Jason was the last to move, pausing at the door, his eyes drifting back to Alley's sleeping form.

She looked worn, fragile—but not broken.

Not anymore.

He swallowed hard, then turned away.

As he stepped into the hallway, he heard Emmy's voice behind him, steady—just for Alley.

"It's okay, babe. I've got you."

And Jason knew—

She did.

Chapter 53

A silence that screams

Later that night, betrayal still burned in Steve's veins as he drove under November's chill, which seeped into the air, carrying the scent of fallen leaves and the promise of winter creeping in.

The streets were lined with twinkling lights, the golden glow of Thanksgiving decorations lingering in storefronts, competing with the first hints of Christmas wreaths.

The warmth of roasting turkey, cinnamon, and spices inside the house wrapped the walls in a familiar embrace, laced with the uneasy undercurrent of a family pretending nothing was falling apart.

The house was quiet when Steve stepped inside.

Like the walls themselves were holding their breath.

"Steve, is that you?"

His mother's voice floated from the kitchen, warm but tired.

Maggie stood at the counter, a glass of wine in her hand, her expression unreadable.

Steve let out a breath, stepping toward her. "Wouldn't mind something stronger."

Maggie gave him a knowing look as he leaned down to kiss her cheek. "Your dad's in the living room," she said, gesturing toward the whiskey bottle on the counter. "I'll bring your drink."

Steve nodded and made his way inside.

His father sat in his usual chair by the fireplace, a glass of whiskey in one hand, the other resting on the armrest. Low jazz chords drifted through the room in the background.

He looked up when Steve entered.

Expression unreadable.

A moment passed.

Then another.

Maggie walked in, handed Steve a drink, and settled onto the sofa beside him.

Steve took a sip, letting the warmth burn down his throat.

Then he finally spoke.

"You knew."

His voice was cold. Steady.

But underneath, it was laced with something deeper. Something lethal.

Dale didn't look away. He simply nodded.

"How long?"

A pause.

A breath.

Then—

"Maybe a few months."

Steve went pale.

He couldn't ask the next question, but he had to.

His voice came quieter but sharper. "Is Jason the father of Alley's child?"

Maggie's fingers curled around her wine glass, tension pooling in her shoulders.

Dale didn't flinch. He held Steve's gaze, unwavering.

"Yes."

The single word hit like a gut punch.

Everything inside him froze.

His mind reeled back—Alley's tears, her suffering, her grief that had swallowed her whole.

She had believed her child was dead.

And Jason knew.

His body tensed. His voice cut the silence like glass—sharp and unfiltered.

"And you covered for him."

Dale hesitated, setting his glass down. "It wasn't like that."

Steve laughed dryly.

"Wasn't it?" He glared at Dale, voice shaking with barely restrained anger. "You had weeks to stop this from happening. Days to tell Alley before she completely shattered. And you did nothing?"

Dale didn't flinch. "Yesterday, you came in upset because you thought we showed Alley the pictures of her baby." His tone was steady and measured.

"And today, you're upset because we didn't tell her the baby was alive."

Steve went rigid, frustration flashing across his face. "I don't need you twisting this around, Dad. What I need is the truth."

Dale's expression didn't shift. "I did what I thought was best."

"Best for who?" The words cracked the quiet. "For Alley?"

He drew in a breath, trying—and failing—to keep calm. "Or best for Jason?"

His father's mouth thinned, eyes steady and unyielding.

"You don't understand."

"Then make me understand!" Steve's voice cracked, raw with years of built-up frustration. "Because right now, all I see is a man who took his son and let the woman he claimed to love suffer for seven years!"

The words hung in the air, jagged and unforgiving.

Then Dale spoke in a low, quiet voice.

"Is that what you think happened? That Jason left Alley to suffer, making her believe that she lost her son?"

The firelight flickered across his face.

Dale stood his ground, every word deliberate.

"Jason is as much a victim as Alley is."

Steve frowned, his heart hammering.

Dale's voice dropped even lower.

"Do you want to know what happened in Afghanistan?"

Steve didn't answer.

But he listened.

And when his father finally finished, Steve couldn't breathe.

Everything he had thought he knew, everything he had held onto, had just shifted beneath his feet.

He stood abruptly, the whiskey glass in his hand shaking just slightly before he set it down on the table.

Steve turned away, the weight of everything pressing into him.

He turned toward the door, jaw rigid, fury burning under his skin.

But then he heard her voice—low, even.

"Steve," Maggie said, not rising from her seat. "You have every right to be angry. But don't lose sight of the man you've been to her."

He paused.

"She didn't remember Jason. She didn't remember her son. She barely remembered her own name. And you were the one who stayed."

Steve didn't turn around.

"You're angry because secrets were kept. Fine. So am I.

But don't rewrite your place in her life just because you didn't know everything."

Maggie's voice softened but held firm.

"You weren't chosen because she forgot Jason. You were chosen because you were there when no one else was."

Steve released a slow, trembling sigh.

"She's remembering now," he murmured. "What if that changes everything?"

Maggie's answer came quiet, steady.

"Then let it. But don't forget what was real between you—just because the truth was late getting here."

He needed air. He needed to move. He needed to get the hell out of there.

Maggie watched him, her expression unreadable. She didn't try to stop him.

Neither did Dale.

The cold night hit him as he stepped outside, but he barely felt it.

The wind had picked up since he arrived, sharp and biting, rustling the last of the autumn leaves along the driveway. His coat did little to block the sudden chill creeping under his skin, but he didn't bother pulling it tighter.

His mind was spinning, replaying everything over and over.

Whoever said the truth will set you free had no idea what they were talking about.

Because the truth wasn't freeing him.

It was drowning him.

A gust of wind whipped through the trees, rattling the bare branches above him. Somewhere in the distance, a wind chime clinked, the hollow sound lost in the night.

As Steve got into his car and gripped the wheel, another thought occurred to him.

Alley.

She still didn't know.

The weight of that realization pressed on him like a boulder—heavier than any burden the night had thrown his way.

Because if the truth had shattered him—what the hell was it going to do to her?

His hands locked around the wheel, every muscle coiled with restraint.

She'd gone into shock. Thought the baby was gone.

Her mind had shut down to survive.

Now, the truth was coming.

Steve shifted, tension etched across his face.

Because when Alley finally learned everything—when she learned why Jason never got to tell her—

She might never come back from it.

Chapter 54

A solo night

Jason woke to the sound of muffled voices downstairs, the scent of cinnamon lingering in the air. He turned over, blinking at the dim light slipping past the curtains.

He lay there for a moment, staring at the ceiling, letting the weight of the last few days sink into him.

It had been an impossible week.

Alley knew.

And not just in fragments or dreams—but fully, painfully, completely.

Steve was furious—rightfully so.

And Eaton—He still had no idea.

Jason rubbed his temples, a familiar tightness forming behind his eyes. The kind that came from knowing a storm was coming but not being able to stop it.

Eaton's laughter rose from downstairs—bright, unburdened, unaware. Jason closed his eyes, the sound brushing something tender inside him.

She was going to ask soon.

And he didn't know how he was supposed to answer.

He pulled on a hoodie and headed downstairs. The smell of cinnamon and maple syrup greeted him, warm and familiar. In the kitchen, Margaret wrapped desserts with quiet precision.

She looked up as he entered, warmth touching her lips for an instant, but her eyes searched his face for the unspoken worry there.

She was always good at that. Seeing what others missed.

Despite the exhaustion in his posture, the weight in his eyes, she watched how—without thinking—he leaned down, chuckling at Eaton's joke and passing the orange juice without missing a beat.

He switched like that. From son to father. From man to protector.

And Margaret saw it clearly now: no matter how heavily the past pressed against him, Jason never let Eaton feel the weight.

"I wish you were coming with us," she said, forcing a lightness into her tone as she carefully packed the cake. "Your uncle and aunt would love to see you."

Leaning against the counter, he let out a quiet sigh. "I can't. The hospital's hosting a black-tie dinner. I have to be there."

Margaret raised a brow. "So, you're choosing work over pie and chaos?"

Before she could push further, Robert entered—already dressed for the road, sipping coffee like they were running ahead of schedule for once.

The banter swirled around him. Jason answered when needed, but his attention kept drifting—watching Eaton buzz around the kitchen, blissfully unaware of the gravity waiting just beyond his world.

He felt it then. A jolt. Sharp and fast.

Not fear. Not even guilt. Just grief.

Because Eaton didn't know. Because Alley did.

And the moment those two realities collided, something would shift. Maybe in Alley. Maybe in Eaton. Maybe in him.

Because once she stepped into this—once she saw Eaton, touched his hair, heard him laugh—he wouldn't be just Jason's anymore.

And he wasn't sure how to share that.

But it was coming.

He wasn't ready.

He helped carry bags to the car, his arms strong, his steps steady, though a hint of sadness moved with him.

He held Eaton tighter than usual when they hugged goodbye. Just a second too long. Eaton didn't notice—but Margaret did.

She kissed Jason's cheek, her hand slipping into his for a brief, wordless squeeze.

Then, they were gone.

The house was quiet again.

Jason made himself a cup of tea, standing alone in the kitchen, his gaze fixed on the empty space where Eaton had been moments ago.

He had spent so long building a life around shielding Eaton from pain, from the past.

And now? The past was waking up. With a name. A face.

He carried the tea into the living room and sank onto the edge of the couch. The stillness made his chest ache, too full of thoughts he couldn't quite name.

This used to be sufficient. Eaton. His work. Quiet evenings that didn't ask anything from him. But today, with Alley's voice still echoing in his mind and Eaton's laughter fading into the walls, the warmth of the tea felt thin—unable to steady him the way it used to.

His gaze landed on the invitation again—formal script, careful gold edging. He hadn't RSVP'd with a plus-one. Hadn't even thought to.

But now, alone, the thought crept in.

Maybe it would be easier… just for one night… to not carry all of this.

His mind drifted to Leia.

She was kind. Easy to be around. No hidden ache in the way she looked at him, no silence that carried too much.

He remembered the way she laughed when she got flustered, tucking her hair behind her ear like it gave her a moment to reset.

They'd only shared a few coffees, simple conversations—but with her, there was space to breathe. And maybe that was the appeal.

She didn't know about Alley. Or Eaton. Or the thousand moments he kept folded into himself like fragile paper.

With her, it almost felt like none of it had happened. Like he could choose a different version of himself.

But that wasn't real. Not now.

Alley was remembering. Eaton—off with his grandparents—was still inside a world that would soon crack open. And Jason was the one standing at the fault line.

Even if Leia came—laughing, warm, beautiful—he knew it would be a lie.

But that didn't stop him from wondering if she would come.

He rinsed the mug, set it in the rack, and let the quiet settle.

Leia was light. Tonight was a shadow.

And he couldn't ask her to cross that line just to keep him company.

He grabbed his tux jacket from the back of the chair and turned toward the stairs.

One step at a time, he reminded himself.

The quiet would have to walk beside him tonight.

Chapter 55

A different kind of Thanksgiving

Alley woke up, her mind foggy from the medication. But something was different. The heavy weight she had carried for years seemed lighter—not gone, but not crushing her anymore.

She shifted, feeling Steve's warmth beside her. His steady breathing and mere presence grounded her, and she no longer woke to nightmares or confusion.

She was waking up as someone who finally knew the truth.

Her child was alive.

She turned slightly, blinking at the soft morning light filtering through the curtains. Steve stirred awake, watching her with quiet intensity.

"How are you feeling?" he asked, voice gentle.

Alley paused, turning the answer over in her mind before speaking. "Different."

Steve's hand found hers under the blankets, his thumb tracing soothing circles against her skin. "Good different?"

She swallowed. "Scary different."

"I know," he said, trying to calm her.

Then, hesitantly, she asked, just audible: "Did you know? Before I did?"

Steve didn't flinch. "No. I found out when you did."

Alley studied his face, searching for any hesitation, any sign that he was sparing her from another ugly truth. But there was none. Just quiet honesty.

She said shakily, "What do you feel about it? About... the baby?"

Steve's gaze warmed.

"I feel like I just got back a piece of you I thought was lost forever."

He squeezed her hand. "I love you, Alley. That hasn't changed. And knowing your child is alive? I'm happy. I'm grateful."

Her heart ached at his words. At the weight of everything unsaid between them.

"But what does this mean for us?" she asked.

Steve hesitated, not because he didn't know the answer, but because he wanted to say it right. "It means we take this one step at a time. Alley, I know how much you want to see him, but... we have to be careful. He's a kid. And right now, he doesn't know about you."

Her stomach clenched. "So... he thinks he doesn't have a mother."

"We don't know what he knows," Steve murmured, running his fingers through her hair.

Alley closed her eyes, trying to steady herself. The thought of her child growing up without knowing her—it was unbearable.

She braced herself against the pain, but another question clawed its way forward.

"Why don't I remember his father?" she murmured.

Steve stiffened. Before he could answer, a sudden thud jolted them both.

Elijah leaped onto the bed with a dramatic huff, landing squarely on Steve's legs.

He let out a grunt as the dog began enthusiastically licking his face.

"Okay, okay—Elijah, seriously—" Steve groaned, attempting to shield himself from the full assault of wet kisses.

Alley let out a surprised laugh as Elijah's tail wagged furiously, clearly pleased with himself.

A loud knock echoed. Instinctively, they both answered at once—
"Come in."

The door swung open, and Maggie stood there, hands on her hips, eyebrows raised.

Alley smothered another laugh as Steve scowled, still fending off Elijah.

Maggie sighed, giving them a knowing look.

"As much as I'm sure you two would love to stay here being all emotional, it's Thanksgiving, and everyone's waiting for you. So get up, get dressed, and come eat."

Elijah barked in agreement before happily bouncing off the bed as if personally enforcing Maggie's orders.

Steve groaned, pushing himself up.

"Traitor," he muttered at the dog.

Alley, still curled under the blankets, shook her head. The heavy conversation wasn't over—not by a long shot. But for now, just for a little while, she let herself be pulled back into the present.

One step at a time.

Thanksgiving morning brought a gratitude long absent, steadying her from within.

She was grateful.

For the truth—no matter how incomplete it still was.

For the knowledge that her baby was alive, out there in the world.

There were so many things she wished she could remember: what it had been like to carry him, to hold him for the first time.

She didn't even know what he looked like now—whether he had her eyes, or if his laughter curved the way hers once did.

But he was out there. Living. Breathing. Growing.

And one day, somehow, she would find her way back to him.

She wished she could remember who his father was. So many missing pieces were still waiting to be uncovered. But today wasn't about that. Today was about the fragments that were already falling into place, about the life she was reclaiming, piece by piece.

She was grateful for Steve—for his love, his steadiness, for the way he looked at her as if she hadn't been lost for years. For the way he hadn't let go, even when she had nothing to offer in return.

Grateful for Maggie and Dale, whose concern and unwavering support had carried her through so much more than she could even put into words.

Grateful for Jay and Berry—memories that had resurfaced when everything else had been stolen from her. They were anchors to a past she had once forgotten, but now she held onto them tightly.

But most of all, she was grateful that she wasn't alone in this.

She took a steadying breath, turning toward Steve as he finished buttoning his shirt.

"Ready?" he asked gently.

She met his gaze, feeling the weight of everything between them. "Yeah," she said, her expression softening with quiet certainty. "I really am."

He reached for her hand, squeezing it once before leading her out the door.

She paused at the doorway, clasping Steve's hand. Roasting turkey, warm spices, fresh bread—those scents wrapped the house in home.

Today, she crossed the threshold without feeling like a stranger in her own life, and in that moment, it meant everything.

Chapter 56

When walls reveal their secrets

Eaton burst in the front door, his backpack slipping off one shoulder, Max and Lilly trailing close behind. Hushed, secretive whispers replaced their usual laughter.

Sitting in her usual spot with a book in hand, Margaret lifted an eyebrow as she observed them. There was something about the way they huddled together, talking in excited but hushed tones, that made her certain they were up to something.

Eaton sat with his elbows propped on his knees, looking deep in thought. His brows furrowed in concentration as if he were piecing together something important.

Margaret's voice cut through the quiet. "You alright, sweetheart?"

Eaton finally spoke up, his voice filled with barely contained excitement. "We're waiting for Dad."

Margaret's eyes sparkled with amusement. "Okay, I understand—but why the behind-closed-doors talks?"

Eaton exchanged a look with his friends. Then, lowering his voice dramatically, he said, "It's a secret."

Margaret tilted her head. "For Dad?"

Three heads nodded in unison.

She bit back a laugh at their synchronized enthusiasm. "Well, whatever it is, I hope it's nothing that's going to give him a heart attack."

Jason stepped into the room, the door clicking shut quietly behind him. Strangely still. Too still—especially for a house full of kids.

His eyes shifted toward the living room, where Eaton, Max, and Lilly sat in near-theatrical quiet.

Lilly looked like a coach mid-game, throwing glances at Max, who kept shaking his head as if refusing a risky play.

Raising an eyebrow, Jason made his way to the kitchen, grabbed a glass, and filled it with water.

"What's going on with the little masterminds?" he asked, taking a sip and nodding toward the trio.

Margaret chuckled, shaking her head. "They've been huddled in deep discussion for over an hour."

The kids exchanged a look. Then Lilly said something to Max, who let out a dramatic sigh, the kind that only comes with great internal conflict.

Jason squinted. "Okay, now I'm really suspicious."

"Join the club," Margaret muttered with a smirk.

He set his glass down and strolled into the living room, hands sliding into his pockets. For a moment, he just watched them—three kids squirming under the weight of his attention.

"Alright," he said, rocking back on his heels. "Who's gonna crack first?"

Lilly folded her arms. Max nudged Eaton.

A twitch of amusement touched Jason's lips. "Eaton?"

The boy hesitated, then found his voice. "Dad... we have something important to talk to you about."

"Okay," Jason said, voice steady. "I'm listening."

Before Eaton could continue, Max and Lilly exchanged a quick look.

"Eaton, this is private," Max blurted out, shifting awkwardly. "Maybe we should go outside and wait for my mom."

Lilly shot him a glare, clearly disagreeing with his choice to bail, but after a moment, she turned back to Eaton with concern.

"Will you be okay?" she asked, her voice sincere. "Do you need me to be here?"

Eaton hesitated, fingers twitching at his sides. Then, with a deep breath, he straightened his shoulders. "I can handle it," he said—more to himself than anyone else. "It's okay. You guys can wait outside."

Lilly still looked unsure, but she respected Eaton's choice. She and Max exchanged one of those silent, best-friend glances before slipping toward the front door.

As they left, Jason turned back, amusement fading into curiosity. "Alright, buddy. The floor is yours."

He shifted, hands brushing his sides as if steadying himself.

Then, with all the sincerity in the world, he began.

"Uhm, it's not Max's fault, so I don't want you to be angry with him or tell on him to his mom," says Eaton nervously.

Jason asked, concern creeping into his voice, "What is it? You can trust your dad, you know that, right?"

Eaton's fingers curled into the fabric of his jeans, gripping tightly. His throat felt dry, and he swallowed once before speaking. He opened his mouth, hesitated—and then finally said it.

"Max overheard his mom and Dad talking... He heard her say that Alley was my mom. He said his mom was crying."

Jason stopped dead. He pressed his fingertips lightly against his palm, and for a moment, he stared without blinking. A single swallow, almost inaudible, broke the quiet.

He had dreaded this moment for years—but not like this.

Silence stretched between them—thick, heavy, expectant.

Margaret lowered her book onto her lap and slid off her glasses. She leaned in, gaze locking on Jason and Eaton, eyes sharp and unblinking, breath held tight with tension.

And in that silence, the weight of the truth settled over them all.

.

Chapter 57

When the secret slips

Robert froze mid-step as Eaton's voice echoed from the hallway. His palm flattened against the door, as if bracing for something he couldn't take back.

Across the room, Margaret sat still, her face drained of color.

The faint whir of the heater kicked in, warming the space as the last traces of daylight faded into a deep, winter-blue dusk. The air smelled of cinnamon and lingering spices from dinner, mingling with the aroma of freshly brewed tea.

He didn't notice Eaton until a tug at his sleeve pulled him out of his thoughts.

"Dad?" Concern shaded the boy's voice. "Is Max going to be in trouble?"

Jason steadied himself, crouching down to meet his eyes. "No, buddy. Max isn't in trouble."

Eaton searched his father's face for confirmation. "Do you want to say goodbye to your friends? Let Max know everything's okay?" Jason asked, meeting his gaze.

Eaton hesitated, glancing toward the door where Max and Lilly waited just outside. Margaret's gaze pinned Jason in place, and Robert's unreadable expression pressed down like a silent verdict.

He just needed a moment. A moment to decide how to handle his son's innocent question without shattering his world.

It was their ride. Max and Lilly grabbed their backpacks without a word.

As he stepped out of the living room, he ran his fingers through Max's hair—a quiet gesture of reassurance.

Max didn't say a word, but the slump of his shoulders said enough.

Jason had been blindsided. Completely caught off guard by the kids.

He leaned against the counter, exhaling. He should have seen this coming.

Small towns had no secrets. Everybody knew everybody's business. And if adults weren't gossiping, kids certainly were. There was a real chance that Eaton could have heard the truth from a random classmate at school, or even in passing at the grocery store.

He rubbed his temple. It wasn't just about what Eaton had learned—it was about how he had learned it. Through whispers, through half-overheard conversations.

Not from him.

Not from his own father.

That part stung the most.

He needed to figure out his next move. Fast.

But right now, all he could do was let the low buzz of kitchen conversation steady the turmoil in his mind, even as his world tilted beneath him.

After closing the door behind Max and Lilly, he turned to find Eaton watching him—expression unreadable. Crouching down, he placed a steady hand on his son's shoulder.

"Eaton, why don't you head upstairs and get ready for bed? I'll come up in a bit and we'll talk, okay?"

Eaton hesitated like he wanted to say something more, but in the end, he just nodded and padded toward the stairs.

He watched him go, his heart heavy with everything left unsaid.

For now, bedtime came first.

The rest?

He'd figure it out later.

Jason crashed onto the sofa the moment Eaton sprinted upstairs, letting out a long, weary groan. The day's weight pressed down on him, his body sinking into the cushions as though he could disappear into them. He scrubbed a hand over his face, exhaling deeply, but it didn't mellow the weight he carried, quiet and unrelenting.

The house had settled into an almost eerie quiet, broken only by the distant sound of Eaton's footsteps thumping down the hall upstairs and the rhythmic ticking of the grandfather clock in the corner. Outside, the wind howled against the windows, a reminder that winter was creeping closer.

Robert entered the room. Without a word, he sank onto the couch beside Jason, his sigh heavy with everything left unsaid.

Margaret stood nearby, arms crossed, her expression thoughtful yet firm. The glow of the kitchen light cast a warm halo around her, but her face remained shadowed with quiet concern.

"I think it's best we address this before it blows out of proportion," Margaret finally said, her tone calm and controlled.

Jason stared at the ceiling. He didn't argue—he already knew she was right.

Robert leaned forward, his elbows resting on his knees. "And it's not fair for Eaton to sit with this, wondering if Max's information is true or not."

The wind rattled the windowpane. The house, so full of life just minutes ago, felt unnaturally still.

Jason glanced away, then back, steady now. "Then I guess we better figure out how."

A hush fell over the room, weighty and still.

Outside, the wind carried on, as if the world itself was waiting.

Chapter 58

Wonder Woman's return

Jason's footsteps felt heavier than usual as he climbed the stairs, burdened by the conversation he didn't yet know how to have.

He paused outside Eaton's door, drew a steady breath, and knocked gently. Jason cracked the door open, and peered inside. Eaton sat in his pajamas, tugging the blankets up to his chin, hair still damp from his shower. The bedside lamp cast a warm glow, shrinking the room into a cocoon of calm. Safe.

Eaton looked up, gratitude flickering across his face.

"Thanks, Dad," he mumbled through the pillow. "For being cool about everything."

"Always, buddy," Jason replied, his voice low. "You know you can talk to me about anything, right?"

Eaton nodded, those trusting eyes tightening Jason's chest with love—and something heavier.

He paused at the threshold, listening to the even rhythm of Eaton's breathing. The night's weight pressed outside, but here it was just them.

Leaning forward, he said, "Eaton, can we talk for a few minutes, buddy?"

The boy blinked sleepily but sat up a little straighter, curiosity flickering across his face. "You mean... man-to-man talk, Dad?"

Jason let out a chuckle. "Yeah, man-to-man."

Eaton's lips curled into a mischievous grin as he adjusted against the pillows. "Okay," he said, eyes bright despite the sleep tugging at them. "What's up?"

He hesitated—just for a second—then rubbed his hands together like he was warming up. This was it—the first step.

Eaton mirrored his serious expression, crossing his arms. "Come on, Dad. You can tell me anything."

Jason gave a faint shake of his head, amused despite everything—this kid.

"Alright, alright," he said with a half-laugh. "So… remember how I told you your mom was this amazing, brave, superhero-type person?"

Eaton nodded eagerly. "Yeah! You always made her sound like Wonder Woman."

"Yeah, well," he said, tilting his head with affection, "she is Wonder Woman. Want to hear a story about her?"

Eaton sat up a little straighter. "A real story?"

He gave a nod. "A real story."

Eaton lit up, eyes wide with anticipation.

With a slight lean forward, Jason dropped his voice to a whisper, like he was letting his son in on something sacred.

"Seven years ago, a war broke out in a country called Afghanistan. Your mom, Uncle Berry, and I went there with a team of doctors to help people who were hurt. There were lots of people who needed help—kids, families, soldiers. It was a dangerous place."

Eaton's fingers twisted in his blanket; his mind was fully locked into the story.

"Then, one day—the day you were born—some evil guys attacked the hospital where we were helping people. They had lots of guns and tried to take over the building. The army came, there was fire, and bombs went off."

Eaton's jaw dropped.

Jason continued in a steady, compassionate tone.

"Your mom? She didn't run away. She went back to save people. She saved a bunch of women first, but then she realized the kids in the hospital were still inside. So she ran back—straight into the fire."

Eaton's eyes widened. "Like an actual superhero?"

Jason glanced down, then back up, his voice rough with feeling. "Like a superhero."

"But then—" Jason hesitated, exhaling.

"Then, a bomb went off. Everything blew up. And your mom got hurt badly."

Eaton's eyes darkened with worry.

"When she woke up…" Jason ran a hand over his face. "She had forgotten everything. When terrible things happen, sometimes people's brains make them forget."

Eaton was utterly still. His small hands gripped the blanket.

"She lost her memories?" The question came quietly, almost afraid to land.

"Yeah, buddy. She forgot me. She forgot you. She forgot her whole life."

His lips parted, but no sound came—just the soft clutch of his fingers in the bedsheet.

Reaching out, Jason gently squeezed his hand. "She was sad for a long time. And then… another good guy came along. He helped her. Took care of her. She married him."

Eaton blinked, absorbing that.

Jason hesitated, watching his son closely. "She's getting better now, Eaton. And… I think she might want to see you."

Eaton was silent for a long moment.

Then, finally, he looked up.

"So, is it Alley?" His voice was quiet but sure.

His heart stuttered. The room seemed to shrink around him, the weight of years collapsing into a single, crushing instant.

He nodded. "Yeah, buddy. It's Alley."

Eaton's brow furrowed. He seemed to be processing a million things at once.

Then, his lips twisted in thought. "Does she have scars like you, Dad? Like the heroes in the war movies?"

Amusement lit Jason's eyes. "You bet." He gave Eaton a quick nod. "You'll have to ask her about them if you see her again."

Eaton bit his lip. Then, tilting his head, he asked, "Did she beat up the bad guys with machine guns?"

Jason chuckled. "I'll let her tell you that story."

The space between them was filled only by the steady rhythm of the heater and Eaton's thoughtful breathing.

Then, Jason's heart pounded a little harder as he asked, "Do you… want to meet her, buddy?"

Eaton released a long sigh. His small shoulders rose, then fell.

"I already met her lots of times, Dad." He yawned, rubbing his eyes sleepily. "She's nice. I don't mind seeing her again."

The words stalled. He had spent years dreading this conversation, carrying its weight like an anchor.

And yet here was his son—young, but unshaken.

Eaton stretched and burrowed deeper under the covers. "Just... no big mushy hugs, okay? Like Max's mom. That's a boundary."

A laugh escaped him as he leaned down and pressed a quick kiss to Eaton's forehead. "Got it, kid. No surprise attacks."

"Cool," Eaton mumbled, his eyes already drifting shut.

He sat there a while longer, just watching.

Outside the room, Margaret stood silently by the door, listening.

His voice filtered through the crack—steady—carrying a story that was so much more than words. It was truth. The kind he had carried alone for far too long. A truth of war, of loss, of sacrifice... and of love.

Tears slipped down her cheeks as she pressed a hand to her heart.

He had made Alley the hero—the fearless Wonder Woman who ran into fire and saved lives.

But to Margaret, there was no question.

The real hero was Jason.

The son who had sacrificed everything.

The man who had saved the world, only to walk away from it quietly, never waiting for accolades.

He had done the impossible—saved Alley, saved their child, and now, somehow, was piecing it all together, one step at a time.

Margaret closed her eyes and steadied herself. Her son had always carried too much, always given more than he took. And now, hearing the quiet strength in his voice as he spoke to Eaton—with patience and love—she had never felt prouder.

Inside the room, Eaton drifted into an easy sleep. Jason lingered on the edge of the bed, realizing that he might be the one who wasn't ready to let go.

The glow of the bedside lamp cast a halo over his son's face—so peaceful, so unaware of the burden just eased from his father's shoulders.

He'd finally said it.

Alley was his mother.

These past few months, Jason had rehearsed that moment in his mind a hundred ways—sometimes fearing it, sometimes longing for it. Always wondering if he'd know when the right moment had come.

And now it had passed. Quietly. Gently. Just a story at bedtime.

There was no turning back. Eaton knew. The door that had stayed closed for so long was now open. And oddly… Jason didn't feel the panic he thought he would.

He felt… relief.

A kind that seeped into his bones.

But with that relief, something else stirred. Something quieter, harder to name. Not grief, exactly—but close. Maybe it was the finality of it all. The acknowledgment that Eaton's world would never be just the two of them again. No matter how it unfolded from here, Jason had let go of being Eaton's only parent.

And it was right. It was fair. It was what Eaton deserved.

But still…

He let his fingers brush back a lock of Eaton's hair, the way he used to when he was smaller. Back then, Jason was the only one who knew how to calm his fevers, soothe his nightmares, and explain the world.

Jason closed his eyes for a moment.

He wasn't afraid.

But the ache remained—like missing something that hadn't even gone.

He leaned down, pressing one last kiss to Eaton's forehead.

"I love you, buddy." He didn't look up, but the words sat steady in the space between them.

This time, it felt like the words could carry everything—what had been, what was, and what was still to come.

Now, Eaton would begin learning someone else's story, too—another version of love, another kind of home. And this time… Steve would be part of that world. Whether Jason liked it or not, the man who had helped put Alley back together would also be part of Eaton's future.

Margaret wiped her tears, stepped away from the door, and whispered into the quiet night—

"Goodnight, my boy."

And then, she let him be.

Chapter 59

Magical mountains

The next morning, Eaton woke before the sun had fully risen, his excitement bubbling over like a shaken soda. Pepper, his ever-watchful companion, cracked one eye open, grumbling in annoyance.

With a deliberate stretch, Pepper padded toward Jason's room, climbed onto the bed, and curled up beside him with a sigh.

Margaret sat by the kitchen window, cradling a warm cup of coffee, savoring the quiet before the day's bustle began. She barely had a moment to enjoy it before Eaton came bounding in, his energy filling the room like a burst of morning sunlight.

He hopped onto the highchair, his face lit up with excitement. "Good morning, Grandpa!"

Robert set his newspaper aside and glanced over his glasses. "You're up early," he said, brow lifting.

"Of course! I have to get to school early today. We're going to the Mountains Resort!" Eaton practically bounced in his seat.

Margaret slid a bowl of cereal in front of him, amused. "Eat slowly, dear. We have plenty of time."

Eaton, however, had other plans. He attacked his cereal with the enthusiasm of an explorer setting off on an adventure, shoveling spoonful into his mouth at record speed.

Jason stood at the top of the stairs for a moment, listening to Eaton's voice drift up from below. Lighter. Freer.

Last night, he expected tears. Confusion. Maybe even anger.

But Eaton had simply... accepted it.

That acceptance had settled over Jason like a balm.

The truth was out now. He hadn't realized how tightly he'd been holding it all in—until last night loosened something in him. Jason felt like he could breathe again—even if only in small, uncertain doses.

Jason finally came downstairs, rubbing his temples as if shaking off the last traces of sleep. He glanced at Eaton, and after a moment, the memory of the field trip clicked into place. "Dad, are you sure you want to drop him off?" he asked.

Robert folded his newspaper and stood up, adjusting his coat. "It's on my way. You can pick him up at school in the evening," he said with a reassuring nod.

Margaret sipped her coffee, observing both Eaton and Jason closely. She was surprised to find no remnants of last night's drama. Both behaved as if it had been trivial, their interactions lighthearted and unaffected.

The bus pulled into the resort, and the class eagerly piled out.

Max, Lilly, and most of the kids were familiar with the resort and quickly helped Eaton find his footing. He wobbled on his skis, arms flailing as he tried to balance. The others laughed—not to tease him, but in shared amusement as he clumsily slid forward.

"Whoa—how do you guys make this look so easy?" Eaton groaned, barely managing to stay upright.

Max was in his element, confidently showing off his smooth turns and daring jumps.

"Show-off," Lilly teased, shaking her head with a grin.

Eaton and Lilly laughed at Max's dramatic moves, but before Eaton could make a snarky comment, his ski suddenly wobbled beneath him. His balance tipped—and in the next instant, he was sliding.

The world blurred as he raced down the slope, completely out of control.

"Eaton!" Lilly shouted, panic sharpening her tone.

He twisted, trying to stop, but his skis tangled, and he crashed face-first into the snow. A sharp pain shot through his hand as he landed awkwardly.

The ski instructor rushed toward him while Max and Lilly hurried after, their faces pale with worry.

Eaton groaned, wincing as he tried to move his hand. Pain throbbed through his arm..

"Don't move," the instructor said gently, kneeling beside him. "Let's check your hand."

Eaton bit his lip, frustration and pain mixing in his expression. As Eaton was carried on a stretcher to the first aid room in the lodge, Max and Lilly hurried alongside him, their faces tight with concern.

Just as they entered the lodge, Max's eyes landed on a familiar figure. "Uncle Steve!" he shouted, waving urgently.

Steve pivoted their way, his cheerful expression dimming as he caught Max's anxiety. "What's wrong, buddy?" he asked, moving in.

Max quickly explained, "It's my friend Eaton! He fell while skiing and hurt his hand."

Steve's expression turned serious. He gave Max's shoulder a reassuring squeeze. "Stay with your group, okay? I'll go check on him."

Steve headed into the first aid room, where Eaton was lying on the examination table, his face twisted in discomfort. A lodge nurse stood beside him, carefully wrapping his wrist.

"What's the prognosis?" Steve asked immediately.

The nurse looked up at him. "Nothing's broken," she assured him. "But he may have a sprained wrist. I recommend taking him to the hospital just to be sure."

Steve nodded. "Alright." He turned his attention to Eaton, offering a warm smile. "Hey there, champ. I'm Steve Rivers—I run this place."

Eaton looked up at him, still wincing slightly but embarrassed. Before he could say anything, his sports teacher stepped into the room.

"Eaton, your dad is on his way," she informed him gently.

Eaton gave a nod, relief flickering across his face, but his gaze drifted back to Steve.

"So, how old are you?" Steve asked, pulling up a chair and offering a reassuring grin, trying to put Eaton at ease.

"Seven," Eaton mumbled, eyes dropping to his lap, a little embarrassed.

"You know, you're not the only one who's had an embarrassing fall around here."

Eaton raised an eyebrow, momentarily distracted from the dull ache in his hand. "Oh yeah?"

Steve chuckled. "When I was about your age, I fell right off a cliff—well, more like a steep drop. I thought I was being cool, showing off my moves, and next thing I knew, I was tumbling down, face-first..." He paused dramatically. "Right in front of all the girls in my class."

Eaton let out a laugh, his earlier frustration forgotten. "No way!"

A grin tugged at Steve's mouth. "Oh, it was bad. Snow everywhere, even in my ears. They didn't let me live it down for years."

Eaton giggled, shaking his head. "Okay, that's way worse than mine."

Just then, the door to the first aid room swung open, and Jason stepped inside, his expression tight with worry.

Jason barely noticed the lodge's warm air as he stepped inside, his eyes immediately locking on Eaton.

His son sat on the bed, his wrist wrapped, his expression tired but unbothered. Relief unfurled inside him—only for it to freeze the moment he turned to see Steve.

The moment Steve's eyes met Jason's, his face went taut. For a split second, silence deepened around them.

The easy warmth on Steve's face disappeared, replaced by something unreadable.

Steve's eyes met Jason's—and for a heartbeat, the world seemed to stop.

The warmth drained from his face. He looked at Eaton—really looked.

And suddenly, the pieces shifted.

Eaton.

The name. The face.

A flicker of memory surged forward—a photo frame on Jason's desk. It clicked now. Too late.

Jason's son. Seven years old.

There was no denying it.

And that meant...

Eaton was Alley's, too.

Jason, too, stopped in his tracks, his expression mirroring Steve's—a mixture of shock, recognition, and something more profound. Neither of them spoke.

Eaton, still chuckling from Steve's story, noticed the shift in the room. His laughter faded as he glanced between the two men, sensing the tension in the air.

Chapter 60

Adult problems

Eaton sat on the hospital bed, his injured arm resting in a sling, his legs dangling over the edge. The room smelled of antiseptic and fresh linens, the kind of sterile coldness that made hospitals feel uncomfortable.

"So, no broken bones?" Berry asked, his hands on his hips, relief washing over his face.

The doctor gave a reassuring nod. "No, just a sprain. Keep the sling on for a few days, limit movement, and he should heal quickly."

A hint of relief crossed Jason's face. "Good. That's good."

Eaton grinned. "Told you I'm unbreakable."

Berry shot him a look. "Don't push your luck."

Eaton smirked, clearly enjoying the attention, even if his ego was slightly bruised.

He turned to thank the doctor, but he felt it the moment his gaze shifted. A presence. Someone else was in the room. He turned, irritation flickering across his face.

And froze.

Steve.

He stood near the doorway, arms folded, his usually easygoing expression now unreadable.

For a second, everything stilled.

The air in the room seemed to shift, growing heavier by the second.

Jason's body tensed instinctively, old reflexes kicking in. He had hoped, prayed, that this moment would never come. That the past could stay buried. That he would never have to look Steve Rivers in the eyes again.

But here they were.

"Hi," Steve said, his voice even, though there was a slight edge to it. He stepped forward, holding out a few papers.

"Here's the paperwork needed for insurance."

He hesitated for just a fraction of a second before taking them. "Thanks," he said, his tone carefully neutral.

Sensing the strange tension between the two men, Berry glanced back and forth before finally speaking.

"Even doctors can't escape the insurance companies," he joked lightly, his voice carrying a touch of amusement.

Eaton, still perched on the hospital bed, observed the exchange with growing curiosity.

"Wait…" he tilted his head, brows knitting. "You two know each other?"

"Oh, small world, huh?" Berry said with a grin.

Eaton's curiosity didn't let up. "How do you know each other?"

Steve jumped in first—his tone easy. Maybe too easy.

"It's a small town," he said. "Paths cross."

Then, after a beat, he added, "And your dad's a doctor. People tend to know him."

Jason did not look up. He kept his eyes on the insurance papers in his hands as if reading them would make this conversation disappear.

Steve didn't break his gaze. His arms were still crossed, shoulders squared—like a man bracing himself for a storm.

Eaton's eyes darted between them, his curiosity growing.

Steve held Eaton's gaze for a moment, then his features relaxed with quiet ease.

"Get well soon, champ," he said—his voice steady, though something unspoken lingered beneath it.

Eaton nodded. "Thanks."

Steve turned to Berry first, extending his hand. A firm shake. A polite nod.

Then, to Jason.

For a brief second, neither moved.

Then Jason, almost on autopilot, reached out. Their hands met—firm, but tense.

Their eyes met, and understanding passed without a word.

One that neither of them was willing to have.

Steve released his grip first, expression unreadable. Without another word, he turned and walked out of the room.

The door clicked shut behind him.

He exhaled, his grip on the insurance papers just a little too tight.

Eaton glanced between him and Berry. "Dad are you angry with Mr. Rivers."

The boy's voice cut through the tension, interrupting both their thoughts.

Jason met Berry's gaze and gave a slight shake of his head.

Eaton went on, tone casual. "He was nice. And, Uncle Berry, you said you have to break something at my age—it's a badge of honor."

A quiet breath slipped from him, and the tension in the room finally began to ease.

"I'm not angry with Mr. Rivers," he said at last, voice carefully measured. Turning to Eaton, he added, "I was just worried about you."

Eaton seemed satisfied with that answer.

Just then, Robert and Margaret rushed into the room, their faces etched with concern.

Chapter 61

Lifting shadows

As Margaret and Robert left with Eaton, Jason and Berry made their way back to the office. The hallway was quiet, except for occasional footsteps and distant conversations.

Berry glanced over. "You okay?"

Jason rubbed the back of his neck, eyes darting briefly away. "Yeah."

Berry chuckled and gave him a light nudge. "It's only natural to worry when your kid starts breaking parts."

A quiet laugh escaped Jason, his head shaking. "Tell me about it."

Berry grinned. "My boys are practically competing to see who can break something first."

That earned a smirk from Jason. Some of the tension finally eased from his shoulders.

"Let's grab some coffee before that boring conference," Berry said, steering them toward the break room.

They stepped onto the balcony a few minutes later, holding a steaming cup of coffee. The evening air was crisp, carrying the faint scent of rain from earlier in the day. Below, the town stretched a sea of flickering lights and distant car horns.

"For a second there, I thought you were going to punch Steve."

Jason didn't answer—he just watched Berry. Like he still might.

Berry met Jason's gaze, eyes soft. "That moment hit harder than you expected, huh? I would've been shaken too, man."

He gave a slight nod. "Seeing him with Eaton? That had to hurt."

Jason looked off to the side. "When I saw Steve with Eaton, my mind just... blew up. I had no idea he owned that stupid resort."

Berry let out a low whistle, realizing just how shaken Jason still was.

A light breeze swept over them, carrying with it the muffled sounds of hospital staff chatting nearby.

"He was being so familiar with Eaton, I—" Jason hesitated, gripping his cup a little too tightly.

Berry's gaze brimmed with empathy. "That must've felt like a punch to the gut."

His expression hardened. "I thought he told Eaton he was Alley's husband. That he was already playing stepdad in my kid's life."

Berry frowned. "Do you think he would do that?"

A scoff slipped out. "Maybe not. But now that he knows..." He shook his head, gaze fixed on the horizon as the last remnants of sunset faded behind the buildings.

"Everything shifts now. What we had—just Eaton and me—it's already changing."

He stayed still, staring into the dark where city lights shimmered like scattered embers.

Berry nodded, understanding clear in his eyes.

"I get that. It's scary—not because you don't trust her, but because you don't know what's coming next."

Jason nodded, the weight behind his eyes giving him away. "Yeah. For a long time, it was straightforward. Not easy—but at least I knew what I was holding on to. Now? There's Steve. There's everything Alley's remembering. I just don't know where I fit in anymore."

Berry looked over at him, thoughtful. "You're his dad. Someone else can't erase that."

He didn't answer right away—just took a sip of his now-cold coffee and watched the shadows settle.

Berry's shoulders lowered. "When your dad recommended this hospital, I begged you to join me. I was so excited, thinking we could relive old times. I had no idea I'd be inviting you into a pressure cooker."

Jason remained quiet because Berry wasn't wrong.

The coffee between them grew cold as the minutes stretched.

Finally, Jason spoke, his voice quiet but steady. "Some nights, I just wanted to pause everything—shut out the memories, delay what was coming. Still, seeing her like that..." He paused. "I couldn't let her keep living without knowing who she really was."

Berry observed him, saying nothing.

"And for Eaton," Jason continued, firmer now. "Every child deserves to know who their parents are. I'm doing what's best not only for my Eaton but for my best friend, the woman I loved, and the mother of my child."

Berry nodded. "You're doing the right thing, Jason. It's hard—but it's the kind of hard that matters."

Then he turned to Jason.

"Do you?" Berry asked. "Do you still have feelings for Alley?"

His gaze slid over the distant rooftops—where warm hues had already melted into violet and navy—then returned to Berry. He paused, the weight of his answer gathering quietly before he spoke.

"I loved her," he said quietly. "With everything I had. And maybe I still do." His voice gentled, but his expression turned inward. "But I don't think it's the same as before."

Berry watched him, his face unreadable in the dimming light. "What do you mean?"

Jason's shoulders sagged. "If I were still in love with her, I'd want a life with her. But what I want now... is for her to be safe. Whole. Even if it's without me."

My feelings for Alley transcend desire, expectations, and even time. Jason's voice caught. I know it sounds cliché.

He hesitated. His fingertips tapped lightly against his coffee cup. "I love Alley. But I'm not in love with her."

Berry nodded, unsurprised. "You don't have to apologize for feeling something new, Jason. Life doesn't stop just because the past hasn't finished with us."

He eased back in his chair, the scrape of wood against wood breaking the quiet.

"And lately... I find myself looking for Leia and listening for her laugh. Wanting that ease. It's different from what I had with Alley—but it's real."

Just then, both their phones buzzed. The sharp ping sliced through the moment.

Berry glanced down and let out a sigh. "Conference's postponed."

Chapter 62

A moment of reckoning

The conference had dragged on—presentations, polite applause, and a mind-numbing panel on treatment protocols.

Outside, Jason rolled his shoulders, trying to shake free the day's tension. Berry groaned. "My brain is fried."

Jason shot him a look. "At least you weren't the one everyone was staring at."

Berry snorted. "Oh yeah, must be brutal being the star of the show."

They rounded a corner just in time to sidestep the guest doctor's eyeing Jason like he was headlining a rock tour.

"Rock star," Berry muttered. Jason gave a flat look as they picked up pace, dodging another wave of handshakes.

"Jason," someone called behind them.

He paused, resisting the urge to rub his temples. Fatigue weighed on him—but under it, a familiar unease took root.

He turned: Steve stood across the corridor.

The last doctors drifted away, their voices fading.

Steve approached calmly, offering a formal handshake—no hint of rivalry.

"Jason, can we talk? "

Jason nodded. "Sure. My office is just down the hall."

Berry hesitated. "I'll... let you two talk."

"Please stay," Steve and Jason said in unison.

Berry blinked. "Okay..." he muttered in amusement and followed them inside.

Inside, the office was quiet—the heater humming, the floorboards creaking gently.

Jason slumped into his chair, masking tension. *What does he want?*

"How's Eaton doing?" Steve broke the silence.

Jason blinked. "He's good. Insisted on going to school today."

Berry set his coffee down with a quiet chuckle. "Show-off."

A momentary relief—then the weight returned.

Steve stirred his cup. "I didn't know Eaton was your son until I saw you at the resort."

Jason's expression tightened, then softened. Something in the air shifted.

"I know how it looked," Steve continued, voice low and deliberate. "I tell stories to keep kids calm until their parents arrive. That's all it was—nothing more." He tapped the rim of his cup. "I needed you to know that."

Jason set his cup down. "What about Alley? Does she... know?"

Steve swallowed, looking tired. "No—not yet. I've been terrified to tell her." He paused. "Alley is tormented... haunted by forgetting something so intimate. She keeps asking herself how she could forget the man she had a child with, if it was just a casual fling."

Jason's throat tightened.

Steve continued softly: "She's asked Dale and me countless times about her son—who his father is, his name, what he looks like. She even asked Berry."

Berry winced.

Steve exhaled. "Berry... told her it might've been that doctor who volunteered in Afghanistan—just so she had something, anything, to hold onto."

"Afghanistan?" Jason's voice was low, unsteady.

Berry shrugged. "She was desperate. I didn't know what else to say."

Steve leaned forward, palm flat on the table. His voice softened. "Alley's guilt runs deep. She worries the father won't forgive her—or that he's moved on. She's terrified of showing up after seven years, not even sure she remembers her own child's name or face. She fears calling herself 'Mom' would disrupt her child's life more than it would help."

His fingers trembled slightly as he tapped the rim of his cup.

Jason's mind raced, torn between empathy and alarm.

Steve's voice softened to a whisper: "We agreed to wait—for Eaton's sake. She knows she can't just walk in and say, "I'm your mother.""

He met Jason's eyes. "I will share the truth, but only when *you* are ready. I don't want to leave her in limbo, but I don't want to override your role either."

A loaded silence followed.

Jason nodded slowly. "You've been there for her when no one else could. I appreciate that."

Berry rubbed the back of his neck, eyes shifting between the two men.

Steve exhaled as if unburdening months of holding back.

For the first time, he didn't see Jason as a rival—but as a partner in protecting Eaton's well-being.

The heater hummed. A distant clock ticked.

Silence settled—not empty, but pregnant with possibility.

Chapter 63

Through a child's eyes

The house was quiet, except for the faint clock on the living room wall. Traces of baked apples and holiday spices hung in the room.

Outside the window, the glow of holiday lights danced along the fences and rooftops, tiny bulbs twinkling against the dark winter sky. A light dusting of snow coated the sidewalk, reflecting the warm, golden light from the streetlamps.

Inside, heat radiated as the fireplace crackled, its flickering orange embers painting the walls in warm light.

Jason sat on the couch, one arm draped over the backrest, watching Eaton stretch his legs across the coffee table, his injured arm carefully propped on a pillow.

"Are you in pain?" he asked, voice even—though the concern underneath was clear.

Eaton looked up from his book, blinking like he hadn't even thought about it. "Nope." A grin spread across his face as he wiggled his fingers. "I think my hand just wanted a break from writing."

A quiet laugh escaped. "Convenient."

"I know, right?" Eaton grinned wider.

Reaching over, he gently adjusted the sling. "Be careful with it, though. No sudden movements."

Eaton rolled his eyes but didn't pull away. "I got it, Dad. I won't fall off another mountain, I promise."

He smirked, shaking his head. "That's reassuring."

The warmth of the moment settled between them, familiar and grounding.

For all the chaos, all the unanswered questions swirling in his head, this was the one thing that was certain.

His son.

His family.

He leaned back, stretching his legs as the sounds of the world outside filtered in. Christmas was everywhere—cheerful, bustling, alive. But inside, it felt distant.

"We should get a tree soon," Eaton said, breaking the quiet.

Jason turned, catching the reflection of twinkling lights dancing in his son's eyes.

"A real one this time?" he teased.

Eaton nodded eagerly. "Yeah! A big one. And let's do colored lights, not just white ones. Oh, and we should get one of those trains that go around the bottom."

His lips twitched with amusement.

"Well, it's Christmas." Eaton shrugged, like that explained everything.

For Eaton, Christmas meant lights and magic, trains and trees.

For him, it had become a season full of ghosts. A reminder of everything that had shifted, everything that had been lost and remade.

It had been years since he and Alley decorated a tree together. Years since he thought about what their holidays could have been like.

Would they have had traditions? Would they have bought matching pajamas? Would Alley have insisted on baking cookies, even though she was a disaster in the kitchen?

Instead, the woman he once loved had spent her holidays with another man.

A man who had loved her more than he did.

He stood unmoving, eyes fixed on the lights beyond the glass, something unreadable flickering behind them.

He hadn't searched for her. Steve had. He hadn't fought for her. Steve had.

The realization settled into his bones.

His love had been built on the promise of something lasting, of a life together. But Steve's love?

It had survived even when nothing was certain.

Steve had loved without expectations. Without conditions.

He had let go when the future disappeared. Steve had held on—even with no guarantee.

And now, he was left wrestling with a truth he didn't want to face:

He wasn't angry at Steve anymore. Not really.

How could he be? How could he hate the man who had done what he couldn't?

Because deep down, he knew—Steve was the better man.

Not because he won. Not because he has Alley. But because he never stopped loving her.

And Jason? He let her go—not out of indifference, but because he truly believed she had already let go of them.

"Dad?"

The word snapped him back.

He blinked, refocusing on Eaton, who was watching him with quiet curiosity.

"You okay?" Eaton tilted his head. "You got all quiet."

Fingers tapped lightly against his knee as he nodded once, steadying himself before finally speaking.

"Eaton, can I tell you something important?"

Eaton perked up, instantly intrigued.

"Man to man?" Eaton asked playfully, grinning. His serious expression cracked into a grin. "Yes! Man to man, buddy."

Letting the moment settle, he gently steered the conversation where it needed to go.

"That man who helped you at the ski resort…"

Eaton's brow furrowed slightly. "Yeah?"

There was a pause—brief, but heavy—before he continued.

"He's the one who rescued your mom when she was in trouble. Remember I told you…"

Eaton's eyes widened slightly. "Yeah… she married a very nice man who rescued her."

He nodded. "That man was Steve."

Eaton blinked, the name sinking in. "Uncle Steve?"

The corner of Jason's mouth twitched, barely noticeable. Uncle. It was innocent, natural—yet it landed deeper than he expected.

"Yeah," he said quietly. "That's him."

Eaton leaned back slightly, thoughtful. "So… Uncle Steve saved Mom?"

Jason lifted his chin, answering with quiet conviction. "He did. And he took care of her for a long time."

Eaton's gaze drifted to the window, where snow drifted in delicate flurries and Christmas lights twinkled against the glass.

Then he turned back. "That's cool."

Jason waited—for questions, for hesitation, for some flicker of emotion beneath the surface. Something more.

But Eaton sat there, calm, present, and processing in his own time.

But nothing came.

Eaton wasn't conflicted. He wasn't questioning Jason's place in his life. He wasn't measuring the past against the present.

To him, the man who helped his mom was just another part of the story.

Not a threat. Not a missing piece. Just a fact.

Jason stared at his son, trying to understand how something so complicated could be so simple for him.

How could Eaton just... accept it?

Before he could get a word out, Eaton grinned. The shift was so natural, so easy, it caught him off guard.

"I might get extra gifts this Christmas."

He blinked. "Oh yeah?"

Eaton nodded, eyes twinkling with mischief. "I mean, if Uncle Steve and Mom send me something, that's extra, right?"

Jason shook his head, biting back a laugh. "That's what you take from all this?"

"Priorities, Dad," Eaton said, smirking.

The laughter that followed didn't come from Jason alone.

A deep, familiar chuckle came from behind them, and they turned to see Robert standing at the doorway, arms crossed, an amused expression on his face.

"Smart kid," Robert said, shaking his head. "Knows how to make the best of a situation."

He sighed, rubbing his temple. "Yeah, yeah. Real genius in the making."

Eaton beamed. "I know, right?"

Jason watched him—still smirking over the idea of extra presents, already moving on... while he remained rooted, still catching up.

Ghosts or what-ifs didn't haunt Eaton.

He wasn't chasing love, or regret, or lost time.

To him, life was ski trips, and maybe an extra gift or two.

Where Jason carried years of questions and guilt, Eaton had let go—easily.

Maybe that was the lesson.

Maybe he didn't need to untangle every thread of the past.

Maybe it was okay to just exist in the present.

The snow outside continued to fall, blanketing the world in silence.

It had been so long, but now—he could finally release the weight.

Chapter 64

Unraveling the lie

The house smelled of freshly made coffee and toast. Outside, snowflakes drifted lazily past the window, and the streetlights cast a golden glow over the quiet town below.

Alley sat at the edge of her bed, hands wrapped tightly around her phone. Elijah sat obediently by her feet, his warm brown eyes watching her as if sensing something was about to change.

She had meant to call her mother and sister earlier, but had decided to wait. They were visiting her brother-in-law's parents, and she didn't want to interrupt. She had planned to tell them in person, but couldn't hold it in any longer.

She thought of her mother, and emotion rose. Her health had declined—Alley's disappearance, her father's passing, and the years of waiting had taken their toll. And her sister—she had held everything together, for their mother, and for Alley.

Alley's gaze dropped, eyes stinging. How much pain had she caused them? How many nights had her mother lain awake in those early days after the accident, seven years ago—wondering if her daughter was even alive?

And then, when she returned, she wasn't the same person.

She remembered the hollow look in her mother's eyes when she saw her after the accident. The heartbreak of seeing a daughter—once so full of life—reduced to a ghost of herself.

She had insisted that her mother take a break and begged her to step away and live for herself after Alley married Steve.

Because deep down, Alley knew—her mother had been breaking under the weight of it all.

Her fingers trembled as she pressed the call button.

The phone rang once. Twice.

Then a familiar, warm voice filled the line.

"Alley?"

The moment she heard her mother's voice, something inside her cracked.

"Mom... How are you? How was your Thanksgiving?"

Her mother's voice lit up as she launched into a ten-minute retelling of her grandchildren's latest antics.

"Oh, Alley, you should have seen your brother-in-law's face when Matt sprayed whipped cream all over his little sister."

Alley listened, her heart warmed at her mother's genuine joy. Tears welled in her eyes.

She had missed this.

"Sweetie, are you okay?" her mother finally asked, noticing her hesitation.

"Oh, Mom." Alley's voice wavered. "I have some incredible news to share. I wanted to come down and tell you, but... I met Jay and Berry, and I remembered most of the past."

She hesitated.

"Dad. The fire."

Her mother went silent.

Alley swallowed back the lump in her throat.

"Mom, I found out that my baby—my son—he's alive."

Silence.

Then, a gasp.

"But... We thought he did not make it out of the fire."

"No, Mom. He made it out of the fire. Jay rescued him before the building blew up."

"Oh, sweetheart... all those years, thinking, grieving..."

Her mother's voice held so much love and regret it left Alley breathless.

"I'm just so happy your son was with Jay, his father, all this time."

Alley froze.

Her heart stopped.

Her grip on the phone tightened.

"...What?"

"At least your son grew up with his dad, dear," her mom repeated, her tone light, almost relieved. "I'm just glad they had each other all these years."

Alley felt the breath rush from her lungs.

"Mom…" Her voice was barely a whisper now. "Are you saying—Jay—?"

The world tilted.

She had no memory of being pregnant with Jay's child. No moment where it had clicked. No whisper of that truth—not until now.

The room felt too small, the walls closing in.

Jay.

Jay was her son's father.

Her fingers went numb around the phone.

No. That wasn't possible. She would have known. Someone would have told her.

But then—why was Jay always there in the pictures?

Why was he the one in every memory she had of the hospital?

Why had no one ever mentioned another man?

Her stomach twisted, realization crashing over her like a tidal wave.

"Mom…" she choked out. "I didn't know."

"Oh, Alley…" her mother whispered. "Jay never told you?"

"No."

Her mom went silent on the other end.

She stood frozen, unsure if she could speak.

Jay knew. He had raised their son—without her.

Her mind reached for something, anything that made sense—until the image of Eaton's face slammed into her.

His smile. His eyes.

Her mind reeled, shoving against the impossible truth—then came the image: Jay standing beside Eaton, adjusting his collar, ruffling his hair.

Another flash—Jay at the carnival, seated close, their laughter blending.

Oh God.

Her stomach twisted. The memories weren't random. They were pieces.

Is Eaton my son?

Her breathing stuttered. Her heartbeat slammed against her ribs. The image of Eaton's gray eyes staring back at her, so hauntingly familiar, gave her the answer she was looking for.

For years, it made sense—Alley saw flames, then nothing. No one corrected the assumption. And with no record of him taking the baby, grief hardened into fact.

And she didn't know what to do with the truth once she found it.

Chapter 65

When the truth knocks

Jason pulled into the hospital lot, grabbing his coat. Eaton waited while Margaret climbed out beside him.

The wind howled through the lot, carrying with it the sharp bite of winter—not the festive kind filled with holiday warmth, but the bitter cold that foreshadowed the heart of the season.

Bundling up, the three of them hurried inside, the hospital's warmth a welcome contrast to the freezing gusts outside.

As they stepped into the lobby, Jason turned to his mother and Eaton.

"Mom, I'll just drop these papers off with June and come right back down."

Margaret shook her head, already unbuttoning her coat.

"Go to your office, Jason. Eaton and I are perfectly fine."

"Alright, alright." He backed away with a playful look and disappeared into his office.

Eaton dragged his feet toward the pediatrician's office, glancing down at his sling. He wasn't too happy about parting with it—it had given him instant notoriety at school.

As Eaton suspected, the doctor confirmed what he had been dreading—he could do away with the sling.

He frowned slightly, flexing his fingers. Meanwhile, Margaret walked over to the receptionist, who greeted her warmly.

"May I see the insurance card, please?" the receptionist asked.

Margaret reached into her wallet, flipping through its compartments. Then, she realized she had given the card to Jason when Eaton was admitted earlier.

She sighed, excusing herself. "I must have left it with my son."

"No problem. You can email us later," the receptionist replied.

Margaret pulled out her phone and dialed. "I'd rather take care of it now."

The receptionist leaned closer, voice conspiratorial. "Reception is always spotty."

Margaret frowned at the screen. "Why isn't he picking up?"

She dropped her phone into her bag, sighing, "Forget it—I'll just go grab it myself."

Turning to Eaton, she added, "Come on, let's go find your dad."

"Oh, Grandma, can I please stay here? I want to check out the fish tank. Please?"

Margaret gave a nod before hurrying off toward the elevators.

"He just went up to Dale's office," June offered with a nod.

As Margaret reached Dale's office, she slowed her steps. A muffled sound carried through the partially open door—a woman's sobs.

Frowning, she hesitated for a moment before taking a peek inside.

Alley.

She sat across from Dale, her face buried in her hands, the emotion thick in her words.

"Jason... I thought he was my friend. I trusted him with all my heart, but he betrayed my love—my trust."

Margaret stiffened.

"He knew all this time that Eaton was my son. But he kept it from me."

Alley's voice cracked, her body trembling.

She turned to Dale; her eyes filled with anguish.

"Did you know this, Dale? Were you also on Jason's side?"

Dale remained silent.

Alley shook her head, the betrayal in her expression deepening.

"All this time...he was alive. And Jason let me believe my baby was gone."

Margaret went still, the air catching halfway to her lungs.

"Afghanistan?"

Alley's voice dropped to a whisper, thick with grief.

"I lost seven years of my son's life. I lost my memory, believing I had failed to save him.

She faltered. "All this time...he was alive." Her voice wavered. The words clung to the air, too painful to swallow.

"And even after Jason realized I thought he'd died... he didn't correct me. He just let it sit."

A sudden fury burned through Margaret's veins.

"What did you just say?"

Her words sliced through the air. Alley froze.

Margaret stepped into the room, her expression fierce, her posture unshakable—the determination of a lioness protecting her cub.

"Say that again," Margaret said, her tone razor-sharp. "Say it, Jason kept your son from you. From my grandson."

Alley turned, startled.

Margaret's eyes burned into her, daring her to look away.

"Do you even know what Jason went through after you vanished? After that voicemail? After you dumped him and disappeared?"

Alley's eyes filled with guilt. "I didn't know."

"No. You didn't. Because after Jason survived, he spent months trying to find you. He sent letters—no reply. He called every number he had. Nothing. One day, your sister told him never to call again. And you—you—left a message telling him it's over. Doors slammed shut. Messages went unanswered. So tell me—who was he supposed to reach?"

Fingers curled around the edge of the chair, tension winding tighter through her chest. The room seemed to shrink, pressing in from all directions. She wanted to speak, to deny it—but the words wouldn't come.

"Your sister said you had a new life that you didn't want to be contacted. That you wanted him to stop calling."

Alley felt like the air had been sucked out of the room.

"I don't remember..."

Sorrow clouded Margaret's vision. "I still remember the day Jason made his decision. The day he chose to stop looking for you."

She let the memory unfold as if it had happened yesterday.

He was asleep on the sofa; exhaustion carved deep into the lines of his face.

Nearby, Margaret stood cradling four-month-old Eaton in her arms. The baby squirmed, chubby fingers reaching outward.

Jason stirred, eyes heavy as he looked up—just as Eaton leaned toward him, arms outstretched.

Without hesitation, he scooped the baby into his arms.

Eaton giggled, tiny fingers gripping his shirt as he planted wet, joyful kisses on his face, babbling in delight.

And then, of course, he tried to eat his nose.

Jason's features softened—something long dormant stirring behind his eyes.

He bent down and pressed a gentle kiss to Eaton's forehead.

"Mom," Jason said quietly, his voice calm in a way Margaret had never heard before. "I can't keep looking for someone who doesn't want to be found anymore."

He looked down at Eaton, arms instinctively wrapping more firmly around him.

"I am father and mother to my son from now on."

Margaret's gaze sharpened as she looked at Alley, her words laced with quiet, unwavering anger.

"And yet, you sit here, blind to the truth—while my son spent years bleeding for a woman who never wanted to be found."

Her vision swam, the room narrowing around her. A strange, suffocating pressure squeezed her ribs. No. No, this couldn't be real. Jason had spent years thinking she didn't want him. Had her mother… her sister… believed the same? Had they kept him away because they thought it was what she wanted?

She didn't know anymore. The edges of memory—of truth and belief—blurred and tangled until she couldn't trust what was real. What if she had said those words? What if, in the haze of grief and trauma, she'd pushed everyone away without knowing it?

Something inside her cracked. A sob tore free—raw and jagged—as her whole frame shook beneath its weight. Her hands trembled on her lap, fingers curling inward. She had lost so much, and had they all? What had she done?

Chapter 66

Shattered truths and steady hearts

Jason and Berry entered, their steps faltering as their eyes swept the room—Alley, Dale, and Margaret stood like figures on a battlefield, caught between retreat and confrontation.

Jason's gaze landed on his mother.

"Mom?"

Margaret barely turned, her posture rigid.

"I need Eaton's insurance card. And the car keys." Her voice was clipped and controlled. Without hesitation, he pulled out his wallet and handed the card to her.

Margaret took them, her fingers stiff as she turned and walked out. Her heels clicked sharply against the floor, a jarring counterpoint to the silence she left behind.

Jason and Berry exchanged a glance, silently gauging the emotional wreckage.

Alley sat motionless, fists clenched in her lap. Dale eased into a chair, his face drawn.

Berry crossed over to Alley and sat beside her, his presence solid, grounding. He didn't speak—there was nothing to say, not yet. For now, his role was simple: to stay still and let her hold on.

Before he could speak, a knock sounded at the door.

The tension in the room spiked again.

The door opened, and Steve stepped inside. "I'm sorry, I didn't mean to barge in."

He paused, glancing at Alley before continuing carefully.

"Alley's mom called... She accidentally told her that you are..." He hesitated.

"That you're the father of her child".

She was shaken—said she didn't know how Alley would take it and thought I should be here."

Before he could say more, his eyes locked onto Alley, her hand still resting in Berry's.

Jason closed his eyes, steadying himself. When he opened them again, all eyes were on him. There was no more avoiding it.

He looked at Alley. She was in shock and silent. Dale sat on the other side of her.

"Alley, are you okay, dear?" Dale gently took her hand and checked her pulse. She was calm, her pulse steady.

"Why did my family not tell me?" she asked Dale, her words catching in her throat.

Dale, choosing his words carefully, answered.

"Even the mention of Jay, in the years after you returned, would send you into a kind of shock. You'd freeze, or panic, or go quiet for hours.

"Sometimes you didn't sleep for days. I saw—more than once." He paused.

"They made a choice. Not to punish him, Alley... but to protect you. Maybe... maybe you did too. Not consciously. But your mind slammed the door shut just to survive."

Dale gave a quiet nod, his words hushed and careful.

"Of course—like all of us—they believed Eaton didn't make it out of the fire. There was no trace of him. No hope. And in the middle of your own pain, no one dared to ask more."

He paused, then looked at her with quiet intensity.

"You were barely holding on, Alley. Everyone around you was just trying to keep you breathing. The idea of Jay... Eaton... it felt like too much. So they buried it. You buried it."

The truth was heavier than anything she remembered—but in some strange way, it made sense. The blank spaces in her memory, the fear she couldn't name... Maybe no one had lied. Maybe she'd buried it herself.

Chapter 67

Choosing us

Feeling suffocated in the room, Alley walked out onto the balcony. The cold December air hit her—sharp and bracing. She pulled her sweater tighter, as if trying to shield herself from the weight of her own thoughts. Behind her, Steve followed.

Beyond the railing, the town twinkled with fairy lights. The scent of pine and something sweet drifted through the crisp night air. It should have been comforting. It wasn't.

Steve stood beside her, his eyes fixed on her, saying nothing.

Alley leaned against the balcony railing, her gaze locked on the festive streets below. A gust of wind swept past, carrying the distant sound of laughter and the chime of Christmas bells from the town square.

Finally, she turned to him.

"Did you know that Jason was the father of my child?"

Steve shifted, his hands buried deep in his coat pockets. Then, he nodded.

"Dale told me, he said softly. "He thought you deserved to know when the time was right."

He hesitated.

"I wanted to tell you...but I kept waiting for the right moment. I just didn't want to make it worse."

A quiet moment stretched between them, thick with unspoken words. Alley's fingers gripped the railing as if grounding herself, her eyes lingering on the twinkling lights below.

"What did you think would happen if I knew the truth, Steve?" she asked, her tone steady but weighted.

Steve stiffened.

"What do you mean?"

"Did you think I would leave you?" Her words rose, raw with anger and frustration.

"Did you think I'd crumble again? That 'poor Alley' would just fall apart and need to be handled like some fragile thing? Did you think so little of me? That I'd just run back to him the moment I found out?"

Steve hesitated. His chin dropped for a moment, the weight of her anger settling over him. He shifted on his feet, struggling to find the correct response.

"Alley—"

"No." She shook her head, cutting him off—this time with less fire, more weariness. "That was never a question, Steve." She exhaled, rubbing her temple. "I just... I'm tired of being treated like I might break any second."

The hurt in his eyes was unmistakable.

She lowered her gaze. And then memory slipped in—uninvited, but not unwelcome.

She remembered the early days. The ones no one else saw.

Waking in the hospital, disoriented, unable to move her legs. The realization had landed like a stone. She was in a wheelchair. The loss of autonomy, the fog of memory, the ache in her bones—none of it made sense. But Steve had been there—not just once or twice, but always.

He wheeled her down endless corridors of unadorned tile, speaking with steady patience about the weather, favorite songs, and the little stories that always made her grin.

Later, at physical therapy, he settled beside her, cheering each tentative step and clapping when she stood unassisted for the first time, pride shining in his eyes.

He brought soup and old movies in the evenings. They laughed at terrible rom-coms and cried over aching dramas. Somewhere in those long, heavy days, she began to heal. And somewhere in that healing, she fell in love.

That night, beneath a sky blanketed in stars, snowflakes catching in her hair, Steve had taken her hands and said:

"If all I ever have is a handful of days with you—I'd still trade forever for them."

Alley blinked back a sudden warmth in her eyes, steadying herself with a hand on the railing.

She didn't fall in love with Steve all at once. She fell in love slowly. Steadily. Deeply. With the man who stayed.

Steve's voice faltered again.

"Sometimes I wonder…"

He trailed off, eyes fixed on the snow-dusted balcony rail. "If maybe you're choosing to stay because you feel grateful. Because I was there when everything fell apart. And not because you actually want this. Want me." His words hung in the cold air like mist.

Alley didn't answer right away. Instead, she reached for his hand and laced her fingers through his, grounding him. "Steve," she said softly, "gratitude doesn't build a life. It can't hold love in place. I stayed because you became my home somewhere in the blur of recovery and uncertainty.

Not a safety net. Not a duty. A choice. And I keep choosing you— not because I owe you anything—but because I love the life we built. I love you."

"I was scared," he admitted. "Scared that if you remembered everything—if you found out Jason still cared—you'd leave. That you'd see you were always his, not mine. And I didn't know how to stop it."

"So, if Jason had feelings for me, you would have walked away?" she asked, her voice shaky.

Steve didn't answer right away. His eyes drifted toward the horizon—toward the string of holiday lights glowing faintly in the dark. "Alley…" His voice came low, edged with something unspoken.

"It wouldn't have been about Jason. It would have been about you. If there was any part of you that wanted to be with him, I wouldn't have stood in the way.

I made that promise to you all those years ago when I proposed."

"And if I didn't?" she whispered. "If I still choose you?"

"Then I would have fought for you," he murmured. "I just didn't want to be the one you settled for—not your second choice."

Cold air filled her lungs, steadying her.

She had remembered her love for Jason, yes. But memory wasn't a compass—and it didn't define where she belonged now.

"Steve." The name left her gently. "You were never my second choice. Yes, I loved Jason with all my heart. I remember that now. But he is my past. You… you are my present. My future."

He didn't move—just stared.

"Yes, I might break. I might fall sick again. But I'll stand back up. And I want you there when I do—but you have to let me do it on my own."

Steve stepped forward, pulling her into a quiet embrace.

Alley let herself melt into him, her forehead resting against his shoulder. He pressed a kiss to her temple—reverent, steadying.

No promises. No need for words. Just presence.

"Okay." Steve nodded; his reply was barely audible, yet it was enough.

A gentle warmth blossomed across Alley's features, and with it came a relief she hadn't known for years. The wind wove around them, carrying the gentle peal of bells. And at last, she felt she was moving forward—on her own terms.

Chapter 68

After the silence

Memories stirring—some she remembered, most she didn't—as she stepped into Dale's office. The scent of spiced cider and warm pastries drifted through the air, familiar in a way that ached. It felt like returning to something lost, even if she couldn't name it.

Dale glanced at his watch and stood. "I have a lecture in a bit, but I'll check in later, okay?"

He placed a reassuring hand on her shoulder. "Take your time."

With a nod to Steve, he stepped out quietly, leaving space for what needed to come next.

Steve leaned close and softly tucked a strand of hair behind Alley's ear. "Want to come with me to the airport? Your mom lands in an hour."

Berry, catching the exchange, smirked. "The show never stops."

"I've got my car," Alley replied, nodding as warmth glimmered in her eyes. "I'll see you at home."

As Steve left, Jason and Berry exchanged a look. There was something different about Steve—subtle, yet impossible to miss. He leaned in, pressing a gentle kiss to Alley's forehead, and lingered a beat longer than usual. With a quiet wave, he turned and walked out, leaving the three old friends behind—surrounded not by words, but by the burden of everything left unsaid.

A wave of dizziness swept through her. Her cheeks flushed as she sank into a chair.

Jason crossed to her in an instant. "Are you okay, Alley?"

Berry leaned in, worry etched in his brow.

Without waiting, he poured a hot cider and handed it to her. "Have you eaten at all?"

She gave a weak laugh.

"Of course. I never leave the house without eating an entire pig."

That cracked a smile from both men, the tension loosening just a little as they recalled her legendary appetite.

He met her gaze, quiet strength gathering beneath the surface.

"Alley," he said, voice steady though something in him had begun to unravel,

"I'm so sorry. I never meant to hide the truth—about us. About Eaton."

But before he could continue, she stepped forward and wrapped her arms around him. Tears spilled down her cheeks, though her voice held firm.

"After everything, you're still standing here, apologizing—as if any of this was your fault?"

The room stilled.

"I broke up with you," she went on, words laced with regret. "I left you hurting. I didn't even stop to think about what you were going through. My pain blinded me to everything else."

She paused, struggling to steady her words.

"I'm so sorry—for destroying our family... our life."

He offered a quiet reassurance.

"No, Al. You didn't do it on purpose. I should've tried harder." He stared at the floor.

"I should've fought for us. But my ego... my pride..."

He closed his eyes. "That was my mistake."

He pulled her close again, his own walls breaking down. Burying his face in her hair, he let the emotion rise—grief, regret, and the fading memory of what they'd once shared.

She drew back slightly, hesitation flickering in her eyes.

"I remember loving you... But I don't remember having a child. Were we... living together? Or was it... an accident?"

A trace of nostalgia softened his expression.

"Something like that," he murmured.

"It wasn't exactly planned. You didn't want to raise a baby in a war zone, but I talked you into it."

Across the room, Berry looked up, brow creased. There was something too careful in Jason's voice—measured, cautious. Not dishonest. Just not the whole story.

Berry recognized the pause. He'd seen it before.

Jason continued, quieter now.

"And when you were too groggy from the painkillers on the day of the delivery..."

He let the sentence hang—choosing his words.

"The chaplain pronounced us husband and wife," he said with a soft laugh. "Just to make it legal—for Eaton."

Berry studied him for a beat longer. He wasn't lying.

But he was holding something back.

Not out of fear—but because what had begun to mend might not survive the whole truth.

Alley stiffened, taking it in. Her eyes searched his.

Berry shifted in his seat, his gaze flicking between them.

"You found a good guy," Jason said, trying to keep the moment light. "Might not be as handsome as I am, but he's a better man than I ever was."

A grin lingered at the corners of his mouth, but his fingers twitched—something beneath the surface fighting to break free.

Berry caught it—but said nothing.

Alley steadied herself. "Does Eaton know?"

Jason nodded. "Yes … I told him recently."

She drew a sharp breath. "And… what did he say?"

His hands fidgeted, his voice catching before he pushed through.

"He's okay with it. As long as you don't squish him too hard when you hug him," he added with a faint chuckle.

She wiped her eyes. "Does he hate me for leaving him?"

Tears clung to his lashes. "Hate you?" He laughed softly. "Alley, you're the story he always tells."

"Me?" Her brows lifted, eyes wide with uncertainty.

"Yeah, you." His voice dropped—gentle now. Protective.

A tentative laugh slipped from her lips. "What story?"

Jason leaned against the table, easing into the familiar cadence of the story he'd told so many nights before.

"He believes you're a superhero. The kind who travels the world healing people, saving lives. And one day, on a mission to rescue children from terrorists, you got hurt—so badly hurt that you forgot everything."

A jolt passed through her. She held the hem of her sleeve tight, the fabric twisting in her grasp.

He continued, unfolding the story layer by layer—blunting the painful corners of the truth that still hurt.

"But then, a hero stepped in—brought you home, kept you safe, helped you heal."

She squeezed her eyes shut.

Her pulse thudded, insistent—like memory trying to break through.

A wistful edge crept into his tone.

"Then, the hero gets the girl. So, he marries the superwoman… and they live happily ever after."

Her shoulders trembled as the weight of everything—lost time, quiet suffering, and the life of a child she couldn't recall—pressed in.

She looked up, something raw and steady in her gaze.

"No more secrets."

Jason and Berry nodded.

She swallowed hard. "The truth hides in silence—it's worse than a lie." This time, she didn't waver. "We'll deal with whatever comes. But no more pretending."

His lips parted, the words struggling to surface.

Beside him, Berry offered a firm nod.

Jason stepped forward. "Alright." His voice was quiet but firm. "Everything on the table from now on."

He held her gaze for a long moment.

Then he stepped closer.

"No more pretending. No more walls."

"And what happens next?" she asked.

Their eyes held.

When he finally answered, his voice carried no hesitation.

"That's your story to tell."

Years had passed before she dared to believe it.

Outside, the world went on—unmoved, unchanged. But inside, everything had shifted.

The scent of cider still lingered in the air. But now, so did something else: the weight of truth—and the promise of beginning again.

Chapter 69

We found us

The afternoon sun hung low, pale and wintry, offering little warmth against the chill in the air. The wind stirred the bare branches in the parking lot, scattering a few dry leaves across the asphalt.

Jason, Alley, and Berry stepped out of the hospital doors, laughter lingering between them. For a brief moment, it was easy—easy to pretend the weight they all carried didn't exist. The air was cold, but light with something that felt almost like relief.

As they left the building, Berry reached into his pocket and pulled out a crumpled candy wrapper. "Skittles?"

Jason stared at it, then laughed under his breath. "You're never gonna let that go, are you?"

Berry grinned. "Not a chance."

They walked on together, shoulder to shoulder—the past behind them, but carried still.

Then the café door opened behind them.

Margaret stepped out, scarf tucked neatly around her neck, holding a takeaway bag in one hand. Eaton followed, his cheeks flushed from the warmth of the café, a giant rainbow lollipop in his mouth, sticky fingers clutched around its stick.

Margaret stopped in her tracks. Her eyes landed on them—on Alley—and something in her posture changed, stiffened.

Eaton looked up, unfazed, grinning through the candy. "Hi, Alley! Hi Uncle Berry! Hi, Dad!"

Alley's heart jumped at the sound of his voice.

Margaret started to step forward, then hesitated. Alley, sensing it, reached out a hand—not rushed, not dramatic—just a quiet gesture held open between them.

Margaret's eyes darted from the hand to Alley's face. For a beat, neither moved. The cold wind tugged at their coats.

Then—Margaret's hand found Alley's, their fingers curling together. No words passed, but a quiet understanding settled between them.

Alley turned to Eaton.

He stood with his lollipop, amused, waiting for someone to say something. She met Jason's eyes, emotion pooling there, and he gave her a faint, almost imperceptible nod.

Alley crouched slightly, extending both hands toward Eaton with a playful tilt to her lips.

"Your dad tells me you hate hugs," she said lightly.

"Think I can earn a handshake?"

Eaton looked at his hands, then back at her.

"They're sticky."

Alley chuckled. "That's okay. I'm not scared of a little sugar."

He reached out. Their hands met—small and sticky in hers, warm despite the cold—and she held it just a second longer than a handshake would allow.

Eaton tilted his head, thoughtful. "My dad told me you're… my mom. The one who got lost."

Alley's eyes glistened as her lips parted, but no words came. She gave a small, wordless refusal, overwhelmed.

But Eaton merely shrugged, his shoulders lifting in that easy, carefree way.

"It's alright. We found you."

A sound escaped her—something between a laugh and a sob—as she nodded, eyes never leaving his face. Alley didn't know how a seven-year-old could carry so much grace. But Eaton—her son—had somehow offered her the kind of forgiveness she hadn't yet given herself.

And there, in the middle of a frozen parking lot, surrounded by the wind and the faint whisper of passing traffic, something that had been broken began to mend.

Berry turned away, pretending to scan the row of parked cars, but his vision swam. He blinked rapidly.

He'd seen so much—beginnings, endings, grief—but this sticky handshake between a boy and the woman who gave him life felt reverent. Almost holy.

He wasn't even sure why it hit so deep. Maybe because it made him believe that some broken things do find their way back, that, sometimes, life has a way of finding its own. He blinked, wiping at his eyes before anyone noticed.

Jason stood, hands deep in his coat pockets, the wind a reminder not to drop his guard. Yet he couldn't look away. In that instant, a long-buried knot unraveled. Trust didn't come easy anymore, but seeing them—alive, here—awakened something old and cautious in him. Hope.

Margaret watched from the side, the cold forgotten.

The scene in front of her was impossibly tender—too tender for words. She had spent years protecting Jason, carrying him through the moments he was too tired to face. And now, here stood the woman who once disappeared into smoke and memory... returning, not with excuses, but with open hands and eyes full of sorrow.

Margaret's hand instinctively touched her own chest. She had wanted to resent Alley.

But as she watched that fragile, sticky handshake—watched Eaton light up without hesitation—she felt her defenses slip. Maybe love was vast enough to hold space for grief and forgiveness.

It was getting chilly. Margaret glanced upward just as the first flurry began to descend, white flakes drifting from the pewter-shaded clouds overhead.

She gave a gentle nod.

Eaton understood. He gave Alley one last grin, then turned and walked beside his grandmother toward the car, his lollipop still clutched triumphantly in one hand. As they reached the vehicle, both turned to wave.

Alley waved back, her hand hovering just a moment longer in the air.

Even after the car disappeared down the bend of the parking lot, Alley stood still, her eyes fixed on the space it had left behind. She looked down at her palms—still tacky with sugar and the warmth of a boy's trust.

She raised them to her face, pressing them to her lips.

Just like she had the day he was born.

Behind her, Jason and Berry stood together, their laughter rippling between them—quiet, familiar, healing.

The flurries thickened, swirling around the hospital parking lot, covering the quiet town of Apple Creek in a blanket of white.

She no longer felt like someone recovering.

She felt like someone returning.

The snow didn't feel cold.
It felt like a beginning.

Chapter 70

Silent Gifts

Snow drifted outside the diner's windows, clinging to bare branches like icing on sugar cookies. Cinnamon and pine lingered in the room, twining through laughter and the clink of glasses.

Golden Oaks had closed early for the holiday, and the Rivers and Carters had gathered under one roof.

In the dining room, Eaton darted between chairs in his Christmas sweater, trailing behind him a tangle of red ribbon—and two very opinionated dogs. Pepper barked at Elijah, who responded with a dramatic flop under the table.

"Dad, guess what?" Eaton called, spinning around. "They're not being friends!"

Jason raised an eyebrow from his place by the fireplace. "And?"

"Hopefully they'll learn to get along," Eaton said, as if delivering a diplomatic update to the UN.

Steve chuckled from the kitchen doorway, carving ham like someone who'd done it for this family many times before. "We may need to give them a little space."

At the table, Dale poured cider into mismatched mugs. His usual composure had softened, wrapped in the quiet joy of watching his son and daughter-in-law move through a holiday neither of them thought they'd share again.

Margaret and Vicky arranged the final touches on the sideboard—homemade rolls, cranberry compote, and a pie that had already been sneakily sampled. The two women exchanged a glance—no tension left, only the quiet pride of mothers watching their children find their way.

Maggie breezed in from the hallway with a tray of sparkling cider, her bangles clinking as she walked. "Alright, my people," she declared, setting the glasses down. "Before anyone sneaks another slice of pie, I propose a toast."

They turned to her, smiling.

She lifted her glass. "To family. For holding on when things fall apart. For coming back together, even when it hurts."

She looked at Alley, warmth threading through her words. "To second chances—and the stubborn, beautiful hearts that make them possible."

Glasses lifted. "To family," they echoed.

They clinked, and everything felt exactly as it should for a brief moment.

Later, after dessert disappeared and wrapping paper blanketed the floor, Eaton passed out presents like a seasoned announcer, narrating every delivery with a dramatic flair. Pepper chased bows. Elijah guarded the tree like a soldier on duty.

After most of the unwrapping, Jason crossed the room and handed Alley a final box—flat, wrapped in plain brown paper, tied with twine.

She paused, sensing something in his expression. Then opened it.

Inside was a leather-bound photo album. Eaton was embossed on the cover in worn gold.

Her breath caught.

She turned the pages—first steps, crooked crowns, Halloween capes, and messy finger-painting. Eaton in rain boots. At the zoo. On Jason's shoulders at the beach. A lifetime she'd missed, now lay gently in her lap.

"I didn't know what to give you," Jason said softly, kneeling beside her chair. "But I thought… maybe this. So, you could meet him. The way I did. One year at a time."

She couldn't answer. Her throat closed. Her hand reached for Eaton, who leaned against her side.

"Do you like it?" he asked.

She kissed the top of his head. "It's the most beautiful gift I've ever received."

She looked up at Jason, then to Steve—who met her gaze with a quiet nod.

Her eyes found Vicky and Margaret beside one another, both smiling through full hearts. Near the tree, Maggie stood, her eyes glassy and her smile fierce.

Something had shifted in that room.

It wasn't about recovering every memory anymore.

It was about what still remained—and what could still be built.

Chapter 71

Where the heart lands

Later that night, Alley stood at the window in her room, a cup of tea cooling in her hands. Outside, Apple Creek shimmered beneath the moonlight, the town hushed beneath fresh snow.

Inside, the house was still.

She caught the faint rustle of Eaton shifting in his sleep down the hall. Steve speaking low on the phone. Jason's footsteps had long faded from the front steps. The door had closed behind him with something close to grace.

Her fingers grazed the album in her lap. Jason had once told her she'd married him because it made sense—they were in Afghanistan, and a marriage would protect Eaton legally. He'd believed she'd been drugged and disoriented, still reeling from everything they'd survived.

But now, turning the pages of the album, she remembered clearly.

She was the one who asked.

Not for papers. Not for protocol.

She'd asked because she loved him. Because in a quiet, ordinary moment—before chaos, before blood—she had looked at Jason Carter and couldn't imagine a life that didn't include him.

And he said yes.

It hadn't been survival. It had been love. She wanted to remember that clearly—not to return to it, but to honor what it truly was.

She smiled faintly.

To be loved like that once was rare.

To find it again—so different, so steady, so unexpected—was a grace she hadn't dared to ask for.

A knock came at the door—gentle.

Steve.

She didn't answer at first.

Her gaze moved over the room—the folded quilt, the bookshelf by the window, the chair where her coat waited.

She no longer felt like a visitor in someone else's life. Not just in Steve's house—but in her life. In the rhythm of mornings and shared meals and long, quiet nights.

She belonged here.

She set the album aside and rose slowly, smoothing the front of her shirt just as the door eased open.

Steve leaned in, voice quiet. "Everyone's getting ready. Ski festival's underway."

She smiled. "The Rivers and the Carters, still keeping tradition alive?"

"Looks that way," he said. "Your spot on the sled is still open."

She breathed out, light and grounded. "I'll be right there."

He nodded, then stepped back, letting the door fall shut with a soft click.

Outside the door, Steve paused, listening for her steps. Just one breath of stillness—then he turned, a quiet hope steady in his chest.

She stood for a moment longer, her hand resting gently on the album's cover.

Jason had been her past. Steady, devoted, unforgettable. What they shared hadn't been erased. It would always live inside her—tender and intact.

But her heart had moved forward.

Her present—and her future—were with Steve. She loved him with quiet certainty, not just for standing beside her when she didn't even know who she was, but for how he made her feel whole again. Safe, seen, loved.

She was proud of the life they had built together, not as a substitute for what she had lost, but as something entirely her own.

She had loved once in a warzone, and she loved again now.

It was a quieter kind of love—built on ordinary days, shared silence, and trust.

And as she reached for her coat, heart steady, she knew—

She wasn't moving forward alone.

Epilogue

A beginning again

Five winters had passed since Eaton found his mother again. Life hadn't rushed forward—it had unfolded quietly and steadily, one heartbeat at a time.

The fire crackled. When the phone rang, Jason sat in his armchair, emails open but unread. He checked the screen, then stood, already reaching for his coat.

"That was Steve," he said. "It's time."

Eaton shot upright, blinking. "Wait—now?!"

They piled into the car, headlights cutting through the snow. In the backseat, Eaton bounced nervously while Margaret and Robert whispered beside him.

"Is Mom going to be okay?" Eaton asked.

Jason met his eyes in the mirror. "She's a doctor. She'll be just fine."

Eaton nodded, his gaze drifting out the window.

Jason's voice softened.

"This town was never meant to be home. I thought we were just passing through."

Eaton smirked. "And now?"

Jason laughed softly. "Now I can't imagine leaving."

At the hospital, Steve stood waiting, pacing with his phone in hand. Berry and his wife, Jen, arrived moments later, arms full of coffee.

Leia and Emmy followed with balloons and flowers. Margaret and Vicki stood near the entrance, their eyes bright with anticipation.

Steve exhaled. "She's in the birthing room. Still giving instructions between contractions."

Jason laughed. "That sounds like her."

He turned to Eaton. "Ready to meet your sister?"

Eaton grinned. "Born ready."

As he ran to Steve's side, Jason lingered for a moment. Leia stepped beside him. They stood quietly, watching the doors where new life was waiting to arrive.

She handed him a coffee. Their fingers brushed.

He didn't speak right away. Just nodded his thanks, his expression soft.

Leia glanced at him. "Strange how life folds in on itself sometimes."

Jason looked toward the delivery wing, where voices echoed faintly through the corridor.

"Not strange," he said. "Just… right."

Their shoulders touched briefly. No more than that.

Together, they stepped into the beginning of something new.

Golden Oaks Diner stood quiet beneath the midnight sky, its neon sign casting a glow. Inside, chairs were flipped, and tables wiped clean. The scent of coffee lingered in the stillness.

It had seen a thousand nights like this.

Tonight, it waited for her.

Far away, under hospital lights, Alley clutched Steve's hand. Eaton sat beside her, fingers brushing the newborn's tiny ones.

Alley looked at her son, and he looked back with steady, knowing eyes.

For years, she'd believed she'd lost him. For years, she carried the grief of a fire that had taken nothing at all.

Now, here they were.

Whole.

Together.

And across town, the diner waited to receive Erica☐Rehana☐Rivers, just as it welcomed Eaton all those years ago.

The soft buzz of its neon glow mingled with the warm scent of coffee and quiet hope.

The diner remained unchanged

But Alley had changed.

She wasn't lost anymore. She was home.

And as the first light of dawn brushed the diner's windows, a quiet promise awakened.

Author's Note

I began writing Secrets That Hold Us in the months following my father's passing. Grief is more than pain—it's guilt, fear, and blame. But it also reveals what mattered most. In that silence, I was reminded of the greatest gift I've ever known: my father's unwavering love and support.

Writing became my way forward—a space to breathe, reflect, and transform sorrow into something meaningful. Every story I've written during this time has grown from that place of pain, yes, but also from deep love.

This book may be fiction, but the emotions behind it are real. If you've ever struggled under the weight of expectations, carried guilt that wasn't yours to bear, or tried to find your way back to yourself after everything changed—this story is for you.

The rainbow might not appear in the place you expect—but it will appear again.

—Manjula Pothuri

About the Author

Manjula Pothuri is a writer who finds meaning in exploring the quiet complexities of human emotion. With roots in India and a life spent across continents, she now embraces a nomadic lifestyle—drawing inspiration from the cultures, people, and landscapes she encounters. Her stories often center on love, resilience, and rediscovery, offering readers an emotional connection and a space for reflection.

Manjula continues to write from the heart, held up by the unwavering love of her husband, daughters, and close friends. Their presence has not only shaped her stories but also made them possible.

Upcoming titles by Manjula Pothuri

Threads That Weave Us
Between Us And Ourselves
The Souls That Called Us

Visit **www.manjulapothuri.com** to explore blurbs of upcoming titles and stay in the loop.

Dear Reader,

Thank you for spending time with *Secrets That Hold Us*. I hope the characters stayed with you and that their journey meant something to you, however big or small.

If you enjoyed the book, I would be truly grateful if you could take a moment to leave a review on Amazon or Goodreads. Your words help other readers discover the story—and they mean more than you know to authors like me.

You can also follow me for updates on upcoming titles, behind-the-scenes glimpses, and more:

Facebook:facebook.com/ManjulaPothuriAuthor

Website: www.manjulapothuri.com

Thank you again for reading. Your support makes stories like this possible.

With gratitude,

Manjula Pothuri

www.ingramcontent.com/pod-product-compliance
Lightning Source LLC
Chambersburg PA
CBHW070740180626
46818CB00007B/2934